PRAISE FOR
NANCY GARDEN'S
DOVE AND SWORD:

"In the hands of Garden the entire historical period comes brilliantly alive. The pert and plucky Gabrielle delivers readers into a peaceful village life and then vividly summons the carnage of war. In the process, she grows up too soon, just as the Maid dies too young. In a season of plenty for fine historical fiction, Garden's gripping, gritty tale ranks as one of the best."
— *Kirkus Reviews*, pointed review

"[Garden's] strategically plotted novel achieves the highest goals of historical fiction — it vivifies the past, robustly and respectfully, then uses its example to steer the audience toward a more courageous future."
—*Publishers Weekly*, starred review

DOVE AND SWORD

A NOVEL OF JOAN OF ARC

Other POINT SIGNATURE
paperbacks you will enjoy:

The Wild Hunt
Jane Yolen

Beyond the Burning Time
Kathryn Lasky

Jackaroo
Cynthia Voigt

The Wings of a Falcon
Cynthia Voigt

DOVE AND SWORD

A NOVEL OF JOAN OF ARC

NANCY GARDEN

SCHOLASTIC INC.
New York Toronto London Auckland Sydney

ISBN 0-590-92949-6

12 11 10 9 8 7 6 5 4 3 2   7 8 9/9 0 1 2/0

Printed in the U.S.A.

First Scholastic printing, June 1997

For Lorelle, who understands about history

For Isabella, who understands about horses

Acknowledgments

No one has helped me more with this book than my partner, Sandra Scott, who not only helped with the map that accompanies the text and went with me to France to trace Joan of Arc's and Gabrielle's routes, but who also spent many hours translating, poring over old books, taking notes and pictures, discussing Joan's life and era with me, researching the historical and political background of Joan's story, and reading the manuscript and making valuable corrections and suggestions. Without her help, this book could not have been written, and I am very grateful. Any errors of fact that have found their way into print are my responsibility, not hers.

Many other people have helped as well, both in the United States and in France. I would like to thank Jill Erickson, of the Boston Athenaeum, for her interest and for sending me information about equestrian statues of Joan; Robert C. Kaufmann, Associate Museum Librarian of the Irene Lewisohn Costume Reference Library of the Metropolitan Museum of Art in New York City, and his assistant Carol Rathore, for helping us locate many helpful costume books and drawings; Melinda Scanlon, curator of the Joan of Arc Collection of the Boston Public Library, for making John Cardinal Wright's extensive collection of Joan of Arc books, documents, artifacts, and oddities available to us and helping us find specific materials; our friend Midge Eliassen, for her interest in the project and for giving me her copy of Lucy Foster Madison's children's biography *Joan of Arc* (The Penn Publishing Company, 1919), which I treasure; our friend Charlotte Stratton, for her interest and for showing us a wonderful old book about Joan; our friends Dorrie Hutchins and Diann Lehman, for taking us to the Higgins Armory Museum, in Worcester, Massachusetts, and for helping me track down the Wright Collection, which was originally located in Worcester; my aunt, Mrs. Dan H. Fenn, for reading and commenting helpfully on an early version of the manuscript; Madame Marie Claude Person and Madame Monique Profit, for their hospitality at the museum at Joan of Arc's house in Domremy; Father Jean Mengin, at the Basilique Nationale de Sainte Jeanne d'Arc in Domremy, for patiently answering the many questions we put to him in our halting French; Colette Hibon and Olivier Bouzy, at the Centre Jeanne d'Arc d'Orléans, in Orléans, for helping us use their collection's books and documents — and our friends and families in general, for their interest and support. My gratitude also goes to FSG editors Margaret Ferguson, Laura Tillotson, and Karla Reganold for hard work and many thoughtful contributions, and to Jonas Barciauskas of the O'Neill Library at Boston College for doing his best to answer a tricky last-minute question.

Nancy Garden
Carlisle, Massachusetts
West Tremont, Maine

This book is, before anything else, a story. It is a story with a good deal of history in it, but it should be viewed as fiction woven around fact.

Domremy, Joan of Arc's native village, is a real place. Today it's called Domrémy-la-Pucelle, renamed to honor Joan, who was known as la Pucelle — the Maid. According to people I met in the Joan of Arc museum there, the accent was added to the village's name in modern times, so I don't use it in this book.

Gabrielle was not a real person, and it is perhaps unlikely that another peasant girl from Domremy besides Joan would have gone to battle. But there were some amazingly feisty women in Joan's time — Christine de Pisan, for example, who *was* a real person and who really did write a long poem about Joan; in fact, it was probably the last thing she ever wrote. No one is sure where Christine died, or at which convent she lived, but since her daughter was at Poissy, and since Christine visited there, it seems logical to assume that she herself might have gone there when she wished to withdraw from the world. Most of the military and political people mentioned in the book were real, too, as of course were the members of Joan's family, and some of the other people — Father Pasquerel, Brother Richard, and the Demoiselle de Luxembourg among them.

A big problem that faces writers of historical works is whether or not to make up dialogue. This problem is more acute in biography, in which fictional dialogue is severely frowned upon by many critics, than it is in historical fiction. But the question sometimes arises in historical fiction when it comes to historical characters — Joan's words, for example, in this book. Partly because of her trial, of which records were kept, and partly because several chroniclers of the time wrote about her, some of what she said — or was thought or rumored to have said — has been preserved. It is of course not possible to establish whether she actually did say the words she has been recorded as saying, and it is important to remember that anything she said has been subject to translation, often from French to Latin to French and finally to English, and has also been subject to the recorders' and translators' biases. But whenever possible, I have tried to base Joan's lines in this book on those that have been recorded.

Along with everyone else who has written about Joan, I am indebted to a nineteenth-century scholar, Jules Quicherat, for many details of her story and for many of her words. Although some contemporary chroniclers, as I said above, did write about Joan, it was Quicherat who was largely responsible for lifting her story from the obscurity into which it fell after she was pardoned. It was he who translated the trial testimony that forms the core of our knowledge of her — both the trial of accusation and the later trial of rehabilitation. It is important to keep in mind, though, that testimony at both trials tended to be colored by the witnesses and questioners involved, those at the first being largely hostile to her, and those at the second largely friendly. Chroniclers of the time also tended to be biased for or against Joan, depending on their allegiances in the Hundred Years' War.

That was Joan's war, the war she sought to end. It had been raging for many years by the time she became involved. Basically, the argument was over who should rule France: the English or the French. English kings had controlled parts of France ever since the time of William the Conqueror. The actual Hundred Years' War began in 1340, when the English king Edward III took the title King of France, as did several English kings who came after him, even when there were French kings in France. In 1411, civil war broke out in France, between followers of the Duke of Burgundy and followers of the Duke of Orléans. Both factions wanted control of the French throne, which was then occupied by a mentally ill king, Charles VI, known as Charles the Mad. Then in 1415 the English invaded, and conquered the French in the famous Battle of Agincourt. A few years later, the Burgundians seized control of Paris. In 1420, when Joan was probably around eight, came the Treaty of Troyes, in which Henry V of England was officially made heir to the French throne and was given one of Charles the Mad's daughters in marriage to solidify the arrangement. Henry V died in 1422, leaving his nine-month-old baby, Henry VI, as his heir. When Charles the Mad died, little Henry VI, in accordance with the Treaty of Troyes, became king of France. But Charles the Mad had a living son, also named Charles, as well as daughters, and it was that son who was Joan's dauphin — the crown prince — the man whom she and the loyal French wanted as their king.

By this time, the Burgundians, under Philip the Good, Duke of Burgundy, were allied with the English. In Joan's day, although some of what we now know as France was under the control of the French monarchy, there were other areas, like Burgundy, that were not and that were, in effect, independent entities. Some of these were loyal to Burgundy and accepted the idea of having an English king. Others were loyal to the dauphin, Charles, and dedicated to the idea of a France independent of English rule.

The war itself, which had raged on and off during this whole period, had led to great hardship in much of France. Although the Burgundian court was rich and elaborate, the dauphin's — partly through Charles's excesses — fell upon hard times, and was much poorer. The common people in many parts of France, including the area around Domremy, Joan's village, were subject to heavy taxation and to raids during which Burgundian soldiers and brigands burned and destroyed whatever was in their path, and stole food, livestock, household goods, and anything else they could take.

Life in the early fifteenth century was very different from life today. In any era, the lives of poor people, like those in Joan's village, are often less well documented by contemporary chroniclers and shown less clearly in art and literature than are the lives of the rich. Then, too, in wartime, most contemporary chroniclers concentrate primarily on the war and on politics. Largely for these reasons, there's not a great deal of information about the everyday lives of the poor in Joan's period. Also, today's cultural historians (those who write about daily life) have concentrated more on the Middle Ages (before Joan's period) and the Renaissance (after it) than on the early fifteenth century, when Joan lived. Because of all these factors, it's not always possible to be a hundred percent sure what the people around Joan — especially poor people like Gabrielle — wore, ate, and so on. I have tried to be as accurate as possible in my portrayal of everyday life, and when I've had to make something up, I've tried to base it on logic and what I've learned about the period. Also, on the advice of my editor, in order not to burden the story with distracting details, I have simplified such things as clothing, weapons, and the composition of armies. I've used familiar terms when possible — doublet, for example, to refer to a number of more specific garments, like brigandine, *jacque*, and *pourpoint*. I apologize to the real experts for any errors I've made in these or other matters.

N.G.

*Jeanne, sans sepulcre et sans
portrait, toi qui savais que le tombeau
des héros est le coeur des vivants . . .*

ANDRÉ MALRAUX

(Inscription on wall in the Vieux Marché, Rouen, where
Joan of Arc was burned at the stake, May 30, 1431)

*Joan, without sepulcher and without portrait,
you who know that the tomb of heroes is the
heart of the living . . .*

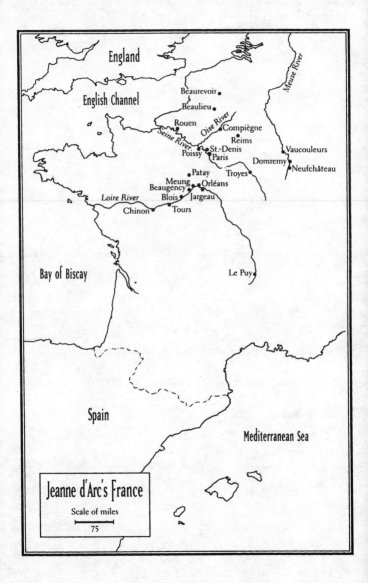

England

English Channel

Beaurevoir

Beaulieu

Rouen

Seine River

Oise River

Compiègne

Reims

Poissy

St.-Denis

Paris

Vaucouleurs

Domremy

Neufchâteau

Meuse River

Patay

Troyes

Meung

Orléans

Beaugency

Blois

Jargeau

Loire River

Chinon

Tours

Le Puy

Bay of Biscay

Spain

Mediterranean Sea

Jeanne d'Arc's France

Scale of miles

75

November 1455

I was asleep when the knock came at the door of my hut on the edge of the convent's walled garden. It was Sister Marie Antoine, who was the same age as I when I had set off on my adventure.

"*Pardon, madame,*" she said, "but there is a man asking for you. He says he knew you in your village, and during the war, and he insists that you see him even though the hour is late. He says he is called — "

Before she could finish, my door was flung open and Pierre d'Arc — Jeanne d'Arc's brother and my dearest childhood friend — burst into the room.

"Gabrielle!" he exclaimed. While Sister Marie Antoine stared, he put out his hands to meet mine and kissed me first on one cheek and then on the other, and then on both again. "So you are still here, still the nuns' healer."

He was heavier than when I had last seen him,

1

more than two decades earlier. I had heard that he had bought his freedom from the prison in which he had spent so many years, and that he and his wife, Jeanne, had had a son — but that was all, and I was hungry, seeing him, for news.

"Sit, please sit," I said as soon as Sister Marie Antoine had scurried out.

He did, then glanced at the bunches of dried herbs suspended from the beams of my hut, and the jars and bottles which I tried to keep neatly ordered on my thick oak shelves. "The nuns must be a sickly band to require so much medicine," he said.

"The villagers consult me as well," I told him. "The women bring their children to me, and come themselves, and farmers come, too, with cuts and broken bones."

"But no soldiers anymore, eh, Gabrielle? No sword cuts or caltrop punctures, no crossbow bolts to probe for, or English longbow arrows to wrench out, no cannon-shattered limbs to mend. Do you miss it?"

"No," I said emphatically. "Do you?"

He sighed and went to the window that looked beyond the fields and woods toward the great city of Paris. "Some," he said. "But I am well content in Orléans with my wife and son, near where you and I were companions in arms so long ago. The good Charles, Duke of Orléans, gave me l'Isle-aux-Boeufs, where there is fertile land, and I have other land now also, and a pension." He smiled proudly. "I am king's chamberlain, and knight. My mother lives nearby. And my son, Jean, has turned out better than his namesake."

"Good," I said wryly, "although it would not be difficult to be better than your brother, who was never to be found when he was needed."

Pierre faced me once more. "Yes," he said, "how well you do remember!" He sighed again. "It is enough, I suppose, my life as it is now. I have grown too old for fighting. And besides . . ." He bent close to me, his eyes burning with fervor. "We are not finished with that time, Gabrielle, and that is the reason I have come to you. The officials are going to study the trial; we may be able to bring honor to Jeannette's name at last, to let her be remembered as the holy heroine she truly was, as the savior of France and a martyr instead of as an evil heretic."

I felt my heart skip. Pierre and I had followed his sister Jeannette — Jeanne la Pucelle, or the Maid, as she came to be called — when she led us French against the English oppressors and Burgundian traitors, and when she had the Dauphin Charles crowned King Charles VII of France. I had seen both Jeannette and Pierre captured at Compiègne, and I had seen Jeannette cruelly burned at the stake despite her brave deeds and her piety. Bring honor to her name? War itself may be wrong; I have wrestled with that thought for many years. But Jeannette joined a war that was already raging, to stop it. I knew I would willingly leave my comfortable convent life if I could help win her the respect she deserved!

But Pierre was still talking, explaining to me that it was the Pope himself who had allowed him and Jeannette's mother, Isabelle Romée, to ask for an investigation into Jeannette's trial. Isabelle had gone to Paris, he said as we settled at my small table and I poured him wine, "and pleaded for Jeannette before many learned men in long robes; she was frightened, but no one save I knew that. I could see Jeannette in her, when Jeannette argued with Dunois and the others — remember, Gabrielle?"

I nodded, and soon we were both remembering the days when we had marched behind Jeannette's white standard. Long after I had agreed to go with Pierre to plead for Jeannette myself, and he had left, I sat remembering still. It had started in, I think, 1425, when I was perhaps eleven, and Pierre a year older . . .

PART ONE

PART ONE

1

"Oui, monseigneur. J'essayerai! I will try!"

That was Jeannette's voice. Pierre and I peered into the d'Arcs' garden and then at each other, astonished. We had just come up from Maxey, the village across the River Meuse from our village, Domremy. Pierre and I, along with some of our friends, had been fighting with the boys of Maxey. There had been real fighting there when I was very small, and now the people of Maxey were Burgundians, loyal to Philip the Good, Duke of Burgundy. But in Domremy we did not think Philip was good at all, and in our battles we village children hurled names at each other along with stones and clods of earth. My mother did not entirely approve of my playing with boys, and some of the boys did not either, but she indulged me on the rare occasions when she did not need me. This morning had been such a time, and so, after I had helped drive the horses to pasture, I had gone with Pierre and the others to ambush the Burgundian children. But they

7

had beaten us, because they had stouter sticks for lances and swords than we. Now Pierre, who was usually cheerful, was in a surly temper.

It was already after noon. The church bells all along the Meuse valley — from our village, and Maxey, and Greux up the river — had long since stopped ringing, and we were late. Pierre would be wanted in the fields, for it was the d'Arcs' turn to watch the village cattle and goats, and I was to look after my younger sisters. Pierre's father and my mother, we knew, would be cross.

Even so, when we reached the d'Arcs' garden, we could not help but stop and stare at his sister Jeannette, who was a little older than we — thirteen, I suppose, although no one kept very careful account of ages. Her everyday dress, of the same coarse red wool as the dresses of all us village girls, was crumpled halfway down its long skirt, as if she had been kneeling. Her lovely straight black hair, which I envied, for mine had such curls that it often stood on end, had twigs in it. But it was not that so much which astonished us, although Jeannette was always neat, much neater than I. It was the look on her plain, honest face that made us stare. An inner light shone from her, despite her troubled — even frightened — eyes. And she was talking, though there was no one with her.

Pierre pulled me into the garden behind his family's stone house, which was better than most others in our village, for Pierre's father, Jacques d'Arc, was an important official. "Try what?"

Pierre demanded of Jeannette. "You said you would try." He put his hands on his hips and made great show of looking around. "And to whom did you say you would try?" he asked. "There is no one here!"

I do not think that Jeannette had ever told a lie until that day. She was so good and pious that she was as often in church as she was at home, spinning with her mother, the devout Isabelle Romée, who had made the grand pilgrimage to Rome. Jeannette loved to hear Isabelle tell about the lives of the saints, especially Saint Margaret and Saint Catherine. And so I did not doubt Jeannette when she told Pierre, "I said I would try to be good, but I addressed no one. It is nothing, Pierre; do not speak of it."

I say I did not doubt her then, and I did not. I wondered, though, as I left Pierre and went home, why a person would make such a promise when no one was there to hear it, and why Jeannette would, when she was already good — better, certainly, than Pierre and I.

We were not bad children, he and I, but we were spirited and mischievous. Even though we were almost grown, we were reluctant to become adults. I did not want to spend my life spinning and cooking, and Pierre, who got no pleasure from tending crops and livestock, wanted to fight Burgundians in earnest, with sword and crossbow, not with sticks as we used in Maxey. I was the second oldest in a house full of girls, and Pierre was the d'Arcs' youngest. Besides Jeannette, he had a lazy brother, Jean, who left much of his own work for Pierre to do, and another brother and sister, who were both married and did not live in Domremy. Pierre's position was worse than mine, because I had special work to do, work that I enjoyed.

My mother was a midwife and healer, and since my older sister Catherine felt sick when she saw blood, it was I who accompanied Maman when she delivered babies. I also went with Maman when she climbed the flat-topped hills and walked into the woods and through the water meadows of our beautiful Meuse valley to gather herbs. She enjoyed this as much as I; she did not like ordinary woman's work either, though she never complained. Breaking clods left by the plow every spring and harvesting at the end of summer were the only women's tasks that I could stomach, for they were out of doors and active. Papa said that I must be a changeling, left by the fairies, for whenever I tried to spin, the thread ran wrong, and when I tended the stew pot, like as not it boiled or burned. But when I put a flaxseed poultice on Papa's head when it ached, he said I had the touch of an angel. "How can she be a changeling," Maman would say, "when she has my hands and your eyes and a gift for healing that surpasses my own?" My mother was always my friend, as Jeannette's mother was hers.

A few days later, Pierre came running to my house at the hour of Compline, as the sky's light faded along with the sweet echoing bells. I was weeding my mother's vegetable plot when I heard him shout, "Gabrielle, Gabrielle! Come quickly; Jeannette is doing it again! Hurry! I think she must be going mad — mad, or else she is very holy. Come!"

He led me — dragged me is more truthful — around the edge of the last house in our row, into the road, and past the church to his house, which was next to it. "Shh," he cautioned, pulling me behind some bushes. His hair, shaggy no matter when it was cut, flopped over his eyes as he ducked his head and whispered, "Look! Look at her!"

I peered out and saw Jeannette on her knees, her face transfixed and glowing again, and her eyes less frightened this time. "*Oui, monseigneur,*" she was saying. "*Oui, mesdames*; yes, my lord; yes, my ladies. I will try, but I am not worthy. I am only a poor peasant girl." She paused then, as if listening. I felt a chill creep over me and did not want to be there, for whether it was madness or miracle, it seemed a private thing.

With Pierre, though, I tried to pretend it was nothing. "She is playing," I told him scornfully. "That is all. She is playing at being a nun or a saint."

"No," Pierre said. "No, she is not." He turned to me, his usually ruddy face pale. "She has been different since that day. She leaves her friends often now to pray, and when she is spinning with Hauviette and Mengette and the others, they talk and laugh and sing, but Jeannette just spins."

"She never sang much with them or talked or laughed," I said, annoyed. In fact, I had always thought Jeannette rather dull, but for love of Pierre I had never said so.

"This is different," Pierre said, his eyes never leaving his sister's face. "As you yourself said, Jeannette does not play much, and I am certain she is not playing now. But what *is* she doing?"

We watched, but she did not speak again. She nodded and remained kneeling, her head bowed, until the sun was all the way down and my legs ached from staying still and quiet. I left then, though Pierre did not.

That summer, Pierre often reported Jeannette's strange actions to me, but I was too busy to spy with him. Many in our village were ill with a quinsy, and Maman had me gather wild columbine to ease their painful throats. Maman was with child also, and needed my help more as the weeks passed.

That July, summer heat lay thickly over our valley and the mist that covered the river at dawn seemed as stifling as the sheepskins we pulled around ourselves on winter nights. Early one morning I was spreading betony thinly on the ground, hoping the sun would burn through the mist soon and dry it, when a great outcry made me drop the stems I was holding. I ran to the street, and it seemed all the village was hastening toward the fields where the cattle and horses usually grazed. "They are gone!" I heard our neighbor Henri shout.

"Who is gone?" I asked, breathless with keeping step with him. Henri had the longest legs in the village and won every race that the boys held on feast days.

"The cattle — driven off in the night! Horses, too, and pigs. And the oxen. Everything."

It was true; I saw no beasts at all. In the fields, the children who had been sent to herd that day clung to their fathers, sobbing. Other village men, including my father and Pierre's, were hurrying people toward the *maison forte*, the stronghold on the island in the river where we kept the village livestock when raiders threatened. But it appeared that this time there had been no warning, and no time to drive the animals there.

Pierre broke away from his brother Jean, who was urging Jeannette and their mother to wade across to the island. "It was Burgundians," he said, running up to me. "Burgundian brigands. They came in the night like common thieves and drove our animals off."

I looked back, still amazed. The flat plains that edged the river were empty. The grasslands above the village were also empty, instead of dotted with the brown-and-white bodies of our gentle cows, without which we of Domremy would be poor indeed. None of the oxen we used for plowing were in sight, nor were the horses that helped us carry goods to Neufchâteau, the market town south of our village, and Vaucouleurs, the city to our north.

"Gabrielle," Pierre cried urgently, "do not linger! The brigands may still be nearby!" He made me wade with him onto the island, where I huddled with our neighbors and wondered where my parents and sisters were.

Soon I felt a strong hand on my shoulder and turned to see Papa with my older sister, Catherine, and my just-younger-than-me sister, Paulette. But my little sisters, Marguerite and Cécile, were not with him, nor was Maman, and fear gripped me.

"Where is Maman?" I cried — but before Papa could answer, a shout went up from those nearest the shore. I gasped to see smoke mingling with the mist. "The fiends," muttered Henri's father to mine. "Some of them must have hidden in the hills after the others drove the animals away, and then moved silently back to burn the village while we fled here!"

Distant laughter came to us across the water, and then carts — many of them ours, pulled by our beasts — rumbled along the road, piled high with goods stolen from our houses. But by the time we reached the village, the marauders were gone — and then we saw smoke pouring from the church roof. Though the building was stone, its roof was not, nor were the furnishings inside. "Stay with Pierre while I look for Maman and your little sisters," my father shouted to me,

Catherine, and Paulette, as he ran toward our house at the far edge of the village.

"We must save the church!" someone cried, so Catherine, Paulette, Pierre, and I helped search for pails and cooking pots — anything that would hold water. The few that we found we took to the river and filled, as did our neighbors. Then we passed them in a human chain from river to church, thus saving the roof from all but a little charring.

I knew that rough soldiers and brigands roamed the countryside, and that they as well as honest folk traveled on the road. I dimly remembered the real fighting in Maxey when I was little, and I knew that some families, including Pierre's, had lost relatives in battle. Lately we had driven our animals to the island more often than before, and sometimes at night when there was a sudden noise, my mother would cling to my father in alarm, and Catherine would grow pale. But never before in my lifetime, though war raged around us and several nearby villages had been sacked and burned, had Domremy itself been attacked, and I had felt that the war and the raids would never touch us.

But on that day, I knew they could. When Catherine and Paulette and I returned to our house, it was to find my father comforting my mother and Marguerite and Cécile. They had been in the hills when the raiders swept down on Domremy, and had hidden, cowering in terror, till the raid was over.

We soon found that most of our hay had been taken, and our house stripped of its few furnishings. The board and trestles for our table, and the benches worn smooth by many generations of my mother's family, were gone, as was the big chest with all our clothes and bedding. The bunches of herbs and baskets of vegetables, both fresh and dried, had been ripped from the rafters. Gone, too, were our parents' big bed and the cradle my father had made for Catherine long ago. But the straw pallets on which we children slept remained, as if they were not good enough for the thieves. Our packed dirt floor was scuffed and pitted, and the very ashes on the hearth were disturbed; perhaps the thieves had sought valuables there. But of those we had none, save a charm against illness my father kept around his neck, and a knife with a carved bone handle which my mother had from her own mother, and used for spearing meat, cleaning fish, chopping herbs — even for trimming the ragged edges of a wound too rough to grow together. She kept it at her waist, and so it, like Papa's charm, was safe. But the lace-edged linen shawl from my mother's wedding day was nowhere to be found, nor were my father's scythe and his spade and hoe and sharpening stone, and the large pewter dish a grateful gentlewoman had given Maman when she had delivered her of twins.

My father put his arms around my mother, and she sobbed onto his chest while my sisters and I stood helplessly by. Papa wiped my mother's eyes with a corner of her long apron. "Do not fret, *chérie* — dear one," he said gently. "Let us thank the good God that they did not harm us. We have four walls and each other, as do our neighbors. And I see that the church has been saved."

"But we have no beasts!" Maman cried. "We cannot live if we have no cattle, and we can go nowhere if we have no horses. We will all be ruined."

"Hush," said Papa. "We lived despite last summer's locusts, and last winter's wolves, and despite the war. We have wheat and rye in our fields and good grapes in our vineyards, and cabbages and carrots and beans in our gardens, and more vegetables besides." He eased Maman — who was now near her time — onto the floor and settled himself beside her.

"Papa," said Catherine, who like me was still standing, though Marguerite and Cécile had drawn closer to Maman and Papa, cuddling against them for comfort. "Papa, why did they take our cattle?"

"To feed themselves, I suppose," he said, "and the horses to replenish their own. It is the way of armies to take what food and goods they find from whomever they can."

"Since they came to Domremy," I asked, troubled, "does that mean the fighting is getting closer?"

"I do not know, my changeling," he said wearily. "Perhaps."

"What is the fighting, Papa?" Marguerite, who was always curious, asked.

"It is complex, *ma petite* — my little one." He smoothed Marguerite's flaxen hair; not only was she curious, but she was also the most fragile of us all and had nearly died the year before of a fever. "The English, who are from across the sea, want their king, Henry VI, who is but a child no older than Cécile, to be our king as well. Philip, Duke of Burgundy, which many think is rightly part of France, wants this also. There is a treaty, called the Treaty of Troyes, that says this must be, but many loyal French think it is an evil treaty, and want a French king."

"What do you want, Papa?" Marguerite asked.

"A French king, of course. The dauphin, Charles."

"Is he a child no older than me, too?" Cécile asked.

Papa smiled. "No, *ma petite*, he is a grown man. And he *is* our king, for he is the old king's son, and his father and older brothers are dead. But many will not consider him king until he has been properly crowned in the great cathedral in Reims. Here we are all true French men and women," he said, easing my mother aside and standing up, brushing off his loosely flowing shirt, "except in Maxey across the river, where" — he glanced at me severely — "our young changeling often plays at war against the Burgundian boys."

I gasped, for I did not know he knew. Perhaps,

18

though, he said it to distract Maman, for she came to my aid, as always, saying, "She does it only when her work is done, and the exercise makes her strong."

"And the boys make her willful, but" — he sighed, and kissed Maman — "she is indeed strong, and as we have no son . . ."

This was the wrong thing to say, for Maman grew morose again, and hung her head. "Perhaps this one," she said softly, dabbing at her eyes with her apron and resting one hand on her large belly, "will be a son."

But it was not. My youngest sister, Brigitte, was born two days later. At least she waited until Jacques d'Arc and the other village officials had appealed for help to one of the ladies whose family, the Bourlémonts, ruled over our region. By the time Brigette came, the lady's cousin had brought back our animals and most of our goods, and Domremy was normal again.

Brigitte came easily and quickly, which was lucky, for Catherine, as usual, felt squeamish and stayed outside with Papa. Maman told me when to cut the cord and reminded me that my work and hers was not over till the afterbirth had come and Brigitte was well swaddled, and till Catherine had taken her to the church to be baptized. Papa smiled when he saw her, kissed Maman, and said cheerfully, "We will never get them all married, for we will never have enough for their dowries, but neither will we fret in our old age, with so many loving daughters to tend us."

That fall and winter passed calmly, with enough food for feast days, though it was not plentiful. On the first spring day, Maman, Catherine, and I, dressed only in our shifts, took all the family's clothes outdoors in buckets, covered them with ashes, and poured boiling water over them. The next day, we beat them and soaked them more — and the third day, as luck would have it, it rained. But on the fourth, the sun shone, so we spread the clothes to dry. They were ready in time for Laetare Sunday, the fourth Sunday in Lent. We called it Sunday of the Springs, for on that day we always visited the Ladies' Tree, a low-branched beech that grew near two springs above the village vineyards near the Bois Chenu — the oak forest.

The buds had swollen early that year, and the grass was unusually green and tender, fed by early warm rains and sheltered by mist from the River Meuse. I woke on Springs Sunday morning long before Prime and went out to a chorus of birds; already the mist was rising and the day was warming. By the time the bells rang, I had finished my morning chores, and with Catherine was readying the little loaves we would eat when dancing at the Ladies' Tree had made us hungry, and the eggs, and the wine — though we would also drink clear spring water. Maman was smiling and happy that morning; it seemed the whole world was, as we hurried up the long hill behind the village with the other families. Catherine went to join the others of her age, and I walked with Pierre and Henri. Maman had the cloth we would spread under the tree, where she would sit and gossip with the women while Papa and the men played at seeing who could throw a nut most perfectly into a distant basket.

From the hills to the south, near the castle of the Bourlémonts, we could see horses drawing a large cart. Up and down, up and down it went over the hills, now appearing, now disappearing. "Even the great ones must think the sun today is especially bright and warm," Henri observed — for usually the Bourlémont ladies did not come to eat under the Ladies' Tree with us until May.

Marguerite, who was almost over the cough she had suffered from all winter, danced up to me and tugged at my hand. "Maman says you will make me a garland," she told me, "and I may put it in my hair before you put it on the tree."

Pierre, who liked children, picked her up. "If you are very good," he said, "Gabrielle will let you keep the garland in your hair instead of putting it on the tree."

Marguerite pursed her lips as if weighing this carefully. "How good must I be?" she asked at last.

Pierre laughed and put her down, giving her a gentle spank. "As good as my sister Jeannette."

Marguerite pouted. "Then I shall never have a

21

garland, for Maman says that no one has ever been as good as Jeannette."

I laughed then, too, and told her, "You will not have to be quite as good."

All that day we danced and sang and played at ball and leapfrog and blindman's buff, and the boys had races, which Henri always won. The Bourlémont ladies sat a short distance from us. They gave Marguerite, who did earn her garland, a little king's cake. Messire Guillaume, our curate, blessed the Ladies' Tree when we had hung it with flowers. Some said the great beech had once been evil, the home of fairies, and was perhaps still. But Maman said Messire Guillaume's blessing would chase away any that remained.

All that day Jeannette sat apart, quietly, though in the past she had danced and sung with the rest of us. And later, on May Day, when we went again to the Ladies' Tree to cut branches to decorate the village, she did not come with us. On the day before Ascension Day, though, she joined the procession when Messire Guillaume took the cross around the village boundaries, ringing the bells and blessing the crops. When he said the Gospel under the Ladies' Tree, and by the springs and in the fields, she had the same glowing look on her face that Pierre and I had seen before.

Pierre had not spied on her much for a while, but he began to again that summer of 1426. When people who had been burned out of their homes by the soldier-brigands stopped in Domremy, Jeannette was always the first, he said, to give up her bed to them and sleep by the hearth. Each time the bells rang for Mass she would leave whatever she was doing and attend; each time the bells rang for any of the day's offices, from dawn to dusk, Prime to Compline, she would stop and pray. She made garlands for the statue of Our Lady in our village church, and went every Saturday to Notre-Dame-de-Bermont in Greux, and lit candles. Sometimes, Pierre told me, she went there even when she was supposed to be in the fields — so the good Jeannette, although good in one way, was less so in another. She grew more solemn daily, but of course she was growing older, toward the time when most girls wed. Indeed, my own sister Catherine was betrothed to Henri's older brother, and my father, though he grumbled at her dowry, was secretly pleased, I think.

It was two years later, in the summer of 1428, that Jeannette changed even more.

2

I was never sure if the first birth in 1428 was a good omen or a bad one, for it could have been either. The mother was carrying twins, Maman was sure, and indeed this was so. One, a boy, came easily, but the next one would not, until we gave the mother carrot seeds and then ergot. When it finally did come, we could not tell if it would have been a boy or a girl. God had mercifully not allowed it to live; it was flat and thin, more like a drawing than a child, and monstrous, with a demonlike face pointing upward — and demon I feared it was, with one leg curled around what was meant to be its body, and the other absent, and the arms the same way. Maman bade me hasten to the church to baptize the living boy, and when I returned, there was no sign of the monster. I did not ask where it had gone, nor did she tell me.

By this time, Catherine had married Henri's older brother and left our house for his, and Pierre and I had grown apart. He planned to wed our neighbor Jeanne Baudot soon, and Maman said it was not seemly for me to spend much time alone with him.

But one day in May I went into the church to pray for Marguerite, who had been very ill the night before, and I saw Pierre there on his knees, at a time when he would normally have been in the fields. He stood when I came in, looking embarrassed, but I ignored that and, touching his arm, asked, "What is it, my friend? You seem distraught."

He gave me a look I had never seen from him. Then he shook his head and went outside.

I followed. "Is it Jeanne Baudot?" I asked as gently as I could.

Again he shook his head. "No, not Jeanne," he said. "My sister Jeannette. She is getting worse. Every evening at Compline she speaks to the thing that is not there and seems to listen to it as well; she goes to the Bois Chenu and the Ladies' Tree to meet it. I have heard her many times, for I have followed her. I do not think our mother knows, or our father, or anyone, and I dare not speak of it to them."

"Is it so wrong?" I asked.

"I cannot tell if it is God or the Devil who comes to her," he said, the words bursting out of him, "but something does *come*, I am sure of it. I heard her say to the thing, 'No, I cannot; I am only a poor country girl and know nothing of armies or of riding a charger into battle.'"

I stared at him, and heard myself whisper,

"What?" She must be mad, I thought, or Pierre is right and the Devil tempts her, for God would not ask a girl to go to battle!

Pierre turned to me; he looked stricken, as if he had seen Death. "I have heard her say this about armies and battles many times. I have also heard her promise the invisible creature that she will remain a virgin. Gabrielle . . ." He hesitated, and dropped his voice, as if he feared he would be overheard. "Gabrielle, I have heard her promise that she will have the dauphin crowned!"

I must confess I almost laughed aloud, for this was even more absurd than leading an army: a peasant girl, one grown up among us, to have the royal dauphin crowned when he and all his nobles could or would not!

"There are prophecies," Pierre said, his face so troubled that it quelled my laughter, "saying that a maid from an oak forest near Lorraine will save France."

"We are not quite in Lorraine," I pointed out to him.

"But we are near," he said. "And we do have an oak forest. Not long ago Jeannette went to Vaucouleurs," he continued, "with our married cousin Durand Laxart. She told our parents she was going with him to his home in Burey-le-Petit to help his wife, but when she came back she told me she had gone with him instead to Vaucouleurs. I fear her going there had to do with what she hears each night when the bells ring."

I still could not believe it, so I said, "I will go with you tonight at Compline, to listen."

And so that night we hid near the Ladies' Tree. This time I felt a tightness in my throat and in my head when I heard Jeannette and saw her.

She dropped to her knees when the bells sounded, and her face had that glowing look I had seen before. Her hair fell back when she raised her head, and the dying light painted silver edges on its blackness. "Dearest Saint Catherine," I heard her say, "blessed Saint Michael, and Saint Margaret. If you wish me to go again, I shall go. But the dauphin's own captain in Vaucouleurs, Robert de Baudricourt, refused me; he would not give me men, or a war-horse, and he laughed when I said I would take the dauphin to Reims to have him crowned."

She paused a moment, her eyes skyward; then frowned and went on.

"Do you not think, beloved saints, that another might be better suited to this purpose than I? I can ride my father's mare bareback and run quickly in my dress, but I have never sat on a saddle or ridden a charger, or worn armor, or handled a sword. I would do God's will in all things, but I am doubtful of this. I am not a knight or a soldier."

She fell silent then, as if listening, and I strained my ears, but all I could hear was the wind and the fading echo of the church bells.

Beside me, Pierre was white and still.

Jeannette spoke again, bowing her head as if in obedience. "Very well. I will go again . . . Yes, you did tell me he would refuse at first; I do remember. And I remember you said I would know how to wear armor, and how to do what must be done . . . Yes, yes, I will have faith. Forgive me that I doubted, gentle saints. I will not doubt again, I promise."

"A madwoman or . . ." said Pierre when Jeannette had gone home and at last we could move our cramped legs.

"Or a saint herself," I finished, shaken and beginning to believe that there might be good reason after all for Jeannette's growing piety. I could not doubt that something came to her, and it certainly did not seem evil. It seemed impossible for such a thing to happen in our own village, and yet I, too, had heard the prophecies Pierre had mentioned. And I had been told of people in other places who heard saints' voices, and spoke to them, and became saints themselves. Such a thing could happen, of course. It filled me with awe that it might be happening here, and to someone I knew.

But happening, of course, it was.

That summer, when the people of Neufchâteau had sent their cattle to graze on our valley's rich grass as they did every year, the war came close to us again. We could not protect both their beasts and ours in our island stronghold, so we fled with all the livestock to within Neufchâteau's protecting walls, and decided to remain there, grazing our herds nearby, till it was safe to go home.

Neufchâteau, with its wide market square and its cloth merchants, its Franciscan monastery, and its grand churches, was the only town I had ever seen. Jeannette and her family stayed at an inn run by a widow everyone called La Rousse — the Redhead — but we lodged with my mother's cousin, and there were so many to help with the chores that I had time to explore Neufchâteau's narrow streets: the street of the bakers, and the cloth merchants' street, and the street where they sold meats to those who had the money to buy. The houses were large and ornate in comparison with those I knew, crossed with timbers and showing stone or plaster walls between, red or brown, or yellowish white. I felt trapped among them, for I could often reach out my hands and touch the houses on both sides of the streets, and their upper stories jutted out and nearly met over my head as I walked. Soon I was eager to return to the Meuse valley's fresh air and open fields, and was glad when at last we all set out for home.

But when we neared our village, Henri, who had run ahead, gave a terrible cry. Soon we saw the reason, and stood aghast at the sight, though perhaps we should have expected the destruction that lay before us. The d'Arcs' stone house still stood, as did the mayor's and a few houses at the far edge of the village, ours among them. But of others there was nothing left save ashes. At first we thought the church was safe, for its stone walls were intact, but when we went inside, we saw that all of its contents had been burned, broken, or stolen. The oats and rye and barley were gone from the fields, and our small crop of wheat as well, and there were few cabbages or carrots left in our gardens. We stared at the naked fields — Maman, Papa, my sisters, and I — and Maman, who was again with child, wept as if she would never smile again.

Once more it was Papa who cheered us all by saying, "They did not harm us ourselves; we are strong and well, and we will start again." That seemed the view of everyone else also. For the rest of that summer, we rebuilt the houses and the inside of the church, and did without the cooking pots and baskets and sticks of furniture that had been stolen or burned. We plowed again, the men at the plows and we women breaking the clods. The men planted the few remaining seeds, and we all prayed for rain to make them sprout and a long warm fall to make them grow.

One day I came in from gathering herbs to find Maman and my sister Catherine laughing together by the fire while they spun. I smiled, for I had not heard Maman laugh since the raid. "What makes you so merry?" I asked as I fell to sorting the herbs by the fire.

"Oh," said Catherine, "have you not heard? Surely Pierre has told you about his sister, the fair Jeannette, who wants to be an old maid!"

I remembered, then, Jeannette's promise to stay chaste. I knew that if she had been chosen by God for some great deed, she would not be able to wed, for the truest servants of God must remain virgin. If she had now made her promise known to others, could it mean that she was indeed the maid of the prophecies?

But aloud I only said, "No, Pierre has told me nothing. What is the news?"

"Why," said Catherine, wiping the laughter-tears from her eyes, "it is said that she was visited by a young man in Neufchâteau while we were all there, and that she promised to wed him — and high time, too, one would think!"

"Catherine," said Maman severely, nodding toward me, "many a good maid weds late. We are not all as fortunate as you."

"Oh, la, it is true, of course," Catherine said quickly. "But in the end Mademoiselle Jeannette refused this man, breaking her promise, and so she was brought to court, in Toul. Think of it, a law court, with Jeannette in her plain red dress, standing before the learned churchmen in their long robes, and saying" — here Catherine put on a high, squeaky voice, nothing like Jeannette's sweet one — " 'No, honored sirs, I do not mean to wed; I told him I would not, and I will not, and there you have it!' Can you not just see her?"

My mother smiled again, and laughed, but

looked nervously at me, and did not laugh as hard as she had been laughing earlier.

"What happened then?" I asked, tying together a bunch of parsley.

Catherine shrugged, spreading her hands, palms out. "I know not," she said, "but since the maid is still unwed, and since no angry man has come to carry her away, I suppose the action against her failed."

I smiled, and turned back to my herbs, rejoicing secretly, for it cheered me to hear of a maid who refused to wed, whatever her reason. And in a court! Perhaps I had misjudged Jeannette; she had never seemed strong to me before. But I admired her now, for I myself had secretly vowed not to wed. Had my family been wealthy, I would have begged to go into a convent, where I could learn to read, and then I would study what books there were about healing. I had no hope of that, for my father could not pay a nun's dowry. But, though I had told no one, I had resolved to learn to tend the sick beyond what my mother knew to do. Jeannette's refusal gave me courage.

That autumn the weather was not as gentle as we wished, and we constantly watched for raiders. We did manage to grow a small amount of grain and to harvest it before the rain came — rain so cold it froze on the houses as it fell, and formed long spears of ice.

That year waned and turned, and my mother's

time came early in 1429. Maman was cheerful when the pains began, and as she sat waiting between them, she said, smiling, "Perhaps next time, my changeling, it will be reversed, and it will be you crouching to deliver and me below, waiting to show you your own little one."

"Perhaps," I said, though despite my love of children, I hoped it would not be, for I knew I would have no time for them were I to perfect my art as healer. I had been hoping that I could travel someday to a great monastery and learn what I could from the monks, if they would teach me.

Once more the birth went quickly. I barely looked at the child when I cut the cord, and then, cleaning him, I nearly dropped him — yes, *him*, for at last Maman had a son!

"It is a boy!" I shouted, so loudly that Papa and my sisters came running in. As Papa seized the baby, who screamed lustily, tears coursed down his cheeks, and down Maman's as well. Paulette and Marguerite and Cécile — Brigitte too — jumped up and down for happiness, shouting, "A boy! A boy!"

I turned back to Maman, surprised at the tears — sad tears, unlike my parents' — that burned my own eyes. Was I not happy that at last Papa had an heir, and I a brother?

I was, but I fled to the Ladies' Tree and let my tears mingle with the cold rain, weeping for my-self and my sisters, my real sisters and my sisters-in-sex — for I saw clearly then that no one rejoiced at our births as at the births of sons. That seemed wrong, for without women to bear sons, and nurture them, and heal them, there would be no sons at all. So was not the one worth at least as much as the other?

3

I spoke to no one of my feelings, but I think my mother knew them. It would have been hard for anyone close to me not to, for thinking of my brother's position had made me see that to which I had been blind before.

But soon, Maman began instructing my younger sisters to do much of my household work, and she taught me more healing lore. She herself dreaded some of it, she told me, like the putting together of broken bones and the stanching of bleeding wounds, fearing she would hurt more than heal. So it was that one day when she was called to a child who had fallen from a loft and hurt his arm, I went with her, carrying her basket of boneset and crushed feverfew and lemon balm in case the child was faint as well. He was screaming with pain when we arrived, and Maman's face grew pale when she saw the arm, bent back in the wrong direction. Her mouth tightened into a firm line that I knew was to disguise her fear.

But the child's pain and terror pushed all fear from my mind. It was as if I did not exist except as a means of helping, almost as if I were a vessel into which God poured, if not knowledge, then at least a sense of what must be done. I knew what an uninjured arm looked like, and had felt the bones of my own shoulder to discover how they went together, as indeed I had studied my whole body in secret to understand how it worked. "Let me," I said quietly to Maman, and when she moved willingly aside, I smiled at the child and said, "I must touch your arm, little one, and it will I think hurt very much worse for a short while and then I think it will be very much better. At least this is what I hope and pray," I added, looking up at the child's worried parents.

They nodded, and the mother held him as I felt his shoulder with my fingers, keeping my eyes closed so that my fingers could see. It was as I had thought. The part of the arm that fits into the shoulder had come out; it did not seem broken off so much as twisted and loose. The child screamed louder when I touched him, exploring, but I had to close my ears and my heart to that — though afterward Maman said I had set my teeth as if to prevent adding my scream to his. I felt the part that had come out, and felt as much as I could of where it belonged. Then I pressed it with the heel of one hand and with the other supported the place in which I knew it should fit. And — I still thank God for this, for had it gone

36

wrong I might never have continued with my work — the bone slipped neatly back.

The child stopped mid-scream and stared at me as if I were not human.

"Is it better?" I asked him, daring to smile. "Hmm?"

He nodded, as if he could not speak, and his mother, with a cry, seized me and hugged me close. *"Merci, merci,"* she said. "Thank you, thank you! It is a miracle your daughter has wrought, madame," she said to Maman.

"She has a gift for healing," Maman said modestly, accepting the eggs the father gave us in payment.

Once we were outside, though, she hugged me, too.

That same winter, Jeannette's friend Mengette told me Jeannette had gone away again with her cousin Laxart, secretly, without telling her parents — "for fear," Mengette said, "that they would stop her." And then Pierre told me that when the d'Arcs had found her gone, Jacques was angry and Isabelle worried, and that word had come to them that Jeannette was staying with a family in Vaucouleurs. "She is determined to see Robert de Baudricourt," he said, "and it seems no one can stop her."

Soon all the village was talking of it, and then Pierre said that she *had* seen Baudricourt and that he had given her a horse to ride and men to follow her. "And armor," Pierre told me outside the church one cold February day. "Laxart came to us and said that she has been given men's clothes — leggings, a tunic, hose — and that she has a horse that cost 16 francs; she will ride on it to Chinon to see the dauphin."

"Men's clothes!" I said in awe and envy, lifting the skirt of my red dress, on which I had often tripped.

Then Jeanne Baudot, whom Pierre was soon to marry and who stood there with us, said, "But surely that is a sin, for a woman to wear men's clothes?"

"If a woman is to ride among men as a soldier," Pierre said sternly, "she had better wear men's clothes. You do not know what beasts men are, my Jeanne." He slipped an arm around her waist and she giggled, raising her eyebrows at me.

"And you, Pierre," she asked, flirting. "Are you a beast?"

He laughed, and pulled her closer to him, and I thought it best to leave them. But all the rest of that day I thought about Jeannette, remembering the prophecies and the time at the Ladies' Tree when we had heard her say that she did not know how to wear armor or ride in a saddle or lead an army.

That night I thrashed on my straw pallet, and more than once Paulette and Marguerite beside me grumbled and asked me to be still or get up. When at last I slept, I dreamed I myself rode a war-horse, in armor, and held a sword. I woke drenched in sweat despite the cold, and knew it was a sinful dream, for no saint had come to me and told me I must do this. And yet, though I knew Jeannette was more pious than I, I felt much more suited than she to lead an army into war. It was I, not Jeannette, who hated to spin and cook; it was I who had played with boys; it was I, alone among the girls of our village, who had fought the boys of Maxey.

But I had not been chosen.

For days I went morosely through my chores, pretending to ignore the rumors that now flew thicker than blackbirds around the village. Jeannette's name was on all lips, with shock and disbelief as well as praise — and under it all, a spark of hope for France.

Only Pierre and my mother seemed to know of my distress, Pierre because he felt it, too, often saying that he wished to go with her, and my mother because she, as always, saw into my heart.

Later that cold spring, Maman said to me, "What do you think, Gabrielle? Jeannette's mother tells me that she herself will go soon to Le Puy, far to the south, to pay homage to the Black Virgin in the cathedral there. The Virgin, Isabelle says, is a famous statue of Our Lady, but with black skin, very old and very holy. And this year, since Annunciation Day falls on Good Friday, it is a year of Jubilee in Le Puy. Many pilgrims will go there, and Isabelle told me she will go herself and would welcome a woman's companionship on the journey. I cannot go, nor can any other wife, it seems, and Isabelle's own daughter must be in Chinon by now, if what everyone says is true." Maman gave me a little poke, as well she might, for I was still mystified. Her words seemed more than gossip, but I could not yet tell what lay beneath them.

"Isabelle will stay," she continued, "as pilgrims do, at inns and monasteries along the way." At this her eyes sparkled like a mischievous child's and she poked me again. "Monasteries, Gabrielle, where the monks grow herbs and study healing!"

I held my breath then. "A woman's companionship?" I managed to ask.

"*Oui,*" she answered, smiling. "Yes. I think I could spare you here if you would like to go, and if your father agrees."

And so it was that I went with Isabelle Romée to Le Puy, and my long journey and my new life began.

PART TWO

4

It was a blustery March morning when we left. Maman gave me her bone-handled knife, the one my grandmother had given her. It seemed too great a gift, but when I protested, she smiled and brushed aside my hair, saying, "You will have more need of it than I. And it will remind you of home."

Soon we were off, me with a square of warm woolen cloth over my shoulders, and a small purse at my waist containing a cross blessed with holy water and a bit of wormwood against fatigue. My mother added a heavy loaf of dark *rousset* bread to the flat twice-baked travelers' loaves Isabelle had put in the pouches worn by Gray Mist, the old horse that carried our goods: sheepskins against the cold, a little common wine, my good dress and Isabelle's, pig's grease for wounds, betony against the Devil, and yarrow for wounds and ills of the head and stomach. Isabelle had our money, a few *sous* and *deniers*.

We left with tears for our families who stayed

43

behind, and high spirits for the adventure. By now I knew it was not only the Jubilee that sent Isabelle to Le Puy, but also her desire to pray for Jeannette there in that holy place. Our guide and protector along the way was a stout, jolly friend of Messire Guillaume — Brother Antoine, who had provided Gray Mist. Brother Antoine was something of a dandy, for instead of a friar's simple garb, he wore a long embroidered robe and leather platforms under his soft pointed shoes.

We went first to Neufchâteau, where we purchased candles for the nights we would spend in monasteries, and salt herring to eat with the *rousset* bread. And there, too, we found many other pilgrims preparing to travel to Le Puy. I had paid little heed to the pilgrims I had seen pass through our village, but now I studied them, and found them to be like most people, young and old, fat and thin, sick and well — though perhaps there were more afflicted among them than in most other groups.

That first night we stopped at the hut of a poor hermit, Brother Antoine's cousin, and I fell asleep wrapped in my sheepskin on the rough dirt floor, dreaming happily of the journey to come.

The days passed, each different from the one before in weather, company, the land, and where we slept. We often walked with other pilgrims, sometimes lodging with them and sometimes

44

lodging or camping by ourselves. The first night that we slept outside, wrapped in our sheepskins at the edge of a field, I could not find a way to lie that would let me sleep, and I spent the whole night shivering and trying to see pictures in the stars. But after that, I found it easier. I liked the freshness of the air and the freedom of lying alone instead of with others, as at home or in an inn.

Gray Mist plodded over land both flat and hilly, passing newly plowed fields and fields lying ready for the plow, and through forests where we lay awake around our fire waiting for wolves or boars that never came, and over mountain passes where we trembled at the thought of brigands whom we never met. But at last Gray Mist faltered, slowing and stumbling, so Brother Antoine led us off our path to an abbey he knew, high on a hill. "Here they have many horses," he said. "And a fine farm as well. The monks may let us exchange Gray Mist for a younger horse."

We toiled up the rocky path, and waited while Brother Antoine knocked at the gate, rousing the porter's dog, who stuck his head out of a hole in the gate's wall to bark at us.

"Oho," said the porter, whose face was very red above his brown robe. "Brother Antoine, you old scoundrel — what, and with women, too? I know not if I should let you in; for all I know it is Satan you seek now and not the Lord."

Isabelle looked alarmed but I could see the

man was joking and I liked him immediately —
his dog as well, who bent his spotted head down
to lick the hand I offered him.

"Now, now, Denis," said Brother Antoine, his
face creased with smiles, "for all *I* know you and
your Cerberus have already admitted Satan, for I
hear great tales of the merry monks who live
here, and of the gaming that goes on behind
these walls."

"Well, then," replied the porter, "it would be
well for me to admit you, so you can see that
these tales are lies and that we are still as sober a
lot here as we ever were." Chuckling, he opened
the gate to let us in.

It was sunset, the hour of Vespers, and the
grounds were quiet except for the warm laughter
of the friar and monk as they embraced, and the
thumping of their hands against each other's
backs and of the gate dog's tail against the wall. I
reached down again and stroked him, and his tail
moved faster.

"So, mademoiselle," said the porter, moving
out of Brother Antoine's embrace and smiling at
me, "you are a friend to animals, I see. Do not be
deceived by this limb of Satan. He is merely
looking for food, not love."

"Then," I said, reaching into the purse at my
waist, "I shall give him food."

"Gabrielle," Isabelle said softly, admonishing
me.

"I will not give him much," I whispered. But I
did give him one small scrap of flatbread.

46

To our right, the porter showed us, was the hostel for pilgrims and other wayfarers. It was a large, long building, with a door at each end, and a window above each door. To the left were more stone buildings, also low and long — the wayfarers' chapel, the porter said, where we could pray, and the bakehouse, from which, even at this late hour, came such a smell of warm bread that it made me nearly faint from hunger, and I almost regretted the scrap I had given the dog.

Across was the abbey church, larger than ours in Domremy but not as large as Saint-Nicolas in Neufchâteau, and nearby were the cloister and chapter house and other private places. The farm was beyond the hostel and, the porter said, the infirmary was there as well, for monks who were ill, with the herb garden close by. I looked up at that and boldly asked, "Might we pilgrims look at how you cultivate your herbs, or see the infirmary?" At this Isabelle blushed crimson and said, in a hushed voice, "Gabrielle!" Then, turning to the porter, she said, "*Pardon, s'il vous plaît* — pardon, please — monsieur; she is but a poor village girl and knows not the ways of the world."

The porter smiled indulgently and said, "I am afraid you cannot see the infirmary, mademoiselle; women are not permitted there. And though *I* would let you see our garden, Brother François, who tends it, is jealous and guards his secrets as a dragon is said to guard treasure." He winked then, and bent closer. "But you would see little in any case; it is merely scratched-up dirt with a few greening patches, this early in the year. Come," he went on, straightening up, "you must all be weary. Let us settle you in the hostel."

We were crowded there, in the one long room, with many other pilgrims, women at one end and men at the other, with a smoking fire in between, and fleas hopping from person to person. So we sat outside to eat, and we ate better than we had so far, for the monks gave us bread, made with oats and rye, that was softer than our flat travelers' loaves. We had cheese also, and onions, and even a soup, made, I think, of barley and dried peas. They gave us *bochet* to drink, which they called hydromel, made of fermented honey and water. I had tasted it only once or twice, on special days. Theirs was sweeter than the drink I knew, and I liked it well.

We stayed outside for a while after eating, for the night was warmer than it had been, and dry, and Isabelle told of her pilgrimage to Rome.

I could not sleep when we went inside, what with the night sounds of snoring, gnashing teeth, and breathing in many rhythms, and the night smells, too, and the itching I had from the fleas. At last I went outside and across to the monks' chapel, although we had been warned that this was not allowed. But I had seen the wayfarers' chapel earlier, and it was a humble church like those I knew, and this other one was not. I could not think that wishing to see a church was sinful.

The chapel was very large and beautiful, with a high vaulted ceiling and a lovely statue of our Blessed Mother, gazing sweetly at the Infant in her arms. I thought Jeannette would like to pray to her, were she here, and I tried to pray also, but instead of a proper prayer all I could say was how happy she looked to have such a fine plump baby, and that I hoped she had had an easy time. Then I thought it might be wrong to speak so familiarly to the Blessed Mother, so I turned to leave, but I heard a sound like groaning, coming from the cloister off the chapel. I followed the sound, and saw a young monk, a boy my age, near a dormant rosebush in the cloister's central garden. He was running, but without moving forward, so that he merely bobbed up and down, up and down, panting and groaning with the effort. It was a comical sight, and I could not keep myself from laughing at it.

The boy started at the sound of my laugh, and looked straight at me.

5

I did not know what to do. People do not like to be laughed at, and this boy was a monk, at least he wore monk's garb.

The boy froze where he stood, and stared as if at an apparition, a smile playing at his lips — or a grimace; I was not sure which. "Who are you?" he demanded of me. "You look — like a peasant girl. How came you here?" He studied me with eyes that were huge and softly brown like a doe's, and dabbed at his sweating forehead with his wide sleeve, which, I could see in the moonlight, was none too clean.

"I *am* a peasant girl," I told him with as much dignity as I could muster. "I am Gabrielle de Domremy, a pilgrim and healer and midwife, accompanying a woman from my village to Le Puy for the Jubilee. I came to the chapel by stealth, for pilgrims are not admitted to it or to the cloister."

"No, they are not," the boy said, but by now he really was smiling. "Did anyone see you?"

"I think not. What were you doing? Are you a monk?"

He sat down on a stone bench, and gestured for me to sit beside him. "I am called Louis, Louis d'Avallon, I suppose, for that is where I am from, and I am a novice here, because that is what my father wishes for me, though I hate it. I am my father's youngest son, and he does not know what else to do with me. My oldest brother is at war, and my next brother manages my father's lands with my father, and my sister is married. That leaves me." He wiped his forehead once more.

"Why do you hate it?" I asked him, astonished. "It is beautiful here — so peaceful."

"Too peaceful," he said fiercely. "I would rather be at war. I was exercising because I am made to sit still all day, indoors. It is very dull."

I nodded, for of course I agreed that it would be. I told him a little about life in Domremy and about my sisters and my infant brother, and how this pilgrimage was more an adventure for me than a holy journey.

"We are both sinners, then, Gabrielle de Domremy," he said, smiling again when I had finished. "I would go with you on your pilgrimage. I would do anything to leave this place."

"Then come with us," I said, surprising myself with my boldness.

He looked startled, then thoughtful.

"Is it not true," I went on, "that if one has no vocation for a cloistered life, one may leave it?"

"It is true," he said, "if one has not yet taken final vows, as I have not. But my father has paid many *écus* for me to be here. And the abbot tells me to be patient, that one cannot know one's vocation until after one has stayed for — well, for a long time."

"Perhaps," I said, feeling mischief rising in me, as if I were with Pierre, "some people are so unsuited for a cloistered life that they must leave sooner. For the good of the order," I added.

"Perhaps." He got up and began pacing. I followed him in under the cloister's stone arches, where he sat on another bench. "Perhaps some people can serve God better by being out of a cloister than in it."

"Brother Antoine, who travels with us," I said quickly, "is a holy man of God, and he goes about in the whole world. He . . ." I stopped, for I had no idea what else Brother Antoine did.

Louis's soft brown eyes had fire in them now. "I *will* go with you," he said. "Perhaps if I leave a letter for the abbot, and tell him that I can do God's work better outside . . ." He frowned; now I was staring at him. "What is it?" he asked.

"You — you said 'leave a letter,' " I answered, barely able to conceal my excitement. "You know how to write?"

"Yes, and read, too," he said cheerfully, as if it were a matter of no importance. "Why?"

"Because," I told him, "I would give anything to be able to read. If I could read, I could study the books that have been written about healing, for I have heard there are some . . ."

"Oh, yes," Louis said airily. "I was copying one just the other day, in the scriptorium. That is why I must sit still all day. It told of certain herbs. Would you like to see it?"

My heart raced, and I could not speak, so I merely nodded.

"Come," Louis held out his hand and put his finger to his lips. "Be very quiet." He started to lead me inside, but then he stopped, saying, "No, it is too dangerous. You stay here. I will bring the book to you — no, I will bring you a sheet I have copied, for the book itself is large and heavy. Wait."

He disappeared, and I sat under the shadowy arches for what seemed a lifetime. Suppose a sleepless monk came outside and found me? By the time Louis returned, I was soaked with fear-sweat, and very cold.

But I forgot it all when he slipped a large parchment page from under his robe, and took me out into the moonlight.

I do not know which moved me more, the gold-and-red-and-blue-and-green drawings of plant tendrils twining in the borders of the page, or the detailed rendering of a sprig of agrimony in the center, with its toothed leaves, or the intricate vines weaving through an angular black-outlined thin gold shape in a square at the beginning, or the rows of black marks that I knew must be words flowing evenly across the page.

"Agrimony," I breathed.

Louis looked startled. "So you can read after all," he said, disappointment in his voice.

"No, no," I told him, pointing to the drawing in the center. "It is a plant I know. My mother uses it for certain pains of women."

"Yes, of course," he said, sounding relieved. "And here it says to use it also for knife cuts, and the fits that seize infants."

I looked in wonder at the black marks; could they indeed convey so much?

"See," said Louis gently, "here are the letters for agrimony. This" — he pointed to the design within the square and traced the gold of it — "this is A, decorated grandly because it is the first letter of the word. The first letter on a page is often thus, dressed as nobility, you could say. The smaller letters after it are *g, r, i*." He pointed to them as he named them. "And *m*, and . . ."

But then a bell rang inside. "Matins," Louis said, snatching the page from me and rolling it up. "Hurry, Gabrielle; you must leave quickly, for the monks will soon come to prayers in the chapel." He paused, tucking the rolled page back under his robe. "When do you leave for Le Puy?"

"I am not sure. Today, I think, unless Isabelle — that is the pilgrim of whom I spoke — wishes to rest. But I think it is far enough still so that we may not linger."

Louis nodded. "I will try to come with you.

Look for me near the big tree outside the gate. If I can come, I will wait for you there. Go" — and I could hear footsteps in the distance — "go quickly."

For the rest of that early morning, I wondered nervously if he would come. But when we left, a while after Prime as the sky was lightening, he was there, wearing, instead of his monk's robes, a nobleman's hose and a short robe lined with fur. The hose were baggy and stained, and the robe was old and threadbare at the elbows of its wide sleeves, as if he had already journeyed in those clothes, and been careless of them.

Isabelle was at first afraid and then cross. Louis told her what he had told me, and then said, "And when I went to the abbot after prayers at Matins, and told him how I felt and that I wished to go to Le Puy, he blessed me and let me go, because it is, after all, a holy pilgrimage."

Isabelle looked as if she did not believe him. "What of your father, monsieur?" she asked. "Will he not be angry?"

Louis scuffed the long toe of his leather shoe into the ground and said, "My father is not fond of me, madame; he loves my brothers more."

I could see the sympathy in Isabelle's eyes as she turned to Brother Antoine as if in supplication, and he said, "Well, well, the boy is a man, it appears, able to make a man's choices, and able to accept his father's wrath if that is to be. Perhaps for the abbot the important thing is the money that the abbey has already received; if the father cares not for his son, what duty is owed may have been discharged well enough. We cannot prevent him from traveling with us, in any case, if he wishes."

At that, Isabelle nodded — and so now our party was four instead of three. We had a new horse, too, from the monks, a young mare who was gentle and able to go faster than Gray Mist, whom I was nonetheless sad to leave. I found a dried apple for him before we left, and bade goodbye to the gate dog as well.

At first as we traveled, Isabelle seemed restrained when she remembered Louis was of noble blood. But he acted so much like us, and was so pleasant and considerate of her, bidding her rest often and fetching water for her, that she soon accepted him. He bought wine for us all, too, out of his small sack of *écus*, kept back from those his father had given him for his journey to the abbey. We told him more about Domremy, and about Jeannette, and he made us laugh with stories of his clumsiness, describing his attempts at matching his older brothers in lance thrusts and sword-play. "I was better than they at the learning that comes from books," he said, "which is why my father sent me to the abbey. I did not ever mind learning, but I wished to be a scholar-knight, not just a scholar, and perhaps one day that is what I shall be, now that you have

56

freed me." He bowed to Isabelle then, and she blushed.

As we neared Le Puy, the air felt cooler. The way grew steeper and the road thicker with other pilgrims, all hurrying to reach the cathedral by Good Friday — Annunciation Day — and eager to behold the blessed Black Virgin. There were more evergreens now, I noticed. We stumbled on rocks as we climbed hills and mountains, and my knees often felt as if they would collapse as we went up, or twist apart as we went down, and my feet slipped dangerously in my wooden *sabots*.

And so it was that one day in Holy Week, when we were at our most tired and hungry and footsore, and had little bread or salt herring left to eat and nothing fresh, and when I thought my right foot would fall off from the blister that I could not seem to heal, and when the road was thronged with silent, plodding pilgrims — on a day when I found myself thinking I had been God's own fool to leave Domremy — on such a day, on a sudden, as the sun neared its highest point over our heads and made Isabelle and me shed our woolen shawls despite the cool air and give them to the mare to carry — a great shout rose from the front of the line, up a small hill.

"What is it?" Brother Antoine asked wearily.

"Shall I run up and see?" asked Louis.

"Yes, do," said Isabelle.

When Louis came back to us, his dirty face was lightened by his smile. "Shall I tell you?" he teased. "Or will you wait yourselves to see a wonder?"

"Oh, tell us," said Brother Antoine crossly, "lest we think you made this wonder up out of your own mind."

"Surely," said Louis, "the crowd ahead would not be shouting with joy at a wonder that was only in my mind."

"Louis," said Isabelle, "if you do not tell us quickly, Gabrielle and I will faint from curiosity."

"I faint?" I said, feigning shocked anger. "I shall never faint, no matter what I see!"

You see how familiar we had all become with one another!

Louis drew us aside to a heap of stones which perhaps had once been a roadside shrine, now fallen apart from neglect or vandals. "It is a marvel, truly," he said, "and I am told it means we are near Le Puy at last."

"And?" urged Brother Antoine, rubbing his foot. "And? What is this marvel? It had better be a fine one, Louis, for I have seen many marvels and can judge them well. If this be not one, I shall — I shall break your head!"

Louis clutched his head in mock horror. I could see both of them were enjoying this banter, but I could also see that Isabelle, who was seated on the ground by now, was tired, and needed reassurance. "If you do not say quickly," I told Louis, "I shall spoil your tale by running forward myself and looking, and then I will have the telling of it."

58

"Very well," said Louis. He knelt and took Isabelle's hands in his. "Up ahead," he said softly, "growing out of the earth and reaching toward Heaven, is a pillar of stone — a very thin mountain — upon the very top of which is a church, scraping against the sky. And a little farther off, high but not as high, rises a great cathedral, and beyond it another pillar-mountain. All those in front of us say the thin mountains and the cathedral are in Le Puy!"

Isabelle closed her eyes, and leaned back against me, for I was standing behind her. "Jesus be praised," she said. "We are there at last!"

6

We were not, of course, quite there, for we had some distance still to walk. By the time we arrived, the sun was well down. We sheltered as best we could outside the city walls, for the gates were closed and there was such a flood of pilgrims that it was said the gatekeepers would open for no one till well after Prime. It was cold, too, the colder because the city was so high. We huddled against one another near our poor fire, warmed more by our sheepskins and the presence of so many people than by its small flames.

At last it was daylight, and the bells rang for Prime. And when the gates were opened, we walked, with all the thousands of others, into the city.

How shall I describe it? The sun was bright on the thin stone mountains that Louis had said rose above the town, and also on the front of the cathedral. The cathedral stood far above us at the head of many steps, which we could hardly see under the crowds that climbed them. Some pilgrims walked upright, others went on their knees, and those who could not do either crawled on their stomachs, pulling themselves up painfully, in constant danger of being trampled.

The cathedral itself was massive, with three arched doorways on a flat façade, framed in alternating light and dark cut stones, the light ones dazzling in the sun. The crowd pressed hard against us as we crossed the large square at the bottom of the steps. For every few pilgrims there was someone selling food or relics or medals. But it was the beggars I noticed most, holding out their grimy hands as we passed, and inching forward on gnarled sticks to tug at people's mantles and cloaks. One woman, dressed in rags, her face pockmarked and her limbs twisted, knelt in our path, and Isabelle gave her bread. On all sides, it seemed, there were people suffering from diseases I knew nothing of. "Do not weep for them, Gabrielle," Louis said to me as I reached in my purse for something to give a runny-nosed child with only one arm. "Most are as well and as strong as you and I; I saw many in the cities I passed on my way to the abbey. If you followed them to their beggar inns tonight, as I did once, you would see them unstrap their bent legs and arms and rub the life back into them." Gently, he moved my hand away from my purse. But I reached in again when he turned aside, and gave the child my few crumbs, for she looked honest enough to me, and I despaired of there being cures for so many who were ill or maimed.

There were other folk, too, of sinister appearance and lewd glance. I clung closely to Isabelle when one, laughing and leering, reached a ruddy hand out to me. Isabelle scowled at the churl and pulled me away. "It is all right, little one," she whispered as we began the long slow climb up the cathedral steps. "Stay nearby and you will not be harmed."

Awe overtook my fear as we climbed, and increased and overwhelmed me when we went inside.

Again, how shall I describe it? I have seen many cathedrals since then, but though some others have rolled together in my mind and become as one, this cathedral remains apart. Inside, it was huge, like a whole world within walls. People surged around us, praying, so there was a constant murmur of voices, broken only by a muted cry when someone was overcome with feeling. What pain humanity must suffer, I thought, with so many here to ask for health or to buy their way into Heaven, or to beg safety from the world's evils, or freedom from sin.

High windows set with colored glass caused the sun to cast red and blue light-jewels with drops of silver onto the stout carved columns that rose to the ceiling, which was painted with wondrous scenes; my neck ached and I grew dizzy studying them. "That is Saint Michael," said Isabelle, who must have been following my glance, "and there are the Women and the Tomb. See, you can find Mary Magdalene there, and there the mother of James, called Mary, and Salome — and the blessed angel, there."

I nodded, and tried to swallow so I could speak, but my neck was stretched so tight that I could not. By the time I turned toward her, the crowd had flowed forward and us with it. Isabelle was on her knees before a wide white altar trimmed with gold. Again I was speechless, thinking how poor and humble our altar at Domremy was beside this one, and wondering which pleased God more. I knelt, and looked up — and then at last I saw the famous Black Virgin, enthroned almost at the altar's peak. Isabelle smiled and squeezed my hand.

"She was brought from Egypt," a man near me murmured reverently, "the blessed Black Virgin. Think of it! All that way!"

"No, no," whispered another man, younger, and balanced on a rough crutch. "From Palestine; I have a monk's word on it."

But a toothless old woman next to me winked and puffed garlic in my face as she said, "Do not believe them, my dear. The Black Virgin was given to the cathedral by Saint Louis himself!"

The argument did not matter to me, only the beauty, and the strangeness of the rich brown faces — not really black — of the Blessed Mother and her Infant, polished and glowing above their red robes.

Both Virgin and Infant wore jeweled crowns, and atop each crown perched a small blue bird. I smiled to see them there, as if nesting, and when

I caught Louis's eye, I could see he was smiling as well. I wanted to speak of them, but with Isabelle praying beside me and Brother Antoine nearby, I dared not.

I heard her whisper, "Blessed Virgin, protect my Jeannette. Guide her in her great and holy journey, and keep her from harm. Watch over her; spare her, and spare France . . ."

Her voice dropped and I could hear no more, but I saw that her lips still moved and her face was transformed with fervor. And suddenly, in that holy place, the meaning of Jeannette's journey swept over me. Perhaps it was true after all that only someone as gently pious as she could save France and crown our rightful king; it seemed fitting.

The envy I had felt for Jeannette diminished, and in me was born instead a wish to serve, to add my strength, perhaps, to her gentleness. I began to pray, but soon the advancing crowd pressed against us and we had to rise and pass farther on, lest we be trampled.

Brother Antoine led us down the crowded steps and through the narrow streets, away from the great throng of pilgrims. We each obtained a medal from a seller in the square as we passed — a five-sided leaden one, rectangular with a triangle above, like a flat miniature house or reliquary, with the image of the Virgin carved in the center. There was a knob at each corner and holy words around the sides. I have mine to this day.

I marveled at the streets of Le Puy. Again, I

have seen many towns since then, but this was the first outside of Neufchâteau, and it was much larger. It amazed me that there could be so many tall houses, so many people living so close together. There were streets for selling bread and other goods, as in Neufchâteau, but longer, and thicker with shops. Unlike our plain dirt road in Domremy, the streets of Le Puy were built of stones set in dirt, rough and slippery, and were so narrow and crowded that I was sure the stone arches that often spanned the space from one house to the house opposite were all that kept the houses from collapsing against each other or falling into the gutters that edged the streets and ran with noxious waste. Instead of the clear clean air of the Meuse valley, there was a smell everywhere of too many people too close together. Carts rumbled noisily by, people hurried past, and sellers shouted their wares. Except for the pigs rooting in the gutters as they did beside our road, too, and the birds flapping overhead, settling on roofs and flying off again, it seemed strange to me, and like a dream.

We found a seller of pies, under a signboard that was itself a wooden pie. Louis, whose purse was still fatter than any of ours, bought two, which we all shared. They were bird pies, I think, some sort of wild bird in sauce, and very tasty. Then we went out of the city to find a place for the night, closer to the gate this time. Isabelle wanted to return to the cathedral in the morning, and Louis and I wanted to climb the pillar-like mountain that had the church on it — Saint-Michel-d'Aiguilhe, it was called. Brother Antoine said he wanted to find a friar he knew who he was sure would have come to the Jubilee.

And so, with plans for the next day and aching limbs and heads from this one and from our journey, we found a spot as comfortable as any, and settled ourselves, hoping the night would be neither cold nor wet.

7

I was awakened the next day, which was cloudy, by Louis shaking me. "Madame and Brother Antoine have long since left," he said, "and I have let you sleep for hours. But I began to fear the Devil had taken your soul and you would never wake. Here." He handed me bread — flat, stale, and hard — but I munched it gratefully, forgiving myself for the double laziness of sleeping late and of eating upon awaking.

Soon we were working our way through the throngs again, this time along the outside of the walls and across a field to the foot of the thin stone mountain at whose very top perched the chapel of Saint-Michel-d'Aiguilhe.

Below, where we were, was a building with a small eight-sided chapel attached, and two monks hurrying toward it carrying an old man between them. The man's head lolled and I could see that he was ill. "How kind of the monks to take him home," I said — for I thought the building must be where he lived.

Louis looked at me as if surprised, then took my hands in his and stretched me out at arm's length from himself. "Why, friend healer," he said, "the house where they take him is a hospital, where monks or nuns tend the sick, and the very old and young, and the infirm. Surely there is at least one such place near where you live!"

"I have not heard of it," I said, gazing in wonder at the building. How I wished that I could go inside and see how the sick were cared for in such a place! But Louis was in a hurry to climb to Saint-Michel — and so was I once we began.

Only a few other pilgrims toiled along the rough-hewn rock steps that led up the narrow mountain. The way was not only steep but also open, with nothing to keep one from falling off the edge; the wind howled more fiercely around us with every step we took. I was ashamed of wanting to crawl like an infant, but after a gust of wind whipped my skirt around my legs and nearly blew me off, I did not mind what anyone thought. Louis, too, crawled a little. I tried to place my knees on the greening spring moss that grew between the loose stones of the path.

"I know not," Louis panted, standing shakily, "how men can have built anything on so high a peak."

We stopped at a tiny chapel partway up, in a cavelike resting place scooped out opposite where the drop at the edge was steepest. From there we could see the red-tiled roofs of Le Puy looking like small scraps of cloth below us. We fell into the scooped-out haven gratefully, both of us pale with fright — at least Louis was pale and I was frightened, and I think he shared my feeling. There were signs that people had stopped there before us: a bit of wool, a few crumbs, and a morsel of moldy cheese. "Too moldy even for birds," Louis said when we left and were struggling to climb the last steps, and I answered, "It is too high and too windy for birds" — and then we were there, rewarded handsomely for our toil.

It was in this chapel, where only two or three others worshipped as we entered, that I began to understand something of what Jeannette must have felt in her parents' garden, for here, atop this thin mountain, I felt closer to God than I ever had before. Saint-Michel-d'Aiguilhe was a simple building, with low stone arches inside, thick and humble and clumsy. Frescoes on the walls showed Christ and Saint Michael and angels and animals — the eagle of Saint John, the ox of Saint Luke, the lion of Saint Mark — and clouds and stars. But I was most drawn to a painted wooden cross, with a Christ so slender his limbs and body *were* the cross, and enormous eyes that looked startled as well as in pain at finding Himself so cruelly tortured. I stood there until Louis made a sign to me that he would wait outdoors. I nodded, but went on looking into those eyes, for I could almost feel the agony and the sadness of His suffering. I remembered what Messire Guillaume had often said about his dying for our sins. Christ was holy, of course, but what would it be like to die for others? Could I do that, I caught myself wondering, and felt myself blush with the shame of my presumption. Then I wondered, could Jeannette, if she went to war to save France?

Louis looked at me oddly when I came out, but he did not ask me what I had been thinking, and I was thankful for it.

The sky was darker by then and in it we could see the moon as well as the sun, a daytime moon, pale and dim. We scrambled back down to the cave-chapel, and sat there watching the sky darken even more and the moon brighten. Then the sun emerged again, and the moon dimmed.

"I sometimes think," said Louis, "that the moon is God's way of smiling on the world, on His sleeping children, and that He is most a loving Father when He shows us Himself in the moon."

A monkish thought for a scholar-knight, I felt, liking him the more for it. "It is a nice idea," I said aloud. "I wonder if Jeannette has such thoughts."

"No," said Louis emphatically. "Your Jeannette is too fierce for them, since she wishes to lead an army to crown the dauphin, and to fight! Though she is a woman, it seems to me she has a soldier's mind."

"But she is gentle," I told him, "more gentle than I." I waited, then dared to say, "I think I should be a soldier with her. I am stronger, and I am not gentle."

"You are gentler than you think," said Louis, as if he knew all the world's knowledge. "And your Jeannette, I think, is not." He looked into my eyes, as no one, not even Pierre or Maman, had ever looked. "I saw your face in there," he said, "in the chapel. I cannot read your thoughts, Gabrielle, but the woman who thought them is strong without being fierce, for fierceness is anger. Your Jeannette is angry at those who keep the dauphin from his crown, and anger is needed now. If God has chosen Jeannette," he said, holding out his hand, "and not you, that is why. Come." He touched his hand to mine. "Let us go."

8

As we neared our spot by the wall, we saw Brother Antoine hurrying there from another direction, with three men behind him. I could tell that one was a friar or a monk, from his robe. The other two were wearing boots and leather doublets. "Men-at-arms," Louis whispered. "My oldest brother's squire has a doublet like that. It looks like leather, and it is, but it is two layers thick, with metal between the layers."

Brother Antoine rushed up to us, clearly bursting with news.

"Well met!" he cried. "What do you think? I have found my old friend Jean — Father Pasquerel — here for the Jubilee. In turn he has found these two worthies, who serve squires attending — wonderful to say! — the very Jeannette from your village, Gabrielle. These two" — he gestured to the men-at-arms — "have been sent to urge Father Pasquerel to go to Jeannette, to protect her and be her confessor. As they have news of her, I am taking them to meet our good

Madame Isabelle, so that she might hear about her child."

So we hurried to our spot by the wall, and found Isabelle gazing out over the fields and plains.

Brother Antoine winked, and put a finger to his lips, motioning us to be silent. He crept toward Isabelle, then seized her arm and shouted, "Oho, sister! And do you search for us, and we right here?"

Isabelle put her hand to her heart as if frightened. I could see Louis was displeased at the jest, and Father Pasquerel as well. I myself was also, for the color drained from Isabelle's face and she looked for a moment as if she might swoon.

" 'Tis you, Brother Antoine; how you did affright me!" she exclaimed, her hand fluttering to her throat.

Father Pasquerel, a dignified man of middle height, with a solemn, kindly face and eyes that were not altogether happy or at ease, stepped forward then. Bowing low before Isabelle, he raised her hand to his lips, a surprisingly courtly gesture, I thought, for a simple friar. "Madame," he said gravely, "I am honored to meet the mother of the holy Maid of whom these men have told me much good."

Isabelle looked confused, but Brother Antoine nodded, and said, "It is true, friend Isabelle. This worthy friar is my old friend Jean Pasquerel, an Augustinian from Bayeux and more lately of Tours, where he serves as lector. He has come

here, like us, for the Jubilee. And these men" —
he gestured to the men-at-arms, who came forward and bowed, one smiling, the other reserved
— "serve men who serve your Jeannette." He
pointed toward the smiling man, who I could see
had a deep scar on his face, as from an old
wound. "This is Claude de Novellompont, who
serves Jean de Metz, one of Robert de Baudricourt's knights . . ."

"And I, madame," said the more reserved man
quietly, "serve Bertrand de Poulengy, who serves
the dauphin, as indeed do we all. I am from Vaucouleurs, which town I think you know well, and
am called Philibert."

"They both, madame," said Brother Antoine
eagerly, "have such good report of . . ."

"Oh, good sirs," Isabelle cried, interrupting.
"What of my child? How does she fare? How
is she received? Is she the butt of humor as I
sometimes fear she must be, or of praise, as I
feel she should be? She is so good, so pure, and
so pious — but it is hard for great men to believe, perhaps, that a poor maid from Domremy
could . . ."

"Be assured, madame," said the scarred man,
Claude de Novellompont, "that she is well received. We traveled together to Chinon, our
masters and the Maid and us."

"At night, madame," Philibert de Vaucouleurs
added quietly, "your daughter slept chastely between our two masters, for protection."

De Novellompont nodded, and resumed the

tale. "When we reached the great castle of Chinon," he said, "the Maid was ushered into the room where the dauphin was. The dauphin contrived to hide among his nobles, for he doubted the Maid's mission, and he had another sit in his place."

"But your daughter, madame," put in his companion, "went straight to the dauphin nonetheless, and knew who he was without sign or signal from any living soul. All who were there much marveled at it, and were sure then that she was sent from God." He turned to de Novellompont as if for confirmation.

"It is so," de Novellompont agreed, and Isabelle gave a little cry, clasping her hands joyfully together.

"She spoke apart to the dauphin for a time," de Novellompont continued, "and he smiled and seemed satisfied that she was as she claimed to be. Even so, the dauphin has sent her to Poitiers, to be examined by churchmen and other officials there, to prove that she is from God. Our masters are sure, however, that she is and that she will . . ."

"As you no doubt know, madame," Philibert de Vaucouleurs interrupted, "the Duke of Orléans is a prisoner of the English in London. And yet the English, who according to the rules of chivalry should not threaten the lands of a prisoner, have put Orléans under siege . . ."

"And if they succeed in taking it," de Novellompont continued, himself interrupting, "they

75

will have a clear route into France along the Loire River, into those lands our own dauphin now holds."

"But," de Vaucouleurs said quickly, "our masters are sure that your daughter will raise the siege of Orléans. Then she will fetch the dauphin, or he will go to her from wherever he is staying at the time — Loches, perhaps, or Tours, or Bourges, for he has many castles. And, finally, she will escort him in triumph to Reims, there to receive his rightful crown."

"The siege of Orléans!" Isabelle gasped. "But surely that is men's work! Lead an army to Reims, yes, to protect the dauphin on his journey, but . . ."

"It is all God's work, madame," said Father Pasquerel, who had been standing quietly by. "Your blessed child is His instrument, if all I have heard is true."

"Our masters," said Philibert de Vaucouleurs, "knowing the Maid to be holy and yet a woman, have asked us to beg this worthy friar to accompany her and be her confessor."

Isabelle turned to Father Pasquerel, her eyes full of tender supplication. "Father, would you?" she cried. "I would be easier in my heart if my Jeannette had you with her. If she is to go to Orléans, and perhaps into battle . . ." She checked herself then, and said instead, "And since you are friend to Brother Antoine, who I know is a just and worthy man of God, surely you must be one also."

Father Pasquerel bowed gravely. "I cannot resist a mother's plea," he said, "especially in this place where we are all come to pay homage to the greatest and most holy Mother who ever lived, the Blessed Mother of God."

"Well said," Brother Antoine pronounced, clapping Father Pasquerel heartily on the back, and the two men-at-arms looked pleased.

Louis, though, seemed thoughtful, and was silent while the others discussed details and reminisced about Jeannette — Jeanne, la Pucelle — Jeanne, the Maid — as it seemed she now was called. And my mind was busy, too, so when Louis called me to one side, I was eager to speak with him, wondering if he had been wrestling with the same thoughts as I.

He had, for when we were apart from the others he said, "Gabrielle, you will remember that I want to go to war, like my elder brother."

"I do remember," I told him. "And you will remember that I do not want to go home to Domremy and spend my life on women's daily chores."

He smiled. "And so . . ."

"And so," I said boldly, "I would go with you when you go with Father Pasquerel."

He squeezed my hand. "I hoped you would say that. But will Isabelle allow it?"

"Perhaps I can find the means to convince her."

When we went back to the others, huddled now by the puny smoking fire in the rapidly chilling air, I had an argument ready in my mind. "Would it not be more seemly," I said primly to Isabelle when the subject of my going had been broached, "for Jeannette to have a woman with her, one she knows and who knows her?"

There was a loud silence.

"I am tempted," Isabelle said, "to go myself."

"Surely," said Brother Antoine to her quickly, "your wifely duty is with your husband."

Isabelle sighed. "Yes," she said, but I could hear the reluctance in her voice and pitied her, even as I rejoiced for myself. "I know it is my duty." She turned to me. "What would I tell your good mother, Gabrielle? And what woman will protect you?"

"As to protection," I said promptly, "I will be with a priest and three good men. And you can tell my mother I was willful and went without your leave."

"Willful you are, *ma petite*, and clever, but I will not lie for you."

"You are right," I said, ashamed. "Say the truth, then: that I felt Jeannette should have a woman with her, and you did, too, but could not go, and that I offered, and you tried to convince me otherwise, for my safety, and that I said — that I said if you refused, I would disobey and go without your blessing, following the men secretly and no doubt falling prey to . . ."

"Enough!" cried Isabelle, laughing. "Enough. I will tell your mother something — and you do have my blessing."

9

I never knew there were so many colors of earth or so many kinds of landscape. I do not remember when I started noticing them, but it was somewhere between Le Puy and Chinon, with Louis and Father Pasquerel and the two men-at-arms. Brown earth, black earth, sand, red clay, almost-white clay — we went from one to the other, and there were other differences as well. Sharing three horses, we crossed plains and gentle hills and mountains — and rivers, too, once swimming the horses, and once on a cleverly contrived raft, pulled by ropes from one side to the other. We dipped into wide valleys and then narrower ones, the trees closer, the land greener — but never as green as our peaceful Meuse valley.

We passed through safe land, but few of the people we met along the way were loyal to the dauphin, so we did not speak of our mission. Once we met a leper, wrapped in a burial shroud though he was alive, beating his clapper to warn all of his approach. He must be lonely, I thought, shunned for fear of contagion by all he met. Each leper is required to wear a shroud, Father Pasquerel told me, and lodge either alone in a hut with a painted white cross to warn all comers, or in a leprosarium with others of his kind. I had been taught that illness comes from God even as health does, and wondered if lepers were grievous sinners. But I had observed that those who fell ill of any sickness in Domremy were no greater sinners than those who did not, and I dared to wonder if the causes of leprosy and other ailments might be other than what I had been taught.

We were weary when at last we came in sight of the river Vienne and saw the walls of the castle of Chinon, with its towers and turrets, rising on a cliff high above us — higher, even, than the tops of the trees that lined the riverbank. I felt small as we climbed toward it, like some insect, perhaps. Kings, I thought, royalty and nobles, are the giants of our world, and we people of Domremy and other villages are the insects, ordered by their whims.

And yet the insect Jeannette had been recognized by a prince as being from God.

"My father's house is large," Louis whispered as we approached the huge gate, leading our horses, "but I think it would fit many times in such a place!"

I smiled, and wondered if Louis had said this

80

to make me feel at ease, for surely, I thought, he is no stranger to great houses.

As we were challenged by a guard at the draw-bridge, a man who had just ridden up to the moat looked toward us, and then stiffened, sliding off his horse and shading his eyes. There was a familiar set to his shoulders and to the angle of his head — and then I knew. I ran toward him, shouting, "Pierre, Pierre!" and threw myself shamelessly into his arms, while my companions looked on, clearly amazed. The guards at the bridge laughed aloud and, Louis said later, poked themselves as if I were some strumpet.

"*Mon Dieu!* My God! Gabrielle! Is it you?" shouted Pierre.

I saw that his shaggy hair was still as unruly as mine, and as he embraced me, his broad and friendly face was creased by the smile I knew so well. He held me away from him, studying me. "Your dress is even muddier now than when we used to play at fighting those Burgundian devils in Maxey. What brings you here and how — and who are these?" He gestured toward my companions, who stood uncertainly by, watching.

I explained, and then Pierre told how he and his brother Jean had traveled to Chinon after monks had gone to Domremy from Poitiers to inquire about Jeannette for the dauphin. "Our father thought we should come," he explained, "since it seemed likely that Jeannette would ride with the soldiers. Jean is at Tours, where Jeannette is now, and where the dauphin is providing men and arms — you have missed them only by days. And I am here, helping to gather still more men for the army she will lead." He pulled himself up to his full height, as if displaying his padded doublet whose thickness I had felt when we embraced. "I am a soldier now, Gabrielle," he said proudly. "What do you think my wife would say to see me?"

So he had married Jeanne Baudot! "I am sure she would like to see you, however you were dressed," I said primly, uncertain as to how I should act toward my old friend now that he was wed. But then Louis came forward, smiling, and put one arm lightly across my shoulders. Pierre, returning his smile when I introduced them, said, "I am grateful to you, brother, for protecting my playmate; she is as precious to me as a sister."

"You have nothing to fear from me," Louis said quietly, and I marveled at this treatment of women by men, as if we were goods, passed from one to the other for safekeeping.

Pierre was well known enough in the castle by this time to vouch for us and have the drawbridge lowered. When it was, he led us inside, our feet and the hooves of the horses echoing on the wood of the high bridge, and resounding off the water in the deep moat below. Within the walls, the castle grounds seemed like a city, with crowds of people but without the press of houses or the darkness of narrow streets. Much of the space there was filled with farriers and laundresses and potters and smiths and cooks and butchers and gardeners — and nobles returning with their dogs from the hunt. Deer and boar and hare were slung across their horses, and the dogs barked and leapt around the horses' legs. All was bustle and rush, as Le Puy had been, yet there was an orderliness here unlike Le Puy's chaos. And here there were no pilgrims.

Pierre led us to a long, somewhat low building, one that would have filled much of our road at Domremy — our little road that I used to think was wide! "This," he said, "is the Château du Milieu, where the dauphin lives when he is here. Inside is the throne room where Jeannette — Jeanne, everyone calls her now — recognized the dauphin. It is said . . ."

"Yes," said Father Pasquerel quickly, interrupting, but politely, "we have heard that miraculous story, proving that your sister was indeed sent from God." He made a little bow to Pierre then; Father Pasquerel could be as gracious as any courtier, I had learned on our journey together.

Pierre nodded. "Our brother Jean is still not convinced, but I am, and so is everyone else. She is a holy person, Father; you should see her with the men. Rough men who are given to oaths and swaggering are as lambs when they are with her."

"Jean is not convinced?" I asked.

Pierre shrugged, dismissing it as he often did when it was a question of Jean, whom he disliked as much as I. "If he is, he hides it well; he does

83

not seem moved by Jeannette's mission. But come — let me show you our lodgings."

He took us to the far end of the castle grounds, where a round tower — he called it the Coudray Keep — rose majestically into the sky. He led us inside, and up a stone staircase to the floor above, where he said Jeannette slept. I would be dizzy, I thought, sleeping so high in the air, for when I looked out of the small slit of a window in Jeannette's round room, I could see the castle grounds as far below me as a bird might see them, and the people — insects again — scurrying busily about.

"Drafty," Louis said disapprovingly. But there were bright tapestries to protect against the drafts, and the room itself, though smaller than rooms I later saw, was as large, nearly, as my parents' whole house in Domremy.

That night Pierre was allowed to let us lodge with him in the Coudray Keep, and I, being the only woman, had Jeanne's chamber. Pierre even managed to bribe two serving women to bring me a bath to wash in. They struggled in, two women no older than myself, bearing an enormous wooden tub bound with iron. They poured hot water into it from huge brass jugs, and finally added a sweet-smelling liquid they called rosewater. On the bottom of the tub was a linen cloth, to protect from splinters!

I felt embarrassed at the attention, and the women were at first surly, since I was no great lady such as they were accustomed to serve. But when I told them I knew Jeannette, whom they had only glimpsed, and that I had played with her brother as a child, they served me as if I were a great lady after all. I would have preferred to laugh and talk with them, and I fell asleep that night longing for my sisters.

I did not see much of the life of the castle. But early the next morning I did see two pages attending a lady as she came out of the Château du Milieu. Although Pierre had told me the dauphin's court was not as rich as some, the pages were dressed almost as elegantly as the lady herself. One wore a sky-blue tunic bordered with gold, pale blue hose, and an odd, tight-fitting red cap with a softly sweeping gray feather. His companion's tunic was red, his hose pinkish, and his hat blue. The lady they served, who was perhaps as old as Maman or Isabelle, wore a full gray gown belted in gold and jewels, trimmed with a white fur I later learned to call ermine. On her head was a thing that looked like a boat with a high prow and an equally high stern, joined together with a shimmering veil draped behind her head, as foamy waves must drape around a boat when it is tossed at sea. I stared at her till she was out of sight, not knowing whether to admire her or laugh at her, and I wished Louis were there to see her, too. But then I realized he must have seen many elegant ladies in his father's house.

Soon after that, clean and rested, we set out for Tours — Pierre, Father Pasquerel, and I. Louis stayed behind with the men-at-arms, to march to Tours with them later, as a soldier; he promised that he would find me there.

10

I will never, I thought, as we arrived in Tours, get used to cities. Father Pasquerel reminded us that all manner of tricksters lie in wait in them ready to take money from unsuspecting country people in exchange for worthless trinkets. I, of course, had no spare money with which to test this. But I did spy someone selling what he claimed was a potion to cure fever, and his liquid was clear as water. I knew well that gooseberry porridge, dried cherries, or burning mugwort was best for that, and I saw no sign of any of them in the cart on which he displayed his bottles.

Pierre led us through the streets, and we found Jeannette outside the house where she was lodging. At first I did not know her, but thought the person there, mounted on a black charger and clad in gleaming silvery armor, with a sword in a crimson scabbard, was a young man. But when Pierre strode up to her and she turned, I saw that this handsome knight was Jeannette — and yet not Jeannette at all, for she was very changed.

Her beautiful long black hair that I had so admired had been cut short and bowllike above her ears, as most men's hair was cut. Its severity made her face look softer and more feminine, though at the same time boyish, if both can be said to be true at once.

I stood gaping at her, trying to convince myself that inside the armor and behind that face was still only Jeannette.

But then I thought, *only* Jeannette, who has spoken to the dauphin, and perhaps to saints?

In front of her, holding her horse, was her brother Jean, his broad back to me, scowling at Pierre, as if he were displeased with both his siblings.

For a moment when I went up to her, tentative and nervous, she, Jeannette — Jeanne — just stared. But suddenly all solemnity vanished and a little smile broke across her face, as a ripple grows in the River Meuse when a child throws a pebble into it. She leaped from her horse, kicking aside the stirrups that encased her booted feet, and moved, awkwardly in her armor, clanking, toward us.

"Plague take this armor," she said crossly, sounding more like Pierre's and my childhood companions than the pious maid I had known in Domremy. "I move like a land snail in it! Gabrielle, what brings you here? Oh, it is good to see a woman I know, one from home who knows me, instead of these fancy town folk!" She made as if to embrace me, her arms moving

88

stiffly in the shiny steel *garde bras* that encased them. Then, lifting her arms toward me as I lifted mine to embrace her, she burst into a laugh heartier than I had ever heard from her. I laughed as well, for I, too, felt how good it was to see a woman from home who knew me. What matter that she had seemed mannish at first? It was clear now that she was not, and I liked her new spirit.

"If I touch you, I will crush you. Come inside." She waved her brothers impatiently off after quickly greeting Pierre. "No, no, d'Aulon," she said to a kind-looking man with very round brown eyes who followed her — her squire, I was to learn. He seemed to have a fatherly concern for her, though I later heard he was only eight or so years older. "We will manage, Gabrielle and I," she said to him. "You may leave us."

D'Aulon glanced at me and inclined his head in a brief nod, and Jeannette, taking my hand as if we were still herdgirls in the fields along our river at home, led me inside the house. It was tall, and each story was faced with wide vertical stripes, for its timbers were set up and down instead of across. "This house belongs to one Monsieur Dupuys," Jeannette whispered as we went in through the low door. "He is as important here in Tours as my papa is in Domremy, and his wife is lady-in-waiting to Marie d'Anjou herself." Jeannette gave me a sideways glance, and then laughed and poked my arm, saying, "Marie d'Anjou is married to the dauphin." She gave me another poke and then said, "She is almost a queen — but I see that to you, Gabrielle, she is just another woman, eh?"

"I — no," I said, confused. "That is impressive. It — I did not know."

Jeannette patted my shoulder, saying, "I am jesting; I did not mean to tease. And I am learning that one person is much like another, regardless of their station, and we are all accountable to God."

She led me into an upper chamber toward the back of the house, where there were a bed and a chest, very elegantly carved, and rushes and herbs strewn on the floor. "Yes," she said, "I sleep in this bed, me and the daughters of the house — whom I will ask to leave tonight so that you may join me and we may gossip undisturbed. Here — a pox on this buckle! — help me remove my shell; I feel like one made of stone in it, though it is splendid, is it not?"

Before I could answer, and tell her that yes, I agreed it was splendid — for I did — she went on, asking, "How came you here, Gabrielle, and why? Oh, it is good to see you! How did you leave them in Domremy? Well, I hope — my mother and father especially. Had the planting begun, when you left? How is Messire Guillaume, and how . . ."

"I will tell you, Jeannette," I interrupted, struggling to undo unfamiliar fastenings, "if you will leave off asking long enough for me to answer."

"A ready wit and a saucy tongue as always," she said merrily. But despite her new and rougher manner, she did not seem hardened, and about her face was that same glow, as if it was with her now always.

At length, we freed her from her armor, from cuirass and vambraces and gauntlets, greaves and sollerets, names I did not know then but was soon to learn. I noticed a ring on her finger, gold, with three crosses and some writing. She must have seen me looking at it, for she smiled, saying, "The writing says, 'Jhesus-Maria,' I am told, and the ring is from my parents, for love and safety."

Then we embraced like sisters, and sat on the great bed while I told her of all that had befallen me, and gave her news of her mother. I explained about Father Pasquerel, whom we had rudely left standing in the street, and said that her mother wished him to accompany her, and that he was willing.

"I will send for him, then," she said, "for it would be good to have a friar at my side, and if my mother wishes it, I will obey. Is she much worried? Is my father angry? He was, for a time . . ."

"Your father I have not seen since I left," I told her. "He did not seem angry then. Yes, your mother is worried. She prays for you constantly, but I think she feels you are on a holy mission, and must accomplish it. Are you, Jeannette? On a holy mission?" I wanted to ask about the times

91

we had spied on her, but I dared not, for Pierre and I had agreed we would let her keep that secret for as long as she wished.

Her face sobered and she said, "Yes, Gabrielle, I am. And surely it is from God that I come, for the dauphin agrees and the men follow me willingly." There was no boasting in her words, despite their sound, only humility. "All except my brother Jean follow willingly," she added, smiling sadly. "He comes because our father asked him to, but he does not approve of what I do, nor does my father, who fears for my safety and my morals. That saddens me, because both of them should know I do this not for myself but because God wants me to do it." She paused a moment, as if reflecting, then seemed to shake the sadness off.

"Listen," she said, "do you see this sword?" She pointed to the one we had put aside, still sheathed in crimson velvet, its hilt topped with five crosses.

I nodded.

"The scabbard," she said, "and another of cloth of gold, are from the people of this city of Tours and the priests at the place where the sword was found." She paused again, looking beyond me, and beyond the sword and the room as if at something I could not see. "Gabrielle," she said, "when I was first here, I was told — I may not say by whom — that there was a sword in a village church, the village of Sainte-Catherine-de-Fierbois, which is not far from here, and that

I should have it. So I sent for it, saying, as I had been told, that it was hidden behind the altar there." Her voice dropped and her eyes shifted to mine as she said softly, "People said no one had ever seen it. But it was there nonetheless."

I realized then that whatever had spoken to her in her father's garden must have told her of the sword.

She stood and, picking up the sword, drew it as easily as if she had been handling swords instead of spindles all her life. "See how bright it shines?" she asked, and it was true; it shone as if the light were coming from within it, instead of reflecting from it.

"When the sword was found," Jeannette continued, sheathing it again, "it was covered with rust. The rust fell away when the priests took cloth to it, *fell away*, without scrubbing. I do not wish to use it to kill," she went on, as if more to herself than to me, "but one who leads an army must have a sword. And" — she smiled now — "a stout leather scabbard, I think, instead of the soft pretty ones I have been given — as if for a courtier's sword, or a woman's plaything."

I nodded, knowing how she must feel, for I would have been sore on that point as well. But to console her I said, "That armor is no plaything."

"No," she said, "it is not." And she stretched then, lean and supple despite the heavily padded doublet and thick hose she had been wearing underneath her armor, and still wore.

"What is it," I asked, "that you will do now?"

"I will wait for the men-at-arms who are coming from Chinon, and take them to Blois, where more men-at-arms will join us. And I will lead them all to Orléans," she added, as if it were nothing, "where the English hold the city under siege, and God will let us vanquish them, so that they may go no farther into France. And then the dauphin will come to us, or we will go to him, and we will take him to Reims to be crowned. That is what I will do. I must do it, for God wishes it, and so I shall. Although" — and here her face softened again, and she looked like the Jeannette I knew — "I miss our quiet valley and my father's house, and I long to sit and spin again with Hauviette and the others. How is Hauviette? And Mengette — how is she?"

"They were well when I left," I said, "but remember that I have been gone nearly two months myself. I miss home, too," I told her, "and yet I would like better than you, I think, to lead an army. But I would not know how."

"You would," she said gently, "if God were guiding you as He is guiding me. You are more suited than I, Gabrielle, to this work — and yet it is I who must do it. And I rejoice in it, for it brings me closer to God, and it brings the dauphin closer to the throne."

We went on in this way, privately, for some time, talking now of war, now of home and those we knew. In every minute that passed, I could see more clearly how much Jeannette — Jeanne —

had changed. She was stronger than before and, as Louis had said, fierce in her anger at the English and Burgundians, transformed with zeal for her mission. I knew that in that way she was indeed stronger than I, and I was sure she was truly guided by God.

But later that night, when we were lying in the great bed and she spoke of her secret fear of weakness in battle and of wounds, and of her annoyance at the tears which she had always shed easily, I told her I had asked her mother if I might go with her, and that Isabelle had agreed, thinking that it would be good for her to have a woman as well as a priest with her.

For a long time Jeannette was silent, and I feared she had fallen asleep or had not heard me. Just as I was about to speak again, she said, very softly, "If you are sure you want to go, and if you will understand that I will rarely be with you, and if you will let Pierre look after you, and if" — here she sat up and looked down at me gravely in the gray darkness of the room — "if you will promise to wear men's clothes as I do, and never reveal that you are a woman — if you will promise all these things, I will let you come with me. I would like you to if you wish it, but I would not want harm to come to you, and it will, if the soldiers think you are a woman. I do not want women following my holy army, as they follow most others, and if it is known there is one woman with us, others will surely come. Do you promise all this, Gabrielle? Do you swear it?"

"I promise," I said, "and I swear."

"We will have need of a healer" — here she smiled — "though, I trust, not of a midwife. It is the custom for squires to help their masters if they fall, I have learned, but what of the men who have no squires — and the squires themselves?" She lay back down again. "It is as healer that you will accompany us. Tomorrow we go to Blois, to prepare ourselves to lift the siege, save Orléans, and make the dauphin truly king."

And that is how I came to go to war with Jeanne d'Arc.

PART THREE

PART THREE

11

I slept like one dead, more tired than I knew from the journey. When I opened my eyes it was to the late morning sun making crossed lines on the floor through the window — a fancy window with real glass in it, rippled like the River Meuse in spring. And Jeannette — Jeanne — was standing over the bed shaking me. "Little friend," she said, "I am glad to see you remember how to open your eyes. I have had a time waking you. But out of bed with you now, for we must hurry to transform you into a boy. Pierre has agreed to make you his page. I have found you clothes," she continued, extending her arm to me and pulling me up, "but first I must be your barber. Come, sit here."

She led me to a bench by the window, and put a roll of cloth around my neck. Then she picked up a pair of sharp-looking shears and, before I could even yawn or wish her good day, she seized my curly hair and cut it off, short, above my ears, like hers.

I did not see the result right away, but I could see it in her eyes, for when she stepped back to survey her work it was with such merriment that I knew she was no barber. "Well, well," she said heartily, "it will do, I suppose, for a peasant boy trimmed by a sheepshearer."

When she took away the cloth, I felt an unfamiliar breeze where my neck was usually protected by my hair and the kerchief I bound it with. My head felt lighter and freer, too, but when I reached up and encountered a mass of short, round curls I knew Jeanne was right to speak of a sheepshearer, for it felt not unlike the back of a ewe.

Jeanne thrust her hand into my hair and tousled it. "It suits you, Gabrielle," she said. "You make a splendid boy. Your hair is curlier than when it was long, like many-leaved vines, all tangles." She took her hand away. "But come, off with that shift. You agree to serve Pierre as his page, do you not? Better gentle Pierre than grouchy Jean, eh?"

"Much better," I said, pulling my shift over my head.

For the next thirty minutes or so, we struggled with garments I had never handled before and that Jeanne had just come to understand. First came short linen braies to put my legs through and tie around my waist. Luckily there was string running through the upper hem with which to cinch them closed, for they were larger than I was. Next there was a loose, long-sleeved chemise, also linen, reaching below the braies. Then came a doublet like Jeanne's, but lighter in weight than hers, with tight buttoned sleeves — heavy enough, though, for it was several layers of thick blue cloth, lined and quilted. It went clumsily around my body and upper legs, and fastened to scratchy woolen hose with points — laces — that went through eyelets on the doublet and tied there.

"You should rejoice," said Jeanne, bending to fasten the same point I was fastening; we bumped heads and laughed.

"Why so?" I asked.

"I have twenty points to fasten; you have less than half as many. And believe me" — here she pulled a point so tight that I curled my leg up to show her I could not move and we laughed again — "believe me, it is a bother tying them whenever you remove your hose. Some hose," she said, "are one piece, unlike these, but I thought since you are not a boy, it would be easier for you to have them separate, for necessity's sake."

I nodded, seeing at once what she meant, though the thought of undoing any of this costume to attend to my daily needs daunted me.

Over the doublet, as an outer cloak, came a short robe of rough brown wool, slit in front, for, Jeanne said, ease upon a horse. It was edged with rabbit fur, and thin in spots, as if it had been much worn, and I wondered who had owned it before me.

Jeanne also gave me a belt and a large purse to

hang from it; I added my own small one, which still held my mother's knife. Finally she handed me a sort of hood for my head, whose long end I could wear wrapped like a turban or slung around my neck as I chose and as the weather dictated.

"And at last these," Jeanne said, presenting me with a pair of soft leather boots, laced up the side. "I tried to get you hose with leather soles, but found none. In any case, your feet will be better protected in these."

"How beautiful they are," I said, turning them in my hands and feeling the softness of the leather. I slipped them on; they made my feet both light and warm, unlike the heavy wooden *sabots* in which I ordinarily clumped. "I could dance in these," I said, and Jeanne, laughing, seized my arm and we whirled for a moment around the room.

It was an odd feeling. It was hard to move at first, for the hose were still so tightly laced to the doublet that I felt my legs constrained. But at the same time it was freer, with no skirt to whip around my legs and catch on things. In a few minutes, I felt I had the knack of it, and I bowed to Jeanne, saying, "My lady, thank you."

"You are welcome, my lad," she said merrily. Then she put on a solemn face. "What would your mother say, and your sisters, and" — she made her eyes round — "Pierre, and" — here her eyes grew rounder still, and she poked me

102

with her elbow — "and that Louis you told me of, eh?"

I felt my face grow hot, for I, too, wondered what Louis would think if he saw me, and I feared secretly that he might not like me this way at all, if indeed he found me again as he had promised.

But I need not have feared. When I emerged from the house with Jeanne that noontime, it was to find Louis, Pierre, Father Pasquerel, and Jean, waiting outside among the men-at-arms who had come from Chinon. Pierre was on a fine charger, leading a smaller, heavier brown mare. "*Bonjour* — good day — my page," Pierre said to me, falling quickly into the fiction of my transformation. Louis gave me a broad wink, so I understood that Pierre had told him what to expect. Pierre's eyes kept going to my hair, where my hood had slipped, and he looked as if he would laugh if he could, and Louis looked so falsely grave I knew he was in the same state. Father Pasquerel, though, seemed puzzled, as if he thought me familiar, but knew not why he should know a page, or how Pierre had acquired one. Jean, I could see, recognized me or had been told of my disguise, for he scowled unpleasantly, and I knew I still had no friend there. "So now we have two *garçons manqués*," he muttered, "two false boys. But men want men to lead them, not maids. This campaign is folly, and no good will come of it."

Pierre ignored him. "I have brought you a horse, Gabrielle," he said — and I was thankful my name sounds the same whether male or female — "to replace the one that was stolen from us."

"Thank you — er — master," I answered, entering slowly into the game. I realized dimly that though no horse had been stolen from us, Pierre of course had to explain why his page had none. But mostly I was still trying to disguise my joy at seeing Louis.

No one, I realized as Pierre pushed the mare toward me, could help me mount, for were I a page, I would be accustomed to mounting on my own. Jeanne, however, grasped the mare's reins and led her and me to a flat stump at the side of the road. "Stand on this to mount," she whispered, "and always have something like it nearby when you mount or dismount; otherwise you will rip your hose or tear the points from them. As to riding, pretend there is no saddle between you and the horse, and you will soon grow used to it, as I did. Perhaps Pierre will teach you more on the way — but a girl from Domremy would not fall off," she added severely.

"Nor," I whispered back, stepping onto the stump after patting the mare's nose to show her I was her friend and hoped she would be mine, "would a page from Domremy."

Jeanne smiled at this, and I reached over the mare's narrow back and somehow threw myself, clumsily I am sure, into the saddle. It felt hard and uncomfortable, not warm and alive like a horse's naked back. But my mare, whom I called Yarrow, for there was a yellow tint to her brownness, like the centers of yarrow flowers, proved gentle and patient. She waited calmly while I arranged myself and while Louis, under the guise of adjusting the straps at her head, instructed me to put my feet in the stirrups. That, too, was an odd feeling, for when I had ridden before, my feet hung freely. In a while, though, I grew accustomed to it, and to my unfamiliar clothes.

And so on a glorious late April day, we set out for Blois to meet the men assembled there to join us. A herald cried, "For Orléans and the king!" as we rode along the Loire, which was wider and deeper than our little River Meuse, and straighter, too — a truly noble river, with islands here and there along its course. I missed Louis, who had to ride behind most of the time with the men-at-arms who had come from Chinon. But since he had owned to being noble and had purchased a horse in Chinon with his father's money, he was respected and well-mounted. He had much to learn, too, even though, as he had told me, he had played clumsily at tilting at a wooden knight with his brothers as a child, and had ridden chargers. But as he had often remarked, he had been better at scholarly pursuits than at such sport.

It was a day blessed by God, Jeanne said. The long wet winter and the cold early spring seemed at last at an end. Larks and thrushes sang to us as we rode, and although I was still struggling with Yarrow's trappings, my spirits were high. I found I was enjoying the masquerade of being a boy. I had taught myself to swagger, and to make my voice squeak so the men would think it was changing, as boys' voices do. Pierre had given out that I had been sickly as a child and so was not strong. But in truth I was stronger than some boys, and lacked few skills country boys possess; I could snare a rabbit or net a fish as easily as they. And since I was only a page, it was not expected that I yet knew the art of war. During the times I needed privacy, Pierre contrived to watch for me, and as for sleeping, a page often sleeps with his master, and none sought to molest me there. My only regret was seeing so little of Louis — and so much at times of Father Pasquerel, who knew by now who I really was and who stayed close to me whenever Louis and I were together, as if to prevent what had not yet begun.

We reached Blois on a bright sunny day with daffodils and wood hyacinths blooming beside the Loire. One moment the way before us was open and empty, but suddenly when we came around a gentle curve, the water meadow was full of men and priests, horses and carts, and bright tents and banners — blues and reds and golds — decorated with family coats of arms or *fleurs-de-lis*, the lilies that stand for France itself. It was as if the world had emptied itself upon the plain, and was peopled only with priests and men wearing armor, or heavy leather or padded cloth, or mail — tight rows of crinkled metal, close as fish scales.

Most men carried shields and weapons: swords, of course, and daggers and axes, and an odd-looking thing I had never seen, called a halberd, which had a curved, hooklike blade on one side for pulling a man off his horse, and a sharp blade on the other. There were maces and pikes as well, and also crossbows, with windlasses for drawing back the string, and metal bolts with square heads to shoot instead of arrows. Pierre showed me a machine for hurling huge stones, and also cannons and bombards and serpentines and culverins. These were all tubes of various sizes, from large to small. Pierre explained that powder was put inside the tube, behind a stone, and when the powder was lighted, it would explode and the stone would be thrust out of the tube.

My mind reeled. The armored men and the horses, the tents and carts and weapons, seemed more like a vision in a dream than something truly there, or like figures painted upon the land. But the figures moved and spoke and shouted, and swords clanked against armor, and heavy carts drawing heavier cannons made the ground tremble as they rumbled along the riverbank.

Into the midst of this throng rode Jeanne's two heralds, named Ambleville and Guyenne, and then Jeanne herself, with no covering over her steel armor, so it gleamed silver in the sun. She held a standard of white *boucassin* with the words — so said Father Pasquerel — JHESUS MARIA emblazoned on it, and painted *fleurs-de-lis* and figures of angels and Our Lord. *Boucassin* is the finest linen; the standard glowed in the sun as if with a holy light, and the images stood out as sharply as the words. She had a pennon, too, a small flag showing an angel, Our Lady, and a dove.

Jeanne rode through the crowd and then turned to face it, drawing her sword from the leather scabbard she had ordered at Tours. It shone as if it had never known rust — and the throng fell silent.

"Welcome, brave Frenchmen," she shouted in a loud, clear voice, and with such gladness that it infected all who heard her. "This is a joyful day, for as you know we meet here, with God's help, to free our good friends the Orléanais and to crown our king."

A lusty cheer went up from the men, so lusty it shook the earth, and I wondered if the wind would carry it to the besieged Orléanais so they could rejoice as we did.

For a few days all was bustle and preparation and organization, and I saw Louis only at a distance, as he worked with the other men, loading carts and herding animals. As for me, I had to learn the duties of a page and gain greater skill in riding. Pierre had already given out that I was adept at healing, so I hunted herbs, filling my two purses and several leather pouches with yarrow for wounds made with iron weapons and to stop bleeding; goatsbeard for closing wounds; sage for healing them quickly; horsetail to shrink swellings; boneset and feverfew and myrtle for healing bones and joints. I even found cabbage in a neglected garden and picked it, for I knew that it, combined with salt from one of the supply barrels, would cure infections, and I feared there would be many of those after the wounds of battle.

Jeanne chased away any women who tried to join us to consort with the men, and twice each day, she and Father Pasquerel made all the priests come together and sing praises to the Blessed Mother. No soldier could attend unless he first confessed. Day and night I stayed as close to Pierre as I could, lest my sex be discovered, or kept to myself with Yarrow, who nickered softly now whenever I approached, and put her head down so I could rub the soft spot between her nostrils. I wondered what she would do when there was fighting, for she was no war-horse, and what I would do myself. Though I was eager, I knew I was not a soldier, and I had no weapon but my mother's knife and a short sword Pierre had given me, which I was unskilled, so far, at using.

The army was really many armies, each group led by its own captain. The day before we were to march, Pierre pointed the captains out to me. First was a grizzled, heavyset man called La Hire, with elegant clothes and a foul tongue. I dubbed him the Blusterer, although he was gentle, Pierre said, around Jeanne, and swore only "By my staff" and other mild oaths within her hearing.

Then came a smaller, lithe, and slippery-seeming man. "He is Gilles de Rais," Pierre told me, "and a marshal of France, which is a high honor, and he is also kinsman to the stout La Trémoille, who is the dauphin's favorite but no one else's, and whom Jeanne says she does not trust."

"Gilles de Rais puts me in mind of a weasel or a river rat," I said, and I called him the Greensnake in my mind, after our nickname for a certain bully in Maxey.

There was a tall captain, too, Poton de Xaintrailles, whom Pierre told me never laughed — the Owl, I named him, for his solemnity. Pierre also pointed out the Archbishop of Reims, named Regnault de Chartres, who, it was rumored, was nearly as close to the dauphin as La Trémoille. "And that man," Pierre continued, "is the Duke of Alençon, my sister's favorite, and well liked by all." He nodded toward a handsome, elegant-looking man only a little older than we but settled in his age, with a sharply chiseled nose and grave eyes. He was standing with Jeanne, in earnest conversation. I could see that she regarded him well and felt warm toward him, for she put her hand on his arm once or twice and laughed heartily at something he said.

"She calls him *mon beau duc*," said Pierre, " — my handsome duke — and sometimes I think she likes him as well as she likes me."

I glanced at Pierre to see if he was jealous, but could not tell. Jeanne's name of *mon beau duc* suited this captain's elegance, and so I borrowed it.

That night I fell to reviewing in my mind the new faces I had seen, and the names I had given them. But what, I wondered again as I fell asleep, will my horse and I, and all of them, be like when we are at war?

111

12

We prayed before we left Blois, led by Father Pasquerel and Archbishop Regnault de Chartres, who seemed to ignore Jeannette whenever he could; I did not like him, despite his high position. And then we set off along the Loire, on the muddy south bank. It was more than a few leagues to Orléans, and we were several thousand strong. The land was flat, which made for easy marching, but it was also marshy, which meant the carts sometimes became mired and had to be pulled free, and many men complained loudly of sodden feet. We pages, who had to wait till everyone else had passed, were in charge of the armor; the men did not wear it to march, for it was too heavy and cumbersome. It was loaded on carts instead, and weighed them down.

First to pass us while we waited were the priests, singing "Veni Creator Spiritus," plus psalms and anthems, and holding high a banner showing a painting of Our Lord. Then came the knights and swordsmen and archers, some on horseback, with squires and heralds as well. Workers came next, stout men to help us cross rivers and scale walls and fences. Then more archers and men-at-arms and infantry, laughing and joking as they passed, with carts bearing the guns and other arms, household goods, and food, most of it for the besieged citizens of Orléans. We left more food for them behind in Blois, to fetch later. Last came the beasts, some for food, but others carrying still more supplies. My gentle Yarrow tossed her head at the huge plodding horses that pulled groaning carts laden with leather boats for crossing rivers, and barrel staves and hoops, and some barrels already assembled, and many ropes. Most barrels we had were for storing goods, but these were for making bridges, with wooden boards laid over them by the workers, on which men and horses could pass.

With the army rode the captains, with their bright standards flying before them. Jeanne wore her armor, again uncovered, so it shone in the sun. I heard one man say she was vain of it, and kept it on even to sleep, but I had seen no sign of that.

Altogether it was a splendid sight, and sound, too, for the men sang with the priests, and all seemed to feel great joy and hope. My spirits were high and happy when we pages finally followed the others. I led Yarrow, who picked her way daintily, as if she were a great lady, lifting each hoof high, away from the mud. I was cheered by the thought that Louis and Pierre were nearby; and as to healing, I had greater hope of that now, for it was said that the dauphin had sent his own surgeon to tend the wounded, and I prayed that I might meet him soon, and learn from him.

We marched for two days before we drew near to Orléans, sleeping in the wet fields at night. That made my muscles ache, but it did not seem much sacrifice to make for the honor of freeing Orléans and keeping the enemy from taking more of France. We lesser people were ordered to eat only food we had brought ourselves or food we found along the way, lest we deplete that which we carried for the besieged city. This was hard on the men, and also on us few pages, who were appointed to guard the beasts and food intended for Orléans. Several times in the night we had to chase hungry men-at-arms away from the pigs, who luckily squealed whenever they were disturbed.

At last on a dismal, stormy morning, the twenty-ninth of April 1429, I saw the men ahead of me swing sharply south, away from the river. "We are nearly there" was on more than one tongue.

"We go south to avoid the English forts," said one man, "for the north side of the river bristles with them."

I felt my throat tighten with sudden fear, and I am sure I was not alone. But soon we were ordered to turn once more, farther away from the city, and I heard the men muttering angrily among themselves. "It is madness," said a page I had befriended, as we slithered along on the wet grass at the edge of the muddy path that the men and horses marching before us had made. "The city itself is on the north bank, and we are on the south. Perhaps this is what comes of having a woman lead an army."

I was angry at his words, and wanted to argue against him, but dared not. As it was, I later learned it was not Jeanne but the captains who had turned us farther south.

So we marched below the city, and partway around it, till we came to a village across the river from Saint-Loup, one of the English forts.

When we halted, it was still rainy and cold. I left my new acquaintance, and found Pierre toward the front of the line, standing a little way from Jeanne, sheltering under a broad-branched tree. She was in heated discussion with a tall man I had not seen before. "That is Dunois," Pierre told me, "called, with affection and respect, the Bastard of Orléans. He is the son of Louis of Orléans and some other man's wife, but no shame attaches to it. Orléans has been in his charge since his half-brother, the Duke of Orléans, has been held captive in London." He held up his hand as I started to protest that I could not follow all this. "It matters only that you remember Dunois is another captain for us to recognize and obey."

"The Lion," I said softly, studying the man's

strong, honest face and his steely gaze; I had heard the lion was the noblest of beasts.

A sword clanked behind us then, and I turned. There at last was Louis, in a tight leather doublet that looked as if at least five others had worn it before him, and with his hair shaggy and wet with rain. "The Bastard Dunois is indeed in charge of Orléans," he said, grinning at me out of a face as grimy as I was sure mine must be — but happy, for I knew he had his wish at last, to be a soldier. I could see that he had learned his lessons well, for he sat his horse with ease, and seemed not clumsy with his sword. Perhaps not having his brothers and father nearby had made him surer of his skill. "And I hear that Dunois is a good man," he went on, dismounting and grinning more broadly, "although the Maid does not seem to agree."

I listened then, and heard Jeanne say loudly, "Was it you, Dunois, who advised me to come here, on this side of the river, instead of going straight to where Talbot and the English are?"

"Madame, it was," Dunois replied with a grave bow. "I and your captain, the Duke of Alençon, we deemed it best because . . ."

But Jeanne gave him no chance to finish. She stamped her foot as well as she could in her heavy armor, and said, "The counsel of the Lord God is wiser and surer than yours. You thought you had deceived me, but it is you who have deceived yourselves. I am bringing you better help

116

than you ever got from any soldiers or any city. It is the help of the King of Heaven."

Here Dunois inclined his head and seemed about to speak again, but Jeanne would not permit it. Louis rolled his eyes and looked askance at Pierre, who reddened as if in embarrassment at his sister's persistence and anger.

"This comes from God Himself," Jeanne was saying, "who, on the petition of Saint Louis and Saint Charlemagne, has had pity on the town of Orléans, and has refused to suffer the enemy to have both the body of your brother the lord of Orléans and his city."

Dunois looked much less lionlike when he smiled. "Madame," he said, "as long as Orléans itself has *my* body, I will not surrender her. With that and your spirit, and God's help, we should do well. But," he added, glancing at the nearly still river, "I fear we are ill-served even so, for the water is low despite the rain, and what little wind there is blows downstream."

"Why do you speak of wind and rain, Bastard," Jeanne asked impatiently, "when there is a besieged city before us? We must cross this river to save her and to prevent those who threaten her from going farther into France."

"That is the very reason that I speak," said Dunois, moving closer to the tree under which they sheltered. "You have brought much aid to Orléans and we are grateful for it. Our plan is — was — to send barges upstream from the city to this shore, load them with food and cannons, and then, while engaging the English at Saint-Loup, which is their only fortification to the east, float them downstream and back across to the city . . ."

"Under the very noses of the English," said Jeanne, smiling at last, "while their attention is on saving their skins at Saint-Loup; I like that, Bastard."

Dunois's smile widened and he looked pleased with himself; house cat now, I thought, instead of lion. "As you see," he told her, "it is not so much a matter of deceit toward you as it is of strategy against the English."

"You would not have deceived me," Jeanne said generously, "but this one" — here she turned to La Hire, who stood nearby — "my lusty friend who has only lately learned how to swear gently, has deceived me."

"By my — staff," roared La Hire, "approaching from the south was the only way, madame, for the northern bank is full of English. But you would have held us in argument had we broached it to you, and delayed the march. We are defeated nonetheless," he said, turning back to Dunois, "for the wind blows strongly in the wrong direction; no barge could make its way against it."

"You are right," Dunois answered, "and so we must wait for a fair wind." The cat-look faded with his smile, and the lion-look returned.

"If it is a fair wind you want," said Jeanne,

"why not pray for it, and it will come." She walked a little away from the men, and went stiffly down on her knees despite her armor and the mud and rain. She had been thus only a moment when the ripples on the surface of the water seemed to stop. Then they turned, and I felt the wind blow against my face, whereas before it had blown on my back.

"It is witchcraft," I heard someone behind me whisper, and Louis, who looked as amazed as I felt, whirled at that, saying angrily, "Do not speak of witchcraft when the wind has changed because of honest prayer." The man fell back, red-faced.

"A fair westerly wind!" cried La Hire. "By my . . ." He snapped his lips together as if to cut off an unseemly oath, and finally spat out, "staff!" Jeanne, returning to the tree, laughed and thumped him on the back.

Dunois looked at Jeanne with what appeared to be a mixture of joy and awe. "It is a miracle," he said softly, "and you are what they say you are — truly from God." He went down on his knees in the mud as if to worship her — although under the tree the mud was less. She raised him up quickly, saying, "Come, there is no time for such fawning. We must prepare to load the barges, La Hire and I and the men — and you."

"I," said Dunois, "go to Saint-Loup, to distract the English. Will you give me men?" he asked La Hire.

"Gladly," said La Hire, "and I will give you

myself as well. I am hungry for those English," he said to Jeanne. "Surely you will not begrudge me the first taste of them. Others can direct the loading."

"It is as you wish," Jeanne said graciously, and, turning, she came closer to where we stood. "Is it not wonderful," she said, as if she did not quite believe her own miracle, "that the wind changed? God is truly on our side!"

I believed her then, with all my heart.

So the barges came up the river in the rain, and were loaded with food for the inhabitants of Orléans, who had been getting some, I learned, from the east through what was called the Burgundy Gate. The English were weakest on that side, and held only Saint-Loup there, about a mile away. But though the open gate kept the Orléanais from starving, not enough food got through to feed them well or even very comfortably, and they sorely needed the supplies we brought.

While the barges were moved and loaded, La Hire took men to Saint-Loup as he promised, "distracting" the English, and came back triumphantly late in the afternoon with few men wounded and a captured English standard, at which we cheered. I had a while to talk with Louis, and to learn that he had found a nobleman from Avallon, who knew his father, under whom to serve, at which he was well pleased.

Not long after, I had my first taste of war healing when Pierre led a gunner to me, with his arm bleeding so heavily from an arrow wound that I was afraid I would be unable to stanch the flow. "This is my page, of whom I told you," Pierre said gravely to the man. "He has some knowledge of healing. Gabrielle, look you at this man's wound; the dauphin's surgeon is somewhere else, it seems."

I wished fervently that the dauphin's surgeon were there with me, though I was glad to hear he had arrived!

When I examined the man's arm more closely, I rejoiced to see that the arrow had only grazed it; the blood must have looked more than it was, spread by the rain. I dressed the wound easily with pig's grease mixed with dried yarrow from my purse.

I went then to where Pierre was huddled near the carts with Jeanne's page, Louis de Coutes, who was so anxious to please he was like a puppy. He was younger than I, and seemed amazed at the people and activity around him, as indeed was I. I tried to disguise it, but de Coutes's eyes bulged out of his head at every new thing, and he was always saying *"Mon Dieu, mon bon Dieu! —* My God, my good God!" We were standing there, exclaiming about the elegant armor a nobleman we did not know was trying to protect from the rain, and complaining, too, of the cold and the wet, when up rode Jean d'Aulon. As Jeanne's squire, he was in charge of managing her household, which now included me, as

Pierre's page. D'Aulon was a good soldier, Pierre said, more honest than most men. Though he looked at me with his round brown eyes in a way that made me suspect he knew who I was, he seemed to respect my need for disguise, and if he guessed my secret, he kept it to himself.

"The Maid enters the city this very night," d'Aulon announced to Pierre — and so we did also, near midnight, while Father Pasquerel and all but around two hundred of the men returned to Blois for the remaining supplies — but Louis was among those who stayed. The rain worsened and thunder sounded as I mounted Yarrow, who seemed glad to march again. I rode at Pierre's side with the others across the river and thence to the Burgundy Gate, which, as I said, was little protected by the enemy. "What a fine group we are," Pierre whispered as we went through. "Jeannette, you, me, and Jean — four peasants from Domremy, going into one of the great gates of Orléans, in procession as if we were royal — for look behind us, Gabrielle!"

I looked and it was true. There was the elegant nobleman, his armor unprotected now despite the rain, and all those who rode closest to us seemed noble. But the townspeople who greeted us were mostly plain folk, and I felt better, seeing them.

Jeanne herself rode right in front of us, with her lion Dunois on her left side, she on a white horse and he on a brown. Her standard was on her right, borne by, I think, d'Aulon. A shout rose as we entered the gate, drowning out the thunder, and the light from the torches the townspeople bore was almost as bright as the lightning that preceded the thunder. Men, women, even small children surged forward, impeding our progress; someone had to walk before our procession, waving a sword to clear the way. There was singing and laughter and shouting and gaiety, as if Jeanne were indeed come from Heaven, or we all were.

Yarrow stepped forward daintily and held her head as high as a noblewoman's palfrey, and Pierre winked at me. I knew he was again thinking "four peasants from Domremy." I was proud to be one of them, but I was angry to see Jeannette's brother Jean bowing in his saddle and waving, as if the crowd had come to see him instead of his sister.

Suddenly there was a cry ahead and a flaring of torchlight. Yellow flames flickered near Jeanne's beautiful white standard and along one edge of her pennon, from, someone said, a torch waving too close. I saw Jeanne put the spurs to her horse and turn him toward the pennon. A moment later the fire was out, extinguished by her, I was told, before it could damage the cloth. Some folk spoke of a miracle, but though I could not see how she did it, it seemed to me that the cloth must have been too wet to burn easily.

At last we came to the cathedral of Sainte-Croix, which had two square towers rising above its entrance, and Jeanne dismounted and went inside to give thanks. We made our horses stand waiting for her; they were more patient than we, there in the streaming rain.

When she returned, we went on, borne ahead by the crowd, who flowed with us as if we were the Loire itself. At length we stopped in a street called the rue du Tabour, where lodgings had been prepared for Jeanne and all her household at the home of the treasurer of Orléans, one Jacques Boucher. The house was tall, five stories, with a peaked roof protected by an arch like that in a church, and cross-timbered with many stout beams. The Boucher family burst into the street to greet us, with smiles as welcoming as sunlight, and Monsieur Boucher himself helped Jeanne from her horse with great respect. We were soon indoors out of the rain, apologizing for the puddles our sodden garments made on the rush-strewn floor, and I was trying not to worry about how long it would be before I would see Louis again, for of course he lodged elsewhere, with the men.

Jeanne was to sleep on the second story, with Madame Boucher or with her daughter, and d'Aulon would sleep nearby. I, being as they thought a very young page, was to stay with their littlest children, two small boys. I was relieved and I could see that Pierre was, too, for had I to lodge with the men, my disguise might not have held.

The children slept at the very top of the house, from which they could see across nearly all the red-tiled rooftops of Orléans. It was from there, while I tried to wring out my wet clothes without removing them, that I got my first sight of the badly damaged twin towers called Les Tourelles, which were in English hands. Before the siege, Les Tourelles, which stood on the Loire's south bank, had been connected to Orléans by a long stone bridge with many arches. But the arches nearest Les Tourelles had been broken, so the Orléanais could not cross the bridge and take Les Tourelles back from that direction. Neither, though, could the English cross there into Orléans.

On the other side of Les Tourelles, I was told, was a mounded earthwork and a wooden draw-bridge leading to a ruined church called the Augustins. The English held those firmly, so the Orléanais could not storm Les Tourelles from that direction either.

The older of the Bouchers' little boys, Charles, who was wide awake despite the hour, pointed all this out to me from the window of the room where I was to sleep. He showed me the fort the English had built around the ruined church, saying, "We Orléanais tore the church down to keep it from the English. There was a great battle there last year, when I was very small. But I saw the smoke, and watched from here, and I didn't cry at the cannons, though they were very loud, and Jacquemin did cry." Jacquemin was his younger brother.

"The English have set up another fort in the river," young Charles went on importantly, "called Saint-Antoine, there under the bridge, in the middle, and there are more enemy forts all around, so you see why we cannot move out of our city, we French. Were you and I on the other side of our house, we could see still more forts, four to the west — more, if you count the river forts."

I began to see why we had gone around Orléans to the south and east in order to enter, and I thought this lad very bright for a child no older than my sister Cécile.

"The English have a huge cannon," Charles told me, moving away from the window and sitting on a carved chest that stood beneath it, "which we cannot see from here. It is at Saint-Jean-le-Blanc, on the other side of the river. It can hurl stones far out into the river, *big* stones. But some of ours are bigger, more than twice theirs. It is true that their big cannon has broken many houses, but it has killed only one person, a woman."

"Is that so?" I said, sitting beside him, for I suddenly felt overcome by tiredness. Still, now that I was somewhat drier, I wanted to go below to the celebration I knew had been hastily planned to welcome Jeanne.

"Yes," he said, "but my father says we have not had a victory since last year. Do you know what that was?" He seized me by the hand and smiled so disarmingly that I could not resist him.

"No," I said wearily. "What was that?"

"It was when the English Earl of Salisbury, who was in Les Tourelles, was looking out. They say a boy — a boy like me, you understand, not very much older — shot off a cannon. His father was a gunner, so he knew how. And the ball hit the window where the earl was, and an iron piece came off the window and took away half his face. And then he died, but not right away. That," Charles said, "was our last victory. So you see how badly we need another, and we will have it now that the Maid has come."

"But not," I said as gently as I could, "if those who follow her are allowed to starve. They say a feast has been prepared for us, and your mother says, I think, that you are to be asleep by now, is it not so?"

"It is so," he admitted sadly, glancing toward Jacquemin, who was breathing deeply and regularly, his eyes closed. "But will you tell me about the feast if I am awake when you return?"

"I will," I promised, "but now you must let me go."

It was indeed a feast, a feast to a soldier anyway, and one that I wished Louis could share, even though Madame Boucher called it poor because of the siege.

There was a long table in the room called the hall, and a shorter one, for servants, coming

127

down from it, so that the whole looked like the letter T, which I now know but did not then. Rushes were strewn on the floor, as they were throughout the house, and two small thin dogs darted in and out, hungry for scraps.

Someone had contrived to roast a pig and to make a thick savory sauce, and had cooked pike and carp and other river fish, and had made a jelly of some other meat. There was soft bread, and wine to drink, and a pudding made of spiced grain and milk. Jeanne ate lightly, only soaking a few bits of toasted bread in wine and water, and I ate only two or three morsels of the roast pig — well, perhaps a little more — and some sweet spiced pudding with my bread. There were pewter spoons for eating soft food like the pudding, and the pig was handed around with a pronged tool I had never seen, nor had most of the others there. It was called a fork, and seemed more useful than a knife for such a purpose, for it held what it speared much more securely.

Musicians played while we ate, and afterwards a jongleur recited *Le Roman de Renart* — *The Romance of the Fox*. That was the first I had heard of the adventures of this clever animal, who seemed much like some people.

When I returned to my room near dawn, young Charles was sleeping as soundly as his brother, so I was spared having to recite the evening's pleasures. I soon fell soundly asleep myself, grateful to be indoors out of the rain, which still pelted down but now lulled me pleasantly, beating against the roof.

For the next few days, little happened. We awaited the return of the army and the remaining supplies from Blois, and I found myself surprised at how often my thoughts turned to Louis, who was busy with the men preparing for the battle that was to come. Pierre said that the captains and Jeanne did not agree about what course to follow, and that most of them thought she could not know how to wage war. This, as I could understand, much vexed Jeanne. But whenever she went out into the city, the people swarmed around her, and there were always crowds outside the house, for it seemed everyone wanted to see her or touch her or speak to her. It annoyed her, I know, and she told me once she longed for Domremy. I was surprised that I did not, for despite my feeling against cities, I found I liked the friendliness of Orléans.

As a mere page, I could go where I pleased once I had threaded my way through the throngs around the house. I left Yarrow in a stable with Pierre's horse, and young Charles accompanied me as I walked. He showed me the churches, and the quarter where meat was sold when there was meat; when we passed it, the butchers were happily cleaning their empty stalls, expecting, they told us, that they would soon be able to fill them. It was the same in other streets, with other merchants. Peasants outside the city had not been able to bring their goods through any but the Burgundy Gate, and since most had to pass by English forts to get there, they had not dared to come — though fish sellers, Charles said, had sometimes been able to fish secretly in the Loire, and thus have goods to sell.

Charles pointed out the public steam baths, two for men and one for women, and I marveled at them, for I had never heard of such. He showed me the great Châtelet, too, from which the city was governed. But best of all were the hospitals, now that I had learned what such places were. There were some for special diseases, like leprosy and plague, though those were outside the walls for fear of contagion. Within the walls, along with almshouses for the poor and homeless, was the Aumône-de-Sainte-Croix, for poor people who were ill. I vowed to visit there, if I could find out how.

On the day after we arrived, Jeanne spent the morning with a scribe on the rue des Ecrivains, dictating a letter to the English. I was there when she did so, and in it she told the English that since she was going to drive them out anyway, they should surrender. She also told them to free her herald Guyenne, whom they had kept when she had sent a letter to them by him from Blois. The other herald, Ambleville, whom she sent with this new letter, returned to the Bouchers' house later that day without Guyenne, so distraught he could hardly speak. "They — they will *burn* him," he said finally, trembling despite Jeanne's hand firmly on his shoulder. "They have set up a stake in their camp ready to tie him to, and piled faggots under it to light. Burn him — and he has done no wrong!" He collapsed in Jeanne's arms then, weeping.

Little Charles Boucher and Jeanne's young page Louis de Coutes, who were nearby, turned to me, clearly frightened. "See," I whispered to them, frightened myself, "war is not an easy thing, nor is it a game." My own voice shook with the words, whose truth I was only just beginning to discover.

"They said they would burn you, too, madame," Ambleville told Jeanne, his voice muffled against her shoulder.

Jeanne gave a short hard laugh at this and said, "In God's name, lad, they will not hurt your friend, or you, or me either. Return to them and tell Talbot that if he arms himself, I will arm myself also. Let him come before the city, and if he takes me, let him burn me, and if I discomfit him, then let the English raise the siege and go back to their own country."

By Talbot, she meant the powerful baron who commanded all the English at Orléans.

Poor Ambleville left, murmuring prayers, and I thought Jeanne cruel to make him go. But Pierre said it was a herald's lot to carry messages, and that since killing a messenger was against all rules of war, the English threat was no doubt an idle one. For safety's sake, though, Dunois — the Lion — imprisoned two English heralds and said he would kill them if harm came to Guyenne or Ambleville.

And so we waited, but Talbot sent no message back.

That evening, Jeanne, with Louis de Coutes, and Pierre, with me as his page, and a few others rode through the gate and onto the broken-arched bridge, going as far as we dared toward Les Tourelles. "In the name of God," Jeanne cried to the English there, "surrender or forfeit your lives!"

There were shouted words and laughter from inside Les Tourelles, and Jeanne turned to one among us who knew English, asking, "What do they say?"

The man looked uncomfortable and replied only, "They refuse." But when she pressed him further, he said, "They ask if you think they will surrender to a woman," at which Jeanne stamped her foot and said, "It is to God and the dauphin that they must surrender."

"They call us your pimps, madame," the man continued, his face reddening as the English shouts continued, "and — forgive me — they call you whore and peasant, a mere girl who herds cows."

I saw Jeanne's lips tighten and her eyes fill with tears; my own face felt hot with shame and anger. There was more shouting from a single loud voice, which our translator said belonged to Sir

William Glasdale, the captain in charge of the English force at Les Tourelles, under Talbot. "And he says what, this Glasdale?" Jeanne asked.

Our translator looked as if he wished the Loire to flood suddenly and sweep him away, but when Jeanne demanded impatiently, "Well?" he replied, "He says he will see you burned, and he calls you witch."

For a moment Jeanne was silent, but I could feel her fury, although for a few seconds she seemed to listen to something none of us could hear. "You are a liar, Glasdale," she shouted at last, "and you will die without having a chance to confess and be forgiven for your sins." Then she turned her horse abruptly and rode straight for the cathedral, where she flung herself off her horse and bolted inside.

This time I followed her into the silent church, nearly empty now of daytime crowds. I gave her a few moments alone, then went to where she was kneeling, and touched her shoulder.

"Leave me," she said, her voice muffled, "in God's name."

"It is only I," I told her. "Gabrielle."

She gave a great sob then, and turned, burying her face against me, and wept.

For a while we stayed there without speaking, and I comforted her as best I could. But finally she lifted her head and said, "I was weak just now, Gabrielle, but I cannot let myself be weak again, for I must do this thing."

"Why?" I asked softly. "Why must you do it?"

"Because I have begun it," she replied, "and because it is God's will."

"Can you be sure of that, Jeannette?" I asked, deliberately using her old name.

"Yes. Oh, yes. I have no doubt." She looked at me oddly, then touched my lips gently with her finger. "Can you keep a secret?"

I nodded.

"Do you remember that long-ago day when you and Pierre came upon me in the garden, and you heard me speaking?"

"I do."

"I told you I addressed no one, but that was untrue. I spoke to the blessed Saint Michael, who came to me when the bells rang and told me to be a good girl. He came again many times after that, as did Saint Catherine and Saint Margaret, and they all told me I must remain pure and a virgin and serve God. It was they who told me I must raise the siege of Orléans and have the dauphin crowned at Reims."

I had suspected that was the way of it, of course, or something like it, but I crossed myself to hear it confirmed.

"Everything has gone as they told me it would, which is why I am impatient, for I know it will continue as they say, and they say the siege will be lifted." She stood up and took my hand. "If the foolish English would only surrender, then we would not need to fight, and I fear that if we do fight, many men will be killed and wounded.

134

But you will help them, will you not, those who are hurt? That is God's work, too, surely."

"If I can, Jeannette," I said, "I will help them."

"And you will speak nothing of this, of what I have said to you here."

"I swear that I will not."

She stooped quickly and kissed me, then strode, warlike again, back outside, and mounted. I followed, and we mentioned it no more.

The Lion, Dunois, and Jeanne's fatherly squire, d'Aulon, left the next day to meet the returning army, and Jeanne rode with Pierre around the English camps, trying again to get them to surrender. But they replied as harshly as before, and as crudely. I did not go with them, for Louis was free of his tasks at last, and I was eager to show him the parts of the city Charles had shown me, and to hear his voice and talk with him again. I longed to tell him of my conversation with Jeanne in the church, but of course I did not. And I found myself wondering at the strength of my joy at seeing him. I had never felt that way about Pierre — but of course Pierre was like a brother to me, and Louis was a friend. Still, that did not seem enough to explain the smile I felt creeping across my face when I saw him or thought of him, or the lightness in my head.

We spent as much time together as we could, Louis and I, but not as much as I would have liked, for we feared gossip, especially since I was still dressed as a page. Then one day he reached for my hand, bent his head to mine, and brushed my lips with his own. I felt a stirring inside that I had never felt before, and I wanted to cling to him and never let him go.

13

I do not like to remember my first battle, or any of the others, but they come back to me vividly — the sounds and smells almost more than what I saw. I do not understand how men can go into battle more than once. Though they cheer themselves with brave words, they must know, all save the youngest and least experienced, that at best they will come out with aching limbs and parched throats, and at worst with torn and broken bodies — or not come out at all, but lie stinking on the battlefield for the enemy and then common scavengers to strip and plunder. Even Jeanne soon felt as I did, I know, but she hid it well, and in time hid it even from herself.

At the beginning, though, until I knew what battle was, I was as eager for it as any young soldier. It was as if we were all in a dream at first, of military glory and of glory for God. The excitement, the talk of courage and conquest, the armor and the horses and weapons and banners — they acted on us like the strongest of wines. And we all thought God would protect us from harm.

How young we all were, and how in love with God and France and Jeanne!

Early on the morning of the fourth of May, the army came back from Blois, by the north bank this time, with Father Pasquerel at its head solemnly carrying the priests' standard, and the other priests with him, singing as solemnly as they marched. With the army was such a swarming of beasts as I had never seen, sheep and pigs and cattle enough to feed a thousand cities. Carts came with them, bearing wine, and grain, and other provisions. The people of Orléans cheered when the men rode through the Burgundy Gate, and the English were nowhere in sight, as if they were subdued by the joy.

Later, while Jeanne and those of us of her household were back at the Bouchers' having the first meal of the day with some of the captains, Dunois came in, his strong jaw firmly set, and strode quickly up to Jeanne. "Madame," he said, "I have news that may be good or ill, depending on how eager you are for battle. The English Fastolf has been seen, bringing men; he is well on his way here, I am told, and will arrive soon."

This Fastolf, I knew, had overcome French troops in February, when they had ambushed him as he carried salt herring and other goods to the English troops in Orléans for Lent.

"He is a good soldier, Jeanne," said Dunois. "Why" — he leaned forward — "he managed to wound me in that February battle, and to chase La Hire away."

"By my — by my sword," shouted La Hire, "he did not chase me! I left of my own will, for supplies, and well you know it, Bastard!"

"Peace, peace," said Jeanne, laughing. "That battle is long over; we must turn our minds to the next."

"I like it not," Jean said darkly, "for this Fastolf is feared much by the men."

"Of whom you are one, brother, and so am I," Pierre said quietly. "We must leave this business to the captains."

"And to me." Jeanne thumped her fists upon the table, then turned to Dunois. "Bastard, Bastard, in the name of God, I order you to let us know as soon as you hear of the arrival of Fastolf. If he gets through without my knowing, I promise that I will have your head cut off."

"I do not doubt it, madame," Dunois answered dryly, and we all chuckled at their exchange.

"So, my brave d'Aulon," Jeanne said, turning to her squire, "and you, my brothers, and my younger brother's page" — here she looked secretly at me, smiling — "what say you to a rest before this battle starts?"

We all agreed, though it was a restless rest for most, I think, with the promise of battle at its end.

Jeanne went to her second-floor room, and d'Aulon with her, and young Louis de Coutes went with d'Aulon. I went to the top floor, empty of children for once, and was still trying to think about the battle to come instead of how my own Louis might fare in it, when a cry rose from outside. I leaned out the window and saw a crowd assembled, shouting and waving, and at first could not tell what was amiss. Then I heard "Saint-Loup!" and "French dead!" and "Dunois!" and "We must fight!" People poured into the street, one or two with the small firearms called culverins and others carrying the long, thin ladders used for scaling walls. For a moment when I saw this I could not move, but my mind said to me, "It is the battle; go!" At last I went down to the second floor, and saw Jeanne struggling to don her armor while Madame Boucher and her daughter fumbled at assisting her. I thrust them aside, for by now I knew which buckle went to what strap, and helped her dress until d'Aulon, rubbing his eyes, burst in and in his turn thrust me aside to finish the task.

"Why did no one tell me French blood is being shed?" Jeanne cried. "Where is my horse? Louis, Louis!" she shouted to her page. "My horse, boy, my horse!"

The young de Coutes, stumbling over his own feet in his haste to obey, was out of the house before she had finished shouting and was soon in front of it again, upon her horse, and leading d'Aulon's. He leapt off as she ran outside, and she leapt on as quickly as her armor allowed. "My standard!" she shouted, and poor de Coutes ran inside again and up the stairs, handing her the standard out the window of her room. As soon as she grasped it, she was off, while d'Aulon, cursing, was still struggling to mount.

Meanwhile, Pierre had raced around the side of the house without waiting for me. He brought up only his own horse, so I fetched Yarrow and followed him as he followed Jeanne. I could see sparks flying from her horse's hooves ahead, and from Pierre's, and no doubt they also flew from Yarrow's.

Crowds of people, many armed and all shouting, ran with us to the Burgundy Gate — and the sight that met us there sobered me greatly, and sobered Jeanne as well. Men came through the gate on foot into the town, carrying wounded Frenchmen, and Jeanne's face was pale and tight as they went by. "I can never see French blood," I heard her say, "without my hair standing on end."

"Here is work for you," Pierre said to me, and indeed there was.

"This is my page," Pierre said to those carrying the wounded. "He has some knowledge of healing and will help you till the dauphin's surgeon arrives. He is young, but able."

In the rush I had left my pouches of herbs behind, and had nothing for bandages, and no tools save my mother's knife; I had even forgotten the sword Pierre had given me.

I slid down from Yarrow, and handed her reins to de Coutes, who had run after us on foot and had just arrived. "Take her," I said to him, "and ride swiftly back to Monsieur Boucher's and fetch the leather pouches you will find in the topmost room, and any old linen that Madame Boucher can spare. Tell her it is for bandages, for wounded Frenchmen."

He nodded, and rode off.

Trembling inside, I said to the men carrying the wounded, "Lay them over there, against the walls away from the crowd, and show me the worst of them first." I know not where I found the strength or the sense to say that, for my mouth was dry and I could not keep my hands from shaking as I bent over the first man and tried to pull his bloody doublet away from his heaving chest.

So it was that I spent my first battle tending the wounded, with what small art I had, stanching blood and binding wounds with cloth torn from ragged garments and from flags. As had happened before, as soon as I actually began, I lost my fear and all sense of myself, and simply worked, letting my hands do what my mind bade it, without questioning why. When a man died — and some few did — I was somehow able to cross myself quickly, and go on. I think it was because I had no choice, and no time to mourn or grieve.

In a while I became aware of a craggy-faced man in the long robe of an academic, his graying hair in a fringe around his bald and shiny head. He stood beside me, impatiently watching, and then his hand came down atop my hand, which probed a heavily bleeding thigh. Brusquely, he said, "No, no, you foolish boy, it is here." I had been searching for a broken-off arrow that was deeply buried, and sure enough, the old man found it quickly and saved the poor soldier much pain.

"I am the dauphin's surgeon," this same man said when he had extracted the arrow and I had bound the man's thigh. He spoke gruffly, as if he were indignant that someone less skilled than he were tending the wounded. "And you are?"

"Gabrielle of Domremy," I said, making my voice as deep as I could.

"Well, my lad," he said, still gruffly, "I know not where you learned our art, but despite your error, you are good at it."

Surprised, I smiled and thanked him, and wondered what he would say if he knew that I probed for crossbow bolts the way Maman had taught me to probe for splinters, and that I fastened most wounds as if they were scythe cuts or the rips childbirth sometimes causes in women's flesh. He — the surgeon, Nicolas d'Amboise, he was called — became the master and I the apprentice that day, though unofficially, and I learned much from watching him. He had no patience for things done carelessly, and I was sometimes awkward with trying to earn his praise. But he did give it, I soon learned, for honest effort and for work done well, and he taught me much, whenever there was time.

I know not how long it was before young de Coutes returned on Yarrow with my herbs and some old linen, or how many men we had served by the time Nicolas had examined the herbs, nodded his terse approval, and shown me a mixture or two I knew not of. But by day's end, when the last men who could be helped were resting, I lifted my eyes wearily from them and saw smoke in the east. We learned from returning Frenchmen that Saint-Loup had seemed lost until Jeanne arrived, but that seeing her had put such heart into our men that they had attacked anew, and won the day. Saint-Loup was captured and burned; there was nothing left — and I marveled, as I stood there, exhausted and bloody, leaning against Yarrow's flank, that so stout a fortress could fall in so short a time. "Some English men-at-arms," Pierre told me as we rubbed our horses down, "tried to escape by donning the robes of priests. The men wanted to kill them, but Jeanne would not hear of it, and took them prisoner instead." He shook his head, as if marveling at her mercy, but I was glad of it, for I had seen enough blood that day, and had begun to think that perhaps I was not suited for this adventure.

But I was in it now, and there was no way to turn back, for me or any of us.

14

When Jeanne returned through the gate, the Orléanais greeted her with joy at the victory. But although she smiled graciously, her smile was taut and small, and there was no triumph in her eyes. When I arrived back at the Bouchers', she was closeted with Father Pasquerel, weeping and confessing. My hostess said, awed, "She is as softhearted as any other woman." I myself, feeling need of consolation and prayer for those who had fallen, went alone to the cathedral, found a quiet corner, and prayed.

The next day being Ascension Day and a holy feast, there was no fighting, but there was a council of captains to which Jeanne was not invited. This angered her, and she stumped about the house, a different Jeanne from the one who had wept the day before. At last she called for a scribe, and dictated another letter to the English, so loudly that I could hear its contents.

"Men of England," she began, "you have no right in this kingdom of France. The King of

Heaven orders and commands you through me, Jeanne the Maid, to abandon your fortresses and go back to your own country. If not, I shall make you such trouble that the memory of it will last forever." She also demanded the return of her captured herald, Guyenne; Ambleville had at length come back to us safely. And then she strode outside, seized an arrow from an archer, and tied the letter to it. Running to the wall, with me and her brothers and the man who knew English anxiously following, she had the archer shoot it into the English camp. "There's a herald for them to keep or burn," Pierre said, chuckling, and I chuckled as well, though Jean scowled, as if he did not approve, as usual.

"Read it! Read it!" Jeanne shouted over the wall. "There is news in it!"

But the English laughed derisively and shouted to each other, saying, our translator reluctantly reported, "News has come from that whore of the Armagnacs!" The Armagnacs, I knew, were other supporters of the dauphin's cause; there were some in Paris, I had heard.

I was alarmed to see Jeanne weep again at the English reply. But by the time we returned to the Bouchers', her hurt had turned to anger, and she was more desirous than ever to do battle.

Later, in the evening when the moon had risen, my own Louis came to me at last. We walked for a while near the city walls, and then beyond the Burgundy Gate, toward the ruin of Saint-Loup.

Louis pointed to the moon, smiling, and asked, "Do you remember our daytime moon?" and I answered, "I do — and God still smiles on us."

"He smiles on the English, too," Louis said wryly. "We shall soon see whom He truly favors."

"Louis," I said, turning to face him, "now that you have fought, are you as eager for war as you were before?"

His face grew more sober. "You are a healer, Gabrielle, and do not have a soldier's fierceness like your countrywoman Jeanne. But think of this: without war, how will we have our king, and how will the Burgundians be quelled and the English persuaded to leave us?"

I thought of the boys of Maxey and of the way the English had replied to Jeanne's letters, and knew there must be sense to his words. But the cries of my wounded echoed in my mind and I wished there were another way.

And yet excitment filled me again the next morning when the streets bustled with battle preparations and everyone spoke eagerly of success. "Today is the day, eh?" said Madame Boucher as I bade farewell to her and the children after hearing Mass.

Young Charles Boucher squeezed my hand and said, "We French will drive the English out today, with the Maid, and then all will be right again. We will have good things to eat and be able to walk outside the walls, and the countryfolk will come into the city again with food from their farms. And I will watch the battle from the walls."

"You will not," said his mother sternly. "If you watch at all, it will be from the safety of your room, well back from your window, for I will not have your head blown off by a stone from a cannon, or your face and life lost to a bit of iron like the English Salisbury, of whom you like so much to tell."

And so, in the midst of an argument between mother and child that reminded me of many I had heard in Domremy, I hurried out with my sword to get Yarrow, find Pierre, and see what my role would be that day.

I rode behind Pierre, who in turn rode behind La Hire, who was joking, and Dunois, who was not, and Gilles de Rais, who was smiling, and the other captains. After us came a huge force of men-at-arms — archers and gunners and knights and their squires. We were many thousand again, as we had been when we left Blois. Somewhere in that vast throng, I knew, was Nicolas, the surgeon, with a cart bearing oils and herbs and greases, linen strips for bandages, and sharp knives and saws. And somewhere also was my Louis. I prayed for his safety even more than for my own and Pierre's and Jeanne's, and for the lives of all our gallant French.

We rode through the Burgundy Gate to the riverbank, and waded our horses across to the island of Saint-Aignan. Yarrow needed urging, and

I wondered as I had before how both she and I would behave in battle. I could see Les Tourelles to my right as Yarrow stepped gratefully up onto the island, and I could also see part of the ruined Augustins church, whose walled yard was full of English troops. I knew we must take it if we were to take Les Tourelles from that direction — from the south. There were also English soldiers on the walls of the blockhouse between the Augustins and Les Tourelles. We would have to conquer them as well — but our French soldiers streamed out of Orléans as if there were no end to them, a vast ever-flowing river of men. It was exciting, but terror gripped me, making my mouth dry and my palms so wet that I feared they would slip away from any wound I had to tend. "This is war," I whispered over and over to Yarrow as I bent to rub her neck. *"This is war."*

A cart soon came up and I watched while men removed two leather boats from it, set them in the water, and lashed planks between them, quickly making a bridge from the island to a spot facing Saint-Jean-le-Blanc, the small fortress the English held on the southern bank. Jeanne and La Hire were first across and then a small party of men-at-arms. When he left, Pierre bade me stay behind, but I pretended I did not hear, and followed him, for my fear was less when he was in sight. Besides, I knew that to tend the wounded, I would have to go where they would be.

By the time I reached Saint-Jean-le-Blanc,

there were no longer any English there, as if they had fled in fear as Jeanne approached. But I could see them to the south and to the west, where they had gathered by the Augustins. And then, before our other forces could leave the island and assemble, the English thundered toward us, attacking with shouts and cries and stamping of hooves. The noise was so deafening I dropped Yarrow's reins and grabbed at my ears, and I was so horrified to see the sudden avalanche of men bearing down upon us that I could not move. Yarrow was horrified, too, I think, for I felt her trembling under me, though she bravely did not flee.

"Go back, Gabrielle!" Pierre shouted, wheeling his horse around to face Yarrow, whose nostrils were flaring with terror. "This is no place for you! You should not have followed me. Go back!"

But I was too frightened to leave his side, and I urged poor Yarrow closer to him, till her flank touched his leg. An odd metallic taste filled my dry mouth and throat and I wondered if Jeanne felt the same, or if she was stronger in this than I. The English swirled around us, lances, swords, and arrows thickly thrusting, flying, and cruelly piercing when they found their marks. Then an Englishman near me turned his horse so sharply to face me that the horse reared. The man waved a mace, and I closed my eyes and lay against Yarrow's neck, crying out silently — at least I think I was silent — to God and Our Lady to save us.

The next thing I knew, Yarrow moved, and I opened my eyes to see that Pierre had seized her bridle and pulled her away. The Englishman and his horse were no longer in sight; I was surrounded by Frenchmen again, and, much to my relief, we all galloped back across the boat-bridge to the island, where most of our men were still waiting. The English did not follow, and I wondered if the battle was over and we had lost it. I am ashamed to say I hardly cared, but wished that it was done. Then a shout rose from the southern shore, and I saw that Jeanne and one of the captains — Greensnake Gilles de Rais, I think it was — had turned toward the Augustins again. "Armagnac whore!" the English shouted, hurling names at Jeanne in bad French, but not so bad that I could not understand: "Cowherd — peasant — limb of Satan!" I saw Jeanne's mouth compress into a thin, angry line — no tears this time — and she called across to us. "Go forward boldly in the name of God!" Our French troops roared back in joy to hear her words and see her, and I was so swept up in their courageous cries and in the motion of their brave charge off the island that my fear dried up inside me and I followed them.

It is hard in the midst of battle to know what happens except in the small place directly around one. I remember poor Yarrow's rearing once as I urged her forward, and my sword coming loose and clattering to the ground when I gripped her mane lest I fall and be crushed. I remember Pierre's thrusting me and Yarrow behind one of the huge war machines, a thing like a screen on wheels that acted as a huge shield, which men had brought up on a cart. "Stay there!" he shouted, "or I will never again let you ride with me. You must remain whole, Gabrielle," he added more gently, "so you can succor those who do not."

I stayed crouched behind the machine, off Yarrow now, but with my arm around her leg. I was shaking with fear, and unable to retrieve my sword. The noise was like no noise I had ever heard, but worst of all were the screams of the innocent horses, forced by their riders into a fray not of their making. The smells of blood and sweat and excrement and vomit and gunpowder mingled into a whole so terrible that it was painful to draw breath.

Another page, the one I had befriended earlier, suddenly appeared at my side panting, with a great gash in his shoulder. "They say the Maid has gained the moat," he cried while I ripped the edge off his chemise to bind his shoulder, "and that she has stepped on a caltrop and wounded her foot. It bleeds inside her *sabbaton*, but she heeds it not."

A caltrop, I had learned, is like a ball with spikes; it pierces the foot of he who treads on it. A *sabbaton* is foot armor, and a caltrop that could pierce that would make a nasty wound, I knew. Screams and smells vanished from my mind, giving way to the thought that if Jeanne were injured, all could be lost, for I knew both from today and from Saint-Loup that it was she who gave the men courage as no one else could. So I handed Yarrow's reins to the page and edged away a little from my machine, intending somehow to find her.

When I peered out, searching, I saw a huge, heavily armed Englishman on the wall of the Augustins, preventing our men from getting inside. Suddenly he vanished, blown apart by a mighty shot which I later learned had been fired by a master culverineer who came from near Domremy. And then two knights, as if heartened by the shot, ran hand in hand into the Augustins fortress. With a great cry, the river of French surged after them, capturing it — and the day at last was ours!

I followed the men into the Augustins yard, but it was some time before I saw Jeanne. I found Nicolas first and his cart of supplies, and he set me to binding wounds, as if he had asked me to be his assistant, though he still had not spoken of it directly. Although the army's work was over for that day, ours had just begun, as he made plain to me in his gruff way. We established a hospital of sorts in the Augustins yard, against one side of its badly damaged wall.

It was as quiet now as it had been tumultuous earlier, except for the moans of the wounded. We worked in silence, and swiftly, but soon I heard noise again, shouting and laughing, not the fierce cries of battle. Men streamed past me from inside the ruined Augustins church, carrying chickens and loaves and turnips and other foods, and some arms as well. La Hire, resting nearby, burst past me and faced them angrily, saying, "By my . . ." — and here, Jeanne being absent, he used a word I will not use myself. "I will strike the head off any man who plunders, for the Maid will have none of it!" Most of the men, shamefaced, dropped their booty — but I saw others gather the food up again and take it away.

Then came Dunois, truly the Lion, at the head of a band of sorry-looking French who had been prisoners in the fort. Among them, I was glad to see, was Jeanne's young herald Guyenne, who looked frightened and pale but happy to be among us again. La Hire put his arm around his shoulders, saying he would lead him to Jeanne. "Look you to the wounded, boy," Nicolas ordered me, hurrying to the prisoners, "for I must see to these."

Not long after, Jeanne herself arrived, disheveled, with her beautiful armor spattered with mud. She sat wearily beside me, easing off her *sabbaton* and saying, "I need your tending, Gabrielle, for I have hurt my foot. But I will need more tending by and by, for I will be wounded again, soon, above the breast."

I glanced up at her in wonder that she should

know this, but I said nothing, and fell to examining her foot. Her *sabbaton* had saved it from much damage; it was more pinched that cut, but I dressed it and instructed her to keep it moist with wine until it healed.

Dunois, who had stood by as if ready to spring to our aid if needed, came closer then and said, "Come, Jeanne, I shall cross the river with you, for you must rest well this night."

"I will stay with the men, Bastard," she said, but then La Hire, also nearby, offered her his arm gallantly, bowing as if at the dauphin's court. "Come, lady," he said, "and have this victory dance with me — across the river." Jeanne laughed heartily at this, and left for Orléans with them both.

And there was I, among my few wounded, suddenly aching for sleep. Pierre was nowhere to be seen, nor Nicolas, nor Louis, nor my sweet, brave Yarrow, nor anyone I knew, and I still had not found my sword. But more men soon gathered, and lit fires, and roasted meat, some taken from the Augustins, and some brought by the grateful Orléanais, who had crossed as we had to Saint-Aignan Island. They also brought bread and a little cheese and wine, along with much cheer and gratitude. Before long, everyone was telling stories of the battle just fought, as calmly and cheerfully as if it had been a mere tournament, but with great relief that it was finished, at least for now, and that such progress had been made. And soon I fell wearily asleep among my wounded, with no feeling about the rightness or wrongness of what we were about. My last thoughts were worried ones, for Louis and for my horse, before sleep prevented me from fretting more.

15

I woke, stiffly, before Prime, as it was getting light. When I rose, I examined my wounded, cheering them as best I could, and giving them water from a muddy well in the Augustins yard. Nicolas returned and, quickly looking over the wounded men, said roughly, "Good. I see no errors here, and no carelessness." He surprised me by giving my shoulder a friendly squeeze before he left again to be near the other men when they attacked.

I still had not seen Pierre or Louis, or Yarrow, or the page I had entrusted her to. I surmised that Pierre was with Jeanne, but wondered why he had not sought me out. Later I learned that he had looked for me, then thought I had returned to the city, and so gone back there, where he soon fell asleep from exhaustion.

I climbed cautiously up part of the ruined Augustins walls. Les Tourelles, where the English were, was uncomfortably near, no more than a bowshot away, with only trenches and earthworks between us and the blockhouse on the riverbank, from which the wooden drawbridge led to Les Tourelles itself. But all was quiet. Perhaps the English were exhausted, too, and still slept.

Beyond Les Tourelles, across the river, I could see many Orléanais near the broken bridge, bustling about with carts. A party of them moved out onto the solid part of the bridge with a weapons cart, and others followed, as if they had found a way to cross the broken spans. Not far from the bridge, I saw boats crossing the river, laden with supplies, and a party assembling on the shore near where we had crossed to Saint-Aignan Island the day before. Then the English stirred in Les Tourelles and I dared stay on the wall no longer.

Soon the men from Orléans began to arrive. Jeanne came also, none the worse, it seemed, for her wounded foot, and the better, I would say, for having slept in a bed the night before. She held council with her captains in one corner of the Augustins yard. Pierre, who arrived with her, told me that it was she who had called them to meet, and that they had, for the first time, done her bidding willingly. "It is important," he said, "for it shows the captains trust her now."

"What will happen today?" I asked him.

"Why," he said, smiling, "we will take Les Tourelles, and it will be ended."

I asked him then if he had seen the page with my horse, or Louis, and he said he had not seen the page or Yarrow, but that Louis had spent the night on Saint-Aignan Island, to be ready to assist with the supplies brought by boats from Orléans. I was much cheered, knowing he was well, but worried still about Yarrow, whom I sorely missed.

Suddenly trumpets sounded and our men bestirred themselves, rushing forward with the men who had come in the boats from Orléans. They all swarmed into the trenches and onto the earthworks protecting Les Tourelles. But the English defended their fortress strongly, with arrows and crossbow bolts and huge round stones shot from cannons. There was terrible chaos again, and screams and heat and the acrid smell of fire. I found myself wanting to run away, or to shout, "Stop! Stop!" — but I could not leave my wounded, whom I tried to soothe while the battle raged only a short distance away. It seemed to me that as fast as our men attacked they were beaten back, over and over. At last, though, they came close enough to put their scaling ladders against the blockhouse walls, to be climbed by the bravest of men. A cruel fate awaited them despite their metal helmets, for the English beat them down with burning pitch and axes and maces and buckets of stones and slingshots and *guisarmes*, which are spears with curved blades, like scythes. The ground was soon slick with blood, and I was busy with new wounded. Here were broken heads as well as broken limbs.

When I tended one man, a common gunner,

whose shoulder had been laid open with an ax, my doublet opened, and the chemise I wore under it pulled awry, revealing my breast. Before I could conceal it, the man leered despite his pain and grabbed me to him, saying, "What, are the other pages wenches as well?"

I tore free of him, which opened his wound further, and adjusted my garments, swallowing my fear and wishing that I had not lost my sword. Luckily, we were a little apart from the others, but I whispered nonetheless, spitting out the words in anger. "If you touch me, I will let you bleed to death. And if you reveal to your companions what you have learned, I will seek you out and poison you, for I am a healer and know how."

He grinned, showing black stumps of teeth, and his hand strayed again.

"I follow the Maid," I said, moving away and drawing my mother's knife, pushing his hand aside with its point, "as do you. You serve her ill by doing this. I also assist the dauphin's surgeon, who serves the Maid on the dauphin's behalf."

The gunner seemed ashamed then, or frightened. He fell back upon the bloody earth, and let me dress his wound in peace.

I had not feared discovery for some time, concealment had become so natural to me. But after this I bound my doublet as closely around me as I could, and thanked the Blessed Mother that I was small, for with my garments fastened, there was truly no curve to betray me.

All morning I saw men coming from the attack, achingly tired, their faces caked with dirt and blood and sweat. Each time I asked one how it went, he replied, "As before," and I began to fear God had deserted us, or did not favor our cause as Jeanne had promised. The air was thick with smoke and the red glow that comes from many flames, but still the men pressed on, scaling the walls and being driven back, and scaling and being driven back again. Some of their wounds were terrible, and there were more broken heads than my poor supply of betony could mend, and I had no hot beer to mix with it. Soon my share of the thorn apple salve that Nicolas had made for burns was gone, so I could not ease the men who suffered those most horrible of wounds.

At last, though, all fell quiet, and word came that Jeanne had urged the men to rest and eat what food they could find. All around me in the Augustins yard men sat slumped against the broken walls and ate or slept or conversed or moaned or stared emptily at nothing. Never had I seen such exhaustion or discouragement. But then Jeanne appeared, and strode among them, her armor freshly cleaned of mud, and gleaming. She smiled and joked and urged them on, saying that an easy victory is not as sweet as one for which one has sorely fought, and saying that they would win if they stayed of good heart. This cheered them, and it cheered me as well; I marveled at her courage and her faith. I remembered what she had told me about her saints, and was much comforted — for surely if she was certain the day would be ours, they had told her so.

In midafternoon, at last, I saw Louis, coming back from an assault, with his face so black with soot and dirt I did not know him till he was nearly upon me. But when I saw it was he under the grime, I ran to him. Luckily he held out his arm, stopping me and saying, "What behavior is this for a page?"

"How goes it?" I asked, clenching my fists to keep from gripping his arm. My voice shook, and I could not steady it, so great was my relief at finding him, and at finding him whole.

"As you see," he said wearily. "They fight hard, those English. But we will not let them win. Have you drink?"

I ran to the well and drew him some muddy water, which he drank as gratefully as if it had been good wine.

"My thanks to you," he said, wiping his mouth on his filthy sleeve. He took my hand and squeezed it quickly, then dropped it. "I must return, but" — he glanced around and I knew he spoke formally to protect my disguise — "I am glad to see you well."

"Stay awhile and rest," I pleaded.

He glanced around again and said, so softly that only I could hear, "What, woman, a nagging wife already?" Then, with me still pondering what he meant, he left.

The day wore on much as before, and I could

not see that it would end any differently from how it had begun, with the English in Les Tourelles and we French holding the Augustins. Then suddenly Jeanne was coming toward me, hand cupped against her shoulder. I saw blood between her fingers, and remembered her words of the day before. As she reached me, a man-at-arms ran up, saying, "I have a charm, madame, that will cure your wound." But she turned to him sternly and said, "I will have no charm. I would rather die than do what I know to be a sin, or to be against God. Here is one that can help me." She nodded toward me as she said this, and when she took her hand away from her shoulder, I saw that in it she held a crossbow bolt, which she had just removed. It had left a clean wound, thank God, between her breast and neck, running upward to her shoulder. I had nothing left to dress it with save some olive oil, but I used that, and bound it firmly.

Some time later, as the stalemate continued, I saw Jeanne kneeling in prayer. Not long after, I heard a trumpet, and a man near me said, "The retreat at last; we are leaving!" But suddenly there was a lusty shout from Les Tourelles. Several of the men climbed the nearest earthwork to look, and I scrambled up with them, in time to see Jeanne running toward the trench around the walls that our men had tried all day to scale. "My standard! My standard!" she shouted, and I knew she realized that if she carried it herself, her soldiers would rally quickly — but I feared for her

163

safety as she ran into the melee. The faithful d'Aulon was ahead of the stout Frenchman who bore the standard, and was already running courageously across the trench. There was such shouting I could not make out separate words, but at last I saw Jeanne seize her standard and shake it as if signaling to our men-at-arms to come forward instead of retreating — and so they did, running bravely out of the Augustins once more. Roaring mightily with joy at following the Maid herself, they surged toward the walls, this time with such vigor and purpose that the English must have trembled to see and hear them. There was an answering shout from the Orléans end of the broken bridge, and I could see men running out on it.

All was confusion for a time — men and horses, scrambling and rearing and thrusting and shouting, and cannons and culverins booming, and arrows falling around us like sharp hail. Even some of my wounded stirred and joined the battle, and I, seeing I was no longer needed by them, moved closer. Unthinking, carried by the men's fervor as a twig is carried by a swift stream, I seized an abandoned crossbow, and put my foot on it, as I had seen bowmen do. I tried to draw its string back with its windlass to prepare it for firing, but I could not get the knack of it. It was heavier than I expected as well, so I put it down and unsheathed my knife instead. For war is like that, too, I was discovering: a passion that seizes a crowd, consuming each individual so that the crowd becomes one person, mindless, bent on a single goal, to kill and maim and take.

There was a great bustle of men at the end of the bridge, near Les Tourelles where the arch had been broken. I could see people from Orléans laying a long wooden rain gutter across, trying to reach Les Tourelles from the other side. The supply carts I had seen earlier were close behind them. A cry went up when the gutter wavered and nearly fell into the Loire; it was too short to span the distance. Then came a man with planks, and others lifted the gutter once more. Somehow they fastened the planks to it, and then to the shore, so creating a thin bridge over which the Orléanais, teetering, managed to cross. This meant Les Tourelles was being attacked on both sides, by our men from the Augustins and by the Orléanais from the gutter-bridge!

While I was watching this, a bowman took the crossbow, which was still lying at my feet. " 'Tis too heavy for you, lad," he said kindly. "Wait till you have more years and can draw it more easily. Here, use this." He gave me a short dagger, and ran forward with the bow.

But I had my mother's knife, so I gave the dagger to a young page who had no weapon.

There remained a final section of river for our men to cross, between the blockhouse and Les Tourelles, on the Augustins side. The English — foolishly, for them — let down the wooden drawbridge spanning it, and ran onto it, ready to attack. But our men-at-arms swarmed toward it, attacking also, having scaled the blockhouse walls at last. Jeanne, standing splendidly in her armor against the flaming sky, shouted, "Glasdale! Glasdale!" to the English captain who had insulted her when she had urged him to surrender earlier. "Yield," she cried. "Yield to the King of Heaven! You have called me whore, but I have great pity on your soul and your men's souls!"

I saw him shake his armored fist at her, and hurl insults at her again. Though I did not understand the English words he said, it was easy to tell their meaning.

While Glasdale was shouting, I saw a boat, all in flames, reach the drawbridge near which he stood. I thought at first it was a boat that had been attacked. But I soon realized it had been set alight on purpose to burn the bridge, for it was full of all manner of stinking things, bones and sulphur and garbage. I could tell that Jeanne saw it, too. As Glasdale and his men stepped upon the bridge, the flaming boat reached it, making it catch fire behind them. Within moments the bridge burned through and broke, dropping Glasdale and the men with him into the Loire. Their heavy armor made them sink quickly, and they drowned — without confessing, as Jeanne had predicted when she had answered Glasdale's insults. I shuddered, and crossed myself.

There is little left to tell. The English stopped resisting after that, and the day again was ours. Prisoners were taken from among the noblemen;

they would be held for ransom, as was the custom. English surgeons tended their wounded and buried their dead. Pierre and I found each other, and then I found Louis, who was still unscathed, as was Pierre. Though I did not like leaving without my horse, they urged me back to Orléans, where the bells rang and the people danced and cheered as we made our way to the Bouchers', too weary to rejoice ourselves. Nicolas came to the Bouchers' soon after we arrived and he also dressed Jeanne's wound, adding pig's fat to my oil. She had preceded us, but had been held back in the streets by people praising and thanking her. We all supped, and then retired. I, of course, had to tell the story of the battle to young Charles, who had indeed watched from his room, and whose account of it was far more glowing than the truth.

16

Later that night, as I slept despite the joyful sounds of the Orléanais dancing in the streets, Monsieur Boucher summoned me. "Another page seeks you," he told me.

I thought: *Yarrow!* and ran to greet him.

But my rejoicing quickly turned to apprehension when I saw the boy's face, dirt- and tear-stained, and the fear in his eyes.

"Your horse," he said in a choking voice as soon as I appeared. "The English . . ."

"They did not take her?" I shouted, grabbing his tattered doublet and shaking him — for that to me would have been the worst fate, to have my Yarrow stolen. How would I know how she fared, and whether they fed or beat her?

"N-no," he said, trembling, so I let him go.

"What then?"

His words came quickly. "When — when the fighting was — was thickest at Les Tourelles, after the Maid led the men to the walls, I took your horse from where we had stayed by that machine, and — and I came into the Augustins yard with her and saw you with a — a crossbow — and just then an English arrow flew toward us and your horse took it in her chest, and fell. And then there was such confusion I could not get to you, or find you. Oh, I am sorry!" he said, seizing my arm and looking at me imploringly. "She was a noble horse . . ."

But I no longer heard him, or saw him, for my eyes were overflowing with tears. I turned away, and shook off his hand.

"It — it was very quick," he told me miserably. "She did not even scream."

Yarrow, Yarrow, my mind was saying, *while I played at soldier with a crossbow, you lay dying and I did not even know . . .*

"I am sorry," said the boy again, and his voice broke as I knew mine would were I to speak.

But speak I knew I must; he had been kind and brave to bring me the ill news, and I knew he was suffering for it.

"Nay, friend," I managed to say, "it was none of your doing. You served me well, and her, and I thank you." My voice failed me then; I whispered, "Leave me now, but in peace; I bear you no ill will." And then I stumbled back to my room, and wept for my sweet mare. Never have I known a dearer or more willing horse than my Yarrow. I miss her still, whenever I think of her.

There was rejoicing all night, and the ringing

of bells, but I heard the glad sounds only dimly through my grief.

The next morning, Sunday, though the English came out of their forts, they did not attack. In a while, Jeanne had Father Pasquerel and the other priests set up an altar, before which they said Mass for the men-at-arms and sang anthems. By the time this was done, the English were in retreat. Almost all of them departed that day, leaving behind only a few wounded men and some goods which the Orléanais quickly took as recompense for the siege.

Jeanne left Orléans soon after the days of celebration had passed, to ask the dauphin, who was at his castle in Loches, for more troops so she could take other towns along the Loire that the English held, and to urge him again to go to Reims to be crowned. I stayed in Orléans, mourning Yarrow and seeking lodging elsewhere, for I wished to put off my disguise, so I could see Louis openly as myself. He had elected to stay behind with me, and with the men-at-arms who awaited Jeanne's return. I wanted to visit the Aumône-de-Sainte-Croix, the place for the poor people of the town who were sick. For that I would need, I felt, to be both woman and midwife.

Pierre found lodging for me at the home of a Monsieur Dupont, telling him and Madame Dupont that I was a friend and countrywoman of his sister's, come to Orléans to await her return, bearing messages from Domremy. They had a grander house than the Bouchers', and daintier food, which grew more plentiful daily, as the countryfolk began to come into Orléans again with their goods. We had roasted goose, capons, and pheasants; cream tarts and sweet wafers; and, once, a whole swan still in its white feathers! That one, I did not wish to eat. Even when it was cut and I could see that it had been well cooked, it still seemed too much like the live bird.

The first two days I was at the Duponts', I rested, walking slowly in the streets where young Charles had taken me, and sitting quietly with Louis on the banks of the Loire, outside the city walls. It was peaceful there, though the ravages of battle were all around — scorched grass and trees, and great round stones shot from cannons, and broken machines of war, and arrows from the English longbows, plus rubble from Les Tourelles and the Augustins. But we blinded ourselves to them, and looked up at the bright spring sky with its soft white clouds, and listened to the birds, who had returned now that the fighting was over. It was these things, and Louis's gentle presence, that slowly dulled the ache I felt for Yarrow.

Once we went to the Isle des Boeufs, where Pierre was later to live, though of course I did not know that then. We walked the entire day there, trying to make each other laugh, I with descriptions of battles with the boys of Maxey, and with my parents' name of changeling for me, and he with accounts of feasts at which each course was more elegant than the last. I had thought that swan in feathers was the oddest dish ever brought to table, but Louis told me of a pie in which a chicken, though cooked, was made to rise up as if alive when the crust was broken! I marveled more than ever that Louis could care for someone as humble as I. But he said that he believed it was not people's station that made them what they were but they themselves, and that I had the makings of a great lady.

"I do not wish to be a great lady," I told him, "for that would be dull. I would rather be a great doctor. But that is not possible, I am sure."

Louis looked thoughtful. "They do not, I think, allow women in the university to study medicine, but perhaps when the dauphin is king and Jeanne is again spinning in Domremy, you and I can go to Paris and I can leave off soldiering for a while and go to the university and teach you what I have been taught. I told you I would not mind being a scholar-knight."

"But you do not care for medicine," I said, not mentioning what had made joy leap within me: that he saw us together when the king was crowned and the fighting was at an end. I dared to remember, then, too, what he had said in the Augustins yard about a nagging wife.

And then he took my shoulders and drew me to him, and held me close to his body, saying softly, "No, my Gabrielle, I do not care for medicine, but I truly would not dislike combining

172

study with soldiering. Most of all, though, I find that I care for you. Why is it, think you, that I stayed in Orléans rather than following Jeanne or going home to my father?"

"To avoid the hardships of travel or hearing your father's anger, I suppose," I said, but my voice was weak and my head was spinning.

Louis pulled me even closer and put his lips on mine as he had done before. For a long time we spoke not, and I learned why it is that women sometimes do not wait to be wed before they get with child. It was hard for me to wait that day, for Louis's touch made my body sing and my whole being rejoice as nothing had before — but fear and shyness made me hesitate; he did not urge me, and the moment passed.

The next day, with Louis, I went to the Aumône-de-Sainte-Croix to see if I could be of service, and found I was welcome because of my knowledge of midwifery. And so every day I went there and gave them what aid I could, delivering several fine infants, two of whom, I am proud and pleased to say, were named for me! I helped with the sick, too, and learned the ingredients for several new unguents, which I was anxious to show Nicolas when he returned — for he had gone with Jeanne to the dauphin. Once or twice after I left the hospital, Louis taught me more letters, but usually I was too weary, and so we would just talk.

May passed into June, and soon Jeanne returned, having at last convinced the dauphin to give her troops to win back the towns the enemy held along the Loire. Pierre was with her, and the surly Jean, and Nicolas. Pierre said — and Nicolas agreed — that the dauphin's advisers, especially the stout La Trémoille and Archbishop Regnault de Chartres, who had ignored Jeanne at Blois, wished to ignore her still. "Their purpose is always to advance themselves," Nicolas explained, in obvious disgust. "I am happier in the field than at court when those two are there, for they will agree with whoever buys or flatters them; they are selfish, dangerous men in the guise of loyal ones."

But despite La Trémoille and the archbishop, the dauphin had put Jeanne's *beau duc* Alençon in charge of the army, and had told him to follow Jeanne's council. I saw Jeanne and Alençon smiling and laughing together more than ever after that, almost as close and easy with each other as Pierre and I.

More troops had come to Orléans this time than I had seen even at Blois, and despite what I had learned of war, my blood stirred once more at the sight of them, though their horses put me in mind of Yarrow. Louis, I saw, felt the same, for he turned and said to me, as we watched them enter the city, "It is time for us to be soldiers once more, you and I, is it not? Will Gabrielle be a page again, and a boy?"

I nodded, and stood on my toes — for he was tall, my Louis — and kissed him, saying, "She

174

will be a boy in garb and in speech and manner, but her heart will remain a woman's," and I hurried off to take my leave of the Duponts and don my boy's clothes, so I could return to Pierre's side as his page.

On the tenth of June, we set out, an army again, for Jargeau, to the east of Orléans, which the English held. I had a small black horse which Pierre had somehow found for me. I think he must have belonged to the English, for he knew the language of reins better than that of speech. I named him Anglais and found him steady, but I decided not to love him, lest he, too, be lost in battle.

We, and the men of Orléans who came with us, marched along the Loire, where it was very flat and so misty we could not see much at all ahead of us. And at last we stopped in a wood not far from Jargeau. The knight commanding Louis's section was old, and did not always notice whether his men were with him, so it was easy for Louis to join me when we all made camp in the woods. Louis and I moved a safe distance from the others, and built our own small fire under the trees.

"It will be hard," mused Louis, chewing a bit of rabbit I had both snared and cooked, "to live again within walls. We are so used to being out-of-doors."

I laughed and poked him. "This is our first night out-of-doors after a month of nights within; do you forget so quickly?"

"That I do," he said, swallowing his meat and seizing me around the waist, "for I prefer being outside, away from watchful eyes, and free as the birds and the beasts and the trees and the flowers . . ." He left off then and looked deep into my eyes. "Gabrielle, Gabrielle, Gabrielle," he whispered, his eyes so full of love that I felt an overpowering softness steal my strength from me. "I am so happy when I am with you! I care not where I am, or who I am; I want only to stay by your side and serve you and talk with you, for" — he traced my brow with his gentle fingertip — "your mind is as wonderful as the beauty of your face."

I knew I was not beautiful, and would have laughed but for the seriousness of his voice and the strength of my love for him — and for what he said next, which was, softly, "Gabrielle, little changeling as some call you, will you lie with me?"

I ached to say I would; every part of me hungered for him. And this time I do not think it was fear or shyness that held me back. But I made myself refuse, choosing my words with care. "I wish to, with all my heart," I told him, "but I cannot lest we be wed, and I say this not to trap you, but because I cannot follow the Maid and do what she and God would deem sinful. Surely you see that; oh, please, my Louis, say that you do!"

He looked hurt and for a moment seemed to withdraw from me, but then he kissed me tenderly and said, "Yes, I do see it, and I love you more for it. But we must wed quickly, then, Gabrielle, for we both long for each other so!"

"What of your father?" I asked then, "and what of mine? I have no dowry . . ."

"Do you think I care for that?" he said angrily. "Or for what my father says, or yours? We are rebels, you and I; they cannot cage us, Gabrielle, and they will not. We will not let them, and *we will wed*!"

Oh, how those words echo in my mind, even now; how they make my heart ache and my eyes fill — oh, my Louis!

Nicolas came to me early the next morning, Sunday, with Pierre, and, taking me aside, said, gently for him, "I have been short with you, my boy, and hard, to test you, and I have delayed speaking until I saw you in battle. But you have proved yourself resolute and calm as well as skilled, and so I have asked your master, Pierre, if he will release you to serve me as my page and assistant — in short, as my apprentice — and he has agreed. What say you?"

I glanced at Pierre, who nodded and said carefully, "Since I have promised your parents to look after you, you will see me still — but it is right for you to serve Nicolas, since you have more skill for healing than for warfare."

So I agreed, my mind racing — for of course Nicolas did not know I was not the boy he thought me, and I could see that Pierre had not told him. What would he do if he found out? I feared his anger, but my eagerness to learn from him overcame my fear — though I knew I would have to be more careful, now, of seeing Louis, for Nicolas would expect me to stay close to him, and it would seem strange to him if I were often visited by a young nobleman!

"Good," Nicolas said with much satisfaction. "I shall inform the captains and the Maid."

Soon after, Jeanne summoned me and Nicolas before the captains and the army, telling them to look to us both should they fall in battle. And at intervals all that day our guns fired at Jargeau's walls, but Nicolas and I, near our cart of herbs and linens and tools, had little to do, for our men were too far back for the English shots to reach them. That night, each time my eyes closed, I heard the guns again, jolting me out of sleep.

When morning came at last, I thought there could be no more rounded stones left for the cannons — indeed, the workers were already chiseling new ones. Later, the trumpets called for an attack, and our men surged forward, those in the front carrying the scaling ladders that had been brought up on the carts. They put these against the walls, though we could all see the English waiting above them, armed with stones and iron balls and hot pitch and flame, which they poured down. And once, when I looked up again at the walls after treating a man whose arm had been burned, my breath caught in my throat, for none other than Jeanne was mounting a ladder, her standard in her hand, beckoning our men to follow. As I watched, more horrified every moment, a man on the wall hurled down a stone, which hit her on the peaked helmet she wore. I know I let out a cry when the stone shattered and she fell. There was, for the space of a few seconds, a ghastly silence from us French, and a great cheer from the English. But as Nicolas and I ran toward Jeanne, the sounds were reversed, with the English falling silent and our men shouting with joy and relief, for Jeanne sprang to her feet, as if the fall had been a mere tumble. "Up, friends," she cried. "Up! Our Lord has damned the English. At this very moment they are ours; be of good cheer!"

And our men swarmed over the walls as if no power would ever be able to stop them. Jargeau was indeed ours.

17

What followed I do not like to remember. The English, fearing rightly for their lives and their safety, fled out of the town. Many ran to the river, rushing so quickly that they fell in and were drowned, for in their heavy armor they sank helplessly. Then, too, the gentle — or so I had thought — Orléanais who had come with us argued with our men over who should collect ransom for some of the prisoners. When they did not get their way, they fell upon the prisoners, massacring them till the ground ran red with blood. No one did anything to prevent the slaughter; it was as if victory had crazed them all. Our men joined the Orléanais in sacking Jargeau, despite Jeanne's pleas that it be left alone. Even the church was pillaged, and I do not like to think of what must have happened to whatever women were in the town. I wondered where God was on that day, and said as much to Nicolas, who looked at me oddly, saying, "You have a woman's tenderness; be careful it does not soften you too much."

We returned to Orléans, but soon marched again, toward Meung and Beaugency, in heavy mist along the Loire, Nicolas and I with the supply carts, leading our horses to keep them fresh. We were at the end of the column, and Jeanne and Alençon were at the head. The guns followed, by boat, on the Loire, and we were a large party again, full ready for war. Louis was in the middle somewhere, with Pierre and other men-at-arms, and Jean had disappeared.

I was sleepy and could only grumble when Nicolas tried to instruct me, as we lumbered along, about the proper way to remove a badly mangled leg. I felt heavy and stupid; my head was buzzing, and I began to think perhaps I was ill. The mist kept us from seeing if any English waited for us, and I was sure that if any were nearby, they could not help but hear us even if they could not see us, for we were so many and so loud. And then I stumbled, hitting my knee hard upon a rock. Tears sprang to my eyes and I rocked back and forth in pain, gripping my knee, while Nicolas watched in apparent surprise, saying, "Come, come, boy; tears are a woman's weakness! It is not so great an injury."

I wanted to shout then that I was a woman, and that tears are not weak, and that I would not have wept at all had I not felt so ill. But I choked back those words with the pain and the tears, stood, and went on.

We were weary with marching when word passed along the line that we had reached Meung, so Nicolas and I made ready to receive wounded. There were sounds ahead of fighting, and then silence; our men, we heard, had taken the bridge to Meung easily, and driven the English into the town, where they remained.

And there we stayed the rest of the day, and camped in the fields. After a damp, nearly sleepless night, I was awakened by Louis shaking my shoulder and saying softly in my ear, "*There* you are! Come, the sun is rising through the mist over the river, and it is very beautiful." He kissed me quickly when no one was looking and pulled me to my feet, but my head felt so heavy I could barely hold it up. At last I realized that I had caught cold, from the damp, no doubt, and the mist, whose beauty I felt too ill to appreciate. But I went, reeling, with Louis to the river. When we reached it, Louis put his arm around me and pointed to where the rising sun made a yellow-pink glow in the sky and on the water. I tried to smile, but instead gave such a sneeze as to almost knock him over.

Clearly alarmed beyond all reason, he stripped off the leather doublet he wore over his mail shirt, and put it around my shoulders, saying, "You shall ride on a cart today; I will speak to Nicolas. Quick, now, come to the cooking fires and get warm." He led me back, and I could not protest.

But Nicolas met us before we reached the fire, his face angrier than I had ever seen it. "What does this mean?" he barked, looking from Louis to me and to Louis again. "What interest have you in my page, monsieur? It is as if you are some Greek lover of boys. That will not do, and I am sure" — here he reached out and put a protective hand on my shoulder — "that my good page likes it not."

I looked helplessly at Louis, and Louis turned bright red. "It is not as you think, monsieur," he said stiffly.

"No?" Nicolas stepped closer, his face inches from Louis's face, and his fists doubling. "Then you will not object if I tell you I will have no more of your skulking around my page, wooing him with I know not what promises of wealth and station — empty promises, for you, monsieur, are in tatters and surely the youngest son of a youngest son, with little to offer . . ."

I could bear no more, and I could see that Louis's anger was about to spew forth in a way that could lead only to drawn swords. So I pushed myself between them, my alarm and fever chasing away whatever discretion I had left, and said, "He tells the truth. It is not as you think, for I am not a boy."

Nicolas stared for a moment and I could see something pulsing at the side of his head. I found myself holding my breath and I think Louis was holding his as well — and then at last Nicolas threw back his head and laughed. "Of course!" he bellowed. "Of course! I saw it and yet I did not see it — and you are lovers, then" — his face took on a stern expression, but a mock one, I was sure — "under the very nose of the Maid, who will have no women following her army. It is a grand joke, surely — but a very dangerous one."

We explained then, Louis and I, how things stood with Jeanne, and with Pierre.

Nicolas shook his head as if in disbelief, and said, "Never have I heard such a tale — or seen such healing skill," he added, looking at me, "on the part of a woman. Very well, then," he continued, "I will keep your secret, Gabrielle de Domremy, and I will try to adjust to having a daughter instead of a son — for, yes," he said, his eyes darting away as if he were embarrassed, "I had begun to think of you in that way, for my wife and I have no issue, and . . ."

And then I sneezed, and sneezed again, and both men fussed around me like mothers, bundling me into the medicine cart, among the herbs and saws and bandages. I made the next march — a short one — riding in it, with Anglais walking along beside. Though it was a bumpy ride, I felt better for it, and better, too, for the tea Nicolas fed me, pungent with sharp herbs that cleared my nose at least while I was drinking it, and soothed my fiery throat. Many of the men, Nicolas said, were in a similar state, and

184

grumbling, too, because of lack of pay — but what they planned to spend it on, along the Loire's desolate banks, I could not imagine!

I roused myself as we approached Beaugency. A massive stone donjon rose above the river, and an abbey's buildings covered the slope leading to the shore. The donjon presented a smooth face save for a few slits of windows, and I did not see how we could take it, unless our guns were stronger than I thought, and could crumble it.

I remember that battle in a fog, for my head was still muzzy despite Nicolas's teas and Louis's loving attention. Nicolas now looked in kindly manner upon Louis whenever he came to me, and winked, as if they shared a joke, and tempered his gruffness. Louis fed me tea, brought me bread and cheese, and even helped me into the woods, standing guard while I relieved myself. He stayed near me that night as well. The cart was well away from the fighting and hidden from the men, but now and then I could hear our guns hammering at the donjon, though later I learned they had done it little harm.

When morning broke, I found myself leaning against Louis's shoulder, heedless of the hard metal bumps of his mail shirt. There was less mist, and I felt both better and warmer, partly, of course, because of Louis's warm body and the protection of his heavy doublet, which I still wore.

"I think you slept," he said, smiling into my eyes and kissing me; Nicolas's back was turned, though it would not have mattered had it not been. Still, we had grown accustomed to being careful.

"Because of you," I said, smiling back. "And you? Have you slept?"

"Now and then," he said. "Off and on. But listen . . ." He told me that more French men-at-arms were coming to help us fight — and he left me then, to prepare for battle with the other men.

That very afternoon we went back toward Meung to meet the French reinforcements, and we all waited for the English between Beaugency and Meung, along a ridge that seemed taller than it was, owing to the flatness of the surrounding land.

Nicolas and I positioned ourselves at one end of the ridge and behind it, with the carts and our horses, ready to tend the wounded. I was thankful to find my head clearer, but my nose still streamed and my eyes watered, so I was somewhat distracted.

I was not so distracted, though, that I did not see the English coming toward us like ghosts out of the mist, which again lay thickly over all the countryside. I felt myself moving toward Anglais and bracing my back against the cart, for I was suddenly so chilled with fear I wanted to run, and knew I could not. No one moved, not Nicolas, or me, or our horses or the captains, who were not far from us, or the men. The silence was eerie, and I knew I was not the only one afraid.

At last I heard Alençon's voice. "They approach, Jeanne," he said quietly. "What will you have us do now? Shall we attack?"

I heard her give a short, hard laugh. "See that you all have good spurs," she said.

"What?" asked Alençon, and I could hear amazement in his voice. "Are we to turn our backs on them?"

"No. It will be the English who will put up no defense. We will beat them, and you will have to have good spurs to pursue them."

I understood then, and Jeanne's confidence cheered me, but at the same time I liked not the thought of our men pursuing the English, lest there be another slaughter as at Jargeau.

And there was not. We and the English spent the day bristling at each other across the short space of flat land that divided us, while flies buzzed around the supply carts and birds flew overhead attending to their affairs, all innocent of the impending battle below them. I had to hop first on one foot, then on the other, to keep both feet from tingling. In the end, without so much as a skirmish, we French marched back to Beaugency, and the English forces went toward Meung; it was said among the men that we would meet them again the next day.

That night, when I fell asleep under the medicine cart, my head was stuffy again with my cold, and dread filled my heart.

18

When I woke, it was to the news that the English holding Beaugency had surrendered in the night, and were even then departing. But while our camp slowly stirred to life, cheered by the English surrender, scouts rode breathlessly up from La Hire, saying that a large body of English was riding in haste toward us.

The camp's quiet motion turned to frenzy, for everyone feared that the arriving English would join with those who were leaving, and then attack. "In the name of God," Jeanne shouted, "we must fight them! Even if they were hanging from the clouds we would beat them, for God has sent them to us that we may punish them. Today the gentle dauphin will have the greatest victory he has ever had. And my counsel has told me that the English will all be ours."

We were quickly formed by the captains into three groups. La Hire led the vanguard, with Poton de Xaintrailles. Then came the largest group, where Louis was, and Pierre, and Jean. And finally came the rearguard, in which I was, with Nicolas and Jeanne herself, who was angry to be last, but still confident of victory.

My stuffy head eased some as I moved, and more when I mounted Anglais and rode with the others over the flat land. Soon we were in woods so thick we could not see what or who might be beside us, and more than one of us, I am sure, was uneasy lest the English take us by surprise.

Suddenly there was a distant cry, and then another, and the sound of horses whinnying. Moments later we were urged forward at a gallop, and the woods echoed with the sound. Word came back to us as we thundered on that some of the English had seen a stag and, unable to contain themselves at the thought of fresh food, had shouted, thus giving away their position to our scouts.

Jeanne spurred her horse ahead out of the woods, and Nicolas and I followed more slowly. Soon I heard sounds of fighting, and when we emerged between two hedges, one higher than the other, and I saw what was ahead, I wanted to retreat into the woods once more. But I could not move, even to urge Anglais to turn. Instead I stared in horror at the scene before me, which looked as if it were out of hell itself.

The field was a mass of moving men, of swords and lances glittering as they rose and fell and rose and fell again — but many soldiers already lay bleeding and moaning on the ground under horses' hooves and armored feet. Human screams mingled with those of innocent horses, making me think again of Orléans and Yarrow, and there were few suits of armor or mail that were not stained with blood. I saw a man with no face, he had been so brutally trampled, and another who stared in surprised agony at his nearly severed hand till a sword thrust in his chest put an end to him. The screams rose over such a yelling and a cursing and a shouting, and such a pounding of hooves and raining of arrows and whirling of maces, that even now it makes me tremble to recall it.

Anglais pawed the ground and snorted. Nicolas, beside me, seized Anglais's reins and pulled his head down, holding it steady. Then he crossed himself and muttered, *"Mon Dieu, mon Dieu,* it is a slaughter — but not of us, my child, not of us French." He moved his horse closer and squeezed my shoulder with his strong surgeon's hand, but it did not comfort me. I did not see how he could tell who was French and who English among the men who writhed upon the ground.

For a moment I saw Louis on his horse, whirling an ax above his head, his face so distorted with hate I almost did not know him. And I saw a man who had fallen to the ground look up at him as if pleading for his life. But Louis's ax fell, and split that man's unhelmeted head in two.

I gasped. I think I cried, "No — no!" aloud, and I think Nicolas looked at me, in surprise or sympathy; I know not which. All I knew then was that Louis, my dearest friend and love, had killed a fallen man who was no danger to him and who had begged for mercy. Was this what becoming a soldier had done to him? Which was the true Louis? The gentle man who wanted to be a scholar-knight, who had cared for me when I was ill, and who supported my wish to learn and heal? Or the cruel warrior who knew no mercy?

I could stay no longer. Horrified, and blinded by tears, I slid from Anglais and ran back into the forest. Soon I tripped, and then sank down upon some moss under a tree, with the sounds of the battle still in my ears, and I wept till I had no tears left.

I do not know how long I stayed there. I know I slowly became aware of silence, and of darkness and then moonlight, and of my own stiffness, and my shivering. I could not breathe through my nose, and my eyes were sore from weeping; my cheeks were caked with salt, and stinging with it.

I pulled myself to my feet and looked around, glad there was no one near me, for I did not see how I could face any of my companions. I had run away, which no soldier should ever do, and no healer either. I had abandoned my horse — though Nicolas, I thought, must have him — and abandoned Nicolas and wounded men as well. Worse, I had lost faith in Louis, in Jeanne, and in our quest. For I was sure now that if this was the way to crown our king, even if it was the only way, it was wrong.

I saw again in my mind the scene I had fled, and moaned aloud, knowing I should return to it to give aid to those who had fallen, even though I had no stomach for it. But that, at least, was peaceful work, separate from the fighting that created the need for it.

And so I returned, finding my way by the direction in which the trampled brush was lying. Soon the forest thinned, and I was in the field between the two hedges, where the ground was dark and spongy with blood and strewn with bodies.

I walked among them, numbly; they were, I quickly saw, all English. Had Nicolas and the living soldiers finished removing our French dead and wounded, then, or were there none? I knew not — but those around me, all, were English, and all were dead.

And why had no one come to bury them?

This was the first time I had looked into an English face. I knew not what I had expected, but their faces were like our men's faces, some round, some long, some old, some pitifully young, some bearded and some plain, with all colors of hair and many shades of complexion. Some were mangled beyond recognition — those whom maces had struck, and those who had been trampled by horses and men — and they lay thickly, so thickly.

As I walked aimlessly among them, sometimes stumbling over an outstretched arm or a discarded sword — but most of those were gone, taken as plunder, I assumed, by our French, and many bodies were naked or nearly so, robbed of their garments — as I walked there, I saw a slight motion at the bottom of a heap of men lying every which way, and heard a soft moan. I ran there and tugged at bodies till I was covered with blood and had unearthed a boy no older than myself, with his side laid open — but he breathed. Congealed blood lay on the wound, through which I could see bone and entrails. The boy's eyes fluttered, and he smiled weakly, saying something in his language. He grasped my hand and, holding it, before I could think how to tend his wound, he died.

I stayed there, holding his head against my breast, till I felt a hand on my shoulder, softly, and I looked up to see Louis. His hose and doublet were in tatters and his mail shirt split; his face was covered with filth and blood. But it is his eyes in that moment that I still cannot forget, for they were hollow — empty except for despair.

"I cannot find him," he said brokenly. "I cannot find him."

I had thought that when I saw Louis again, if indeed I did see him, I would run from him, but now I had no strength to run. And this, though broken, was again the Louis I knew, not the beast I had seen on the battlefield, wielding the ax.

"Who," I asked, "can you not find?"

"Him," he said, sinking to his knees beside me and the boy whose body I still held. "He whom I clove in twain, whose head I broke beyond all healing, whose pleas I ignored. I have killed other men, Gabrielle, but none who pleaded with me for life. His eyes — his eyes . . ." He turned away from me and his body heaved, as if he were vomiting, but nothing came up; he was empty, as if he had already vomited many times.

I laid the English boy down as softly as I could. Then I went to Louis and put my arms around him. We stayed thus all night, alone on the spent battlefield among the English dead, until dawn.

19

I remember being surprised, when I woke, that still no English had come to bury their dead, as was the custom. Later I learned that at least two thousand had died and two hundred more had been taken prisoner; it would have taken many nights to bury them all, had there been enough free men left alive to do it. I do not know if those English dead were ever buried, or if they were left for the wolves and the crows.

When we woke, Louis and I, I saw motion at the far edge of the battlefield, and found that most of our army had slept there, only a short way off, around the edges of the dead. Jeanne and some of the captains had spent the night in the nearby town — Patay, it was called. Father Pasquerel, who was making his way slowly among the dead, came gravely up to us, saying, "It is a sorry sight."

"God cannot be pleased," I said, "at such a slaughter."

"Nay, child," Father Pasquerel said, "war is

cruel, but the ways of evil are crueler. This slaughter is a sign from God that He wishes us to prevail. Think of the holy Crusades, which men have fought for God, to curb the evil infidel." Then he smiled in his courtly way and held his hands out to us, saying, "Come, it will be easier now." When we hesitated, he said, "The Maid herself was moved by the slaughter, for such indeed it was. She wept when she saw it, and when she saw one of our French men-at-arms strike an English prisoner and throw him down, she leapt from her horse and held the Englishman till he had made his confession and was dead."

I tried to be heartened by this, but I could not help thinking that perhaps it was not enough, since it had been Jeanne who had urged us to fight.

Father Pasquerel extended his hands to us once more and again said, "Come. At least take bread with us. You must be hungry."

We *were* hungry. Louis looked as if he would stumble and fall at any moment and I am sure I looked the same. I felt too weak to resist, and so I agreed.

After we ate, for all that long day, as Louis and I first tried to clean the blood off ourselves and then rested away from the others, I thought of what Father Pasquerel had said, and Louis and I talked. I knew that the English, like the Burgundian brigands who had ravished my own Meuse valley, must have been cruel to the French whose towns they had seized. I knew that people in besieged towns often starved, and were not free to go where they chose. And I knew this was our country, not theirs, our small corner of the world, and that the English had theirs across the sea, and should be content with it. As the day wore on and my strength returned, I partway convinced myself that Father Pasquerel was right. I saw that Louis was clinging to his words, and later the elegant Alençon said to him, "Had you not killed that man who begged for mercy, he or one of his companions would have killed you. The lesson, *mon ami* — my friend — is not to look into their eyes, eh?"

I shuddered at Alençon's coldness, but Louis seemed heartened by his words.

Later, too, Jeanne came and led me away from Louis, saying, "It grieves me, too, to see so many dead. But my saints have told me that it must be so. I am glad you tend the wounded, and do not love to fight. We both do God's work, my friend, but we do it differently. You are the dove of peace, and I wield the sword of war. At this time, France needs soldiers, but at war's end, when all of France is France again, she will need the work of peace — your work. Follow me, Gabrielle, to see the dauphin crowned and to aid my wounded when they fall. Perhaps when that is done, you will be able to return safely to Domremy, if that is what you want."

I nodded; I was unable to speak, but her words

made sense to me — though I was not sure I would return to Domremy.

We went back to Orléans, where Louis and I slowly became ourselves again. Jeanne went first to Sully and then to Gien, where she was at last able to persuade the dauphin, despite La Trémoille's reluctance, to travel to Reims to be crowned — on condition that we secure more towns for him along the way. So we mounted and left Orléans once more.

It was in Gien that I first saw our king-to-be, and understood how his advisers were able to influence him so easily, for he was not at all as I had imagined. I had thought of the dauphin as tall and stately, with well-molded features and a dignified, noble bearing — gentle, as Jeanne had often called him when speaking of him, but firm, like a stern but loving father, perhaps even not unlike my own Papa, or Nicolas, or Jeanne's kind squire, d'Aulon.

But he was nothing like that. He was small, especially next to the huge La Trémoille, who rode at his side and dwarfed him, and he was a little bowed, with a thin, petulant face and a weak chin and mouth, and eyes that seemed uncertain of where to look. He reminded me of a child who has been pampered and spoiled, and I was disappointed. But Louis, beside me in his repaired mail shirt and a dead man's leather doublet, whispered softly, "He is the only French king we have, Gabrielle; we must do him homage. Besides, a man's outer look shows neither his soul nor his courage."

Louis is right, I thought, and so as the men in the army cheered with joy at seeing their king at last, I added my voice to theirs. Soon, as is the way with such things, I began to feel joyous, too. But Nicolas stood quietly by without smiling, and I heard him say softly, "Poor uncertain Charles; how weary he looks, and how frightened!"

At Gien, our army grew, though there was scant money to pay those who served in it, and less food, and most men were poorly armed, except with loyalty and good spirits. We reached Auxerre at the very end of June, and camped near that city for three days, until at last the people there said they would shift their loyalty to the dauphin if Troyes, Châlons, and Reims did the same; it was as if they feared to rebel alone.

We left with that promise, and went on to Saint-Florentin, which came to our side eagerly — but the next city, Troyes, held by Burgundians, was reluctant. It was there, while we were preparing for battle, that we encountered Brother Richard, a monk from Paris. At first, thinking Jeanne was a witch, he tried to exorcise her with holy water. "Approach boldly," Jeanne said to him, smiling. "I will not fly away." And soon he was kneeling with her in earnest conversation — but Father Pasquerel did not seem pleased.

We stayed outside Troyes for several days,

with the men grumbling from hunger and inactivity, waiting for word from the dauphin allowing us to fight. And then, when word came and the men were filling the moat with the bundles of sticks and brush called fascines, so they could cross it and storm the walls, men came out of the city, bearing signs of truce, and surrendered! Louis and I embraced, I with considerable joy at his not having to fight.

The next day, Louis and I idled by the river — the Seine — in a thicket where we could be hidden and alone. Louis slept much of the time, his head in my lap, and I stroked his hair and dreamed of the time when we would be wed. Would we have three children or four, I wondered, forgetting I had once forsworn children. I thought of my infant brother and wondered how he was and how my sisters fared, especially Marguerite with her cough, and Maman and Papa, and all our neighbors in Domremy. If I closed my eyes just so, I could almost pretend the Seine was the Meuse, but it took much imagination, for the Seine's course was straighter and its banks less green and misty, and there were no cows lowing nearby or village church bells answering each other across a gentle valley. And besides, closing my eyes made me sleepy.

I eased Louis's head off my lap and lay beside him. With one arm around his waist, I settled my head onto his chest — he wore no scratchy mail shirt now, since we were unlikely to do battle —

and snuggled into the crook where his neck met his shoulders. Thus warmed by his body and the sun, I, too, fell asleep.

We spent two or three days in Troyes, where a young woman made Jeanne godmother to her first child, and named it Jeannette. When we left for Châlons, Brother Richard rode with us. The dauphin, thin and still petulant but on a splendid charger, led the march, and the townspeople, lining the walls, cheered us as we went. We were cheered again when we approached Châlons two days later, and as we drew near the town, knots of travelers, dusty and tired, hailed us and the dauphin. "Long live King Charles the Seventh!" they shouted, lifting their staffs in salute as we passed. Many were simple countrypeople who had traveled great distances to see their king-to-be. And, I thought, what a place is France, to inspire such loyalty.

Then all thoughts vanished from my mind, for by the side of the road was a group with Jeanne in its midst, and Pierre and Jean. With a cry I ran toward them, surprising Nicolas, I am sure — but they were people from our own village, from Domremy: Jean Moreau, Jeanne's godfather, and Gérardin d'Epinal, who, it turned out, had married Isabellette, a girl who used to spin with Jeanne and Mengette and Hauviette. Best of all, Henri was there, Pierre's and my old friend. I embraced him, and then laughed at his shock —

for I was still dressed as a page — until I told him who I was.

We all spoke at once, and at first could make no sense of each other's words. Gradually it emerged that Jeanne's father was no longer angry with her; indeed, her parents were on their way to Reims to see her and to see the dauphin crowned, with others from our village as well — and yes, the village was proud of all we had done, and especially proud of Jeanne, and grateful to her.

"So," said Henri, looking me up and down, "you are still playing with the boys, eh, Gabrielle?"

I laughed again, but sobered quickly, telling him that it was no longer play. I told him about Louis, too, and saw his eyebrows rise that I could love a lord. The more I tried to explain that the distinction did not matter to us, the more I could see that he did not understand, and I felt sadly removed from him, my village, and my childhood.

"Your father," said Henry gravely, "would not like to see you in such clothes."

"It is with me as it is with Jeannette," I told him. "I am among men, and must appear to be a man for my own safety."

"Surely," said Henri, "your Louis could protect you from harm, as could this surgeon to whom you are, it seems, apprenticed — though it is a strange world when a woman learns the trade of a man who is not her husband or her brother or her father."

"Louis and Nicolas are not always with me," I said. "All is chaos in fighting, often." I was aching to ask after my family, and I kept straining my eyes behind us as we walked, for a glimpse of them — for surely, I thought, they would have come with the first group.

But when I was finally able to ask, after having to tell Henri what it was like to be in a real battle, he said, "They are well but they will not come, Gabrielle, though your mother and sisters and small brother send you their blessings and their love."

"And my father?" I asked, noting the omission.

Henri looked at the dusty ground. "Your father, I am sure, blesses you in his heart."

"What of his words, Henri?" I asked, feeling my own heart turn to stone within me. "What does he say?"

"He was angry with your mother for a long time," he said reluctantly, "when you did not return from Le Puy. He was angry at Isabelle Romée as well, for letting you go with that priest, saying your mother needed you at home since Catherine had left. For a long time he went about his work silently, and then when he finally spoke of it, he said he feared you would become a — a whore if you followed the army."

This did not sound like my gentle father, and it pained me to learn how little he trusted me. I felt myself turn red with fury and embarrassment. "I am no such!" I cried. "And if I were, Jeanne would turn me out, for she will not have women with the army, which is another reason why I go disguised. Look yourself," I said, sweeping my arm toward the long column of men. "You will see few women here, and those few who do come, she chases away quickly. This is not like most armies," I continued hotly, "with strumpets and wives among the supply carts. This is a holy army, dedicated to its mission!"

I was amazed at my own vehemence, and Henri seemed also, for he stared at me for some time before saying gravely, "So I see," but the corners of his mouth twitched as if he would laugh.

We fell silent then, and I thought again how far I had come in spirit, as well as in distance, from my people. My eyes stung with the thought that perhaps I could never return to Domremy and live there in peace. I had thought before that I *might* not — but to think that I *could* not was worse.

I went quickly to the medicine cart, pulled a sprig of dried rosemary from one of my pouches, and held it out to Henri. "Give my mother this," I said, "with my love" — for she had taught me it stood for remembrance. "And tell my father that I am no whore. I will contrive to see you again, Henri, but if I cannot, fare you well."

I ran back into the column of marching men, purposely losing myself among them, and searching for Louis. When I found him, I tugged at his stirrup as he rode by, saying, "Pull me up, master," and he, looking surprised but pleased, grasped my arm. Between us, we managed to get me onto his horse. I rode into Châlons behind him, my arms tight around his waist.

20

Châlons came to our side easily, as we expected, and we went from there to the castle of Sept-Saulx. This was the residence of Archbishop Regnault de Chartres, but he still ignored Jeanne as he had at Blois, despite being her host. He fawned on the dauphin as much as did his ally La Trémoille — but both of them, Nicolas had told me, were reluctant to acknowledge Jeanne, fearing that she might become more popular than they, or even more popular than the dauphin. "They want to control him," Nicolas said, "for their own gain." I could see why Nicolas disliked being at court, when it was peopled with such creatures!

At last, word came to us that the Reimois — the residents of Reims — had accepted the dauphin as their king. I had heard cheers from our men before, but never such cheers as those I heard from them that day, nor had I ever heard such joyous prayer from Jeanne or seen such frantic preparations for departure, for the news came on a Saturday and tradition holds that kings must be crowned on Sunday. We rode in haste that very day toward Reims, and the people ran out of the city to greet the dauphin. As he went through the gate, they cried, "Hooray! Hooray!" — but their eyes followed Jeanne with as much joy, and with even greater curiosity. Some Burgundian nobles, seeing this, declared they now wished to be for Charles! And new troops joined us, along with dusty travelers who, like our friends from Domremy, had walked to Reims from their villages and their estates. Soon it seemed that the city could not hold one more soul.

There were many reunions as soldiers found relatives among the crowds, but the greatest of all, I think, was my own and Jeanne's and her brothers' with Isabelle Romée and Jacques d'Arc, who were waiting for their children at an inn called the Striped Donkey, near the cathedral where the king was to be crowned. When I heard they were there, I said my farewells to Nicolas, who went to rejoin the king's household, and to Louis, whom I promised to try to find later. Then I rode Anglais to the Striped Donkey, close behind Pierre, Jean, and Jeanne, and stood quietly by while the d'Arcs embraced, until Isabelle moved aside. Looking kindly at me and cocking her head, she said, "But, Pierre, what feminine page is this?"

Pierre started to explain, saying I had been his page and now was another's, moving as gradually as possible to the fact that I was who I was — but long before he finished, I saw that Isabelle knew me. I ran to her, and she embraced me as if I were another daughter.

"I see you served my child well before going to the surgeon — but," she added with what I soon learned was only mock severity, "perhaps not the child I intended you to serve."

I searched for words to defend myself, but she put her hand on my shoulder and said, "Oh, my poor child, I jest! Things turn out as they turn out, and I can see with my own eyes that my brave Jeannette is well, as are both my sons. But come, let us all take our meal together, and we will talk of home."

We did talk of home, for many hours, and I found I was hungrier for news of my family than for food, especially since I now knew from Henri how deeply I had angered my father. "He loves you still," Isabelle told me, "and I am sure he will be glad to hear of your Louis, and that you have not fallen into looseness, as your mother and I assured him you would not."

"I have taken no vows," I told her quietly, "but you may tell my father — and my mother, too — that I will not lie with Louis till we are wed."

Isabelle nodded and patted my cheek. Then, smiling, she looked into my eyes and said, "That takes great strength, I think," and I nodded back, returning her smile.

My new brother was well, Isabelle said, made much of still by my sisters and father; my mother was well also, and as far as Isabelle knew, not with child. I was to be an aunt, though, for my sister Catherine was soon due, and so large Maman was sure she would be blessed with twins. Marguerite's cough was better, as it often was in summer, and Paulette and Cécile were growing daily. Brigitte was merry and made everyone laugh — but none of them, it seems, had a gift for midwifery or healing, so if I wished to come home . . .

Oh, part of me did, truly — but I still longed for a life other than the one I knew I would have in Domremy, like the warp of a coverlet woven in predictable colors, with as predictable a weft. I could see sympathy in Isabelle's eyes about my desire to learn reading, but when I told her about Louis's noble birth, she gently asked how his parents would feel if we wed, and how we would live together harmoniously despite our differences. I told her our differences did not matter to us, and that I had seen enough of the world to believe one could be easily lost in it, and was sure that if we wished no one to find us, no one would.

The hours passed in talk of home, but when at length Isabelle turned to Jeanne and spoke privately with her, and I politely with Jacques, there was a clatter outside on the cobblestones and we rushed out to see what had made them ring so. The sky was still dark, but I saw torches, and men on horseback, and the dauphin himself, entering the cathedral.

"He must watch there all night," said our host,

who had joined us when we went outside, "as a man watches over his sword and armor before he is dubbed knight. And we," he said, "should perhaps repair to our beds, to be ready for the new day."

We did so, I with Isabelle and Jeanne and the daughters of the house. But I rose before the others, at first light, and went outside again, when the sun was just touching the silent, lofty cathedral. Its carved stone glowed with glory, as if reflecting the joy of France on this day of days. Already there were people in the square in front of it; many had been there all night, I was sure, waiting to go inside or to glimpse the grand procession as it passed.

The front of the cathedral was heavy but many-surfaced, lightened and softened by delicate stonework — leaves and spheres and other curving, graceful shapes — and by tall, narrow, arched windows. As I looked up, I could see statues in every niche, angels and saints and other holy figures. The stonemasons must have hung from the sky with their chisels and mallets — and must have to hang still, I thought, for I had been told their work was not yet finished.

There were three great doors in front, framed by deep, intricately carved arches, and above the center door was an enormous round window — a rose window, I had learned this was called in cathedrals. From the inside, with the light coming through, it was splendid with reds and blues and golds, dazzling the eyes.

At the hour of Terce, when the three doors opened and people streamed in, I feared being trampled or lost among so many, but Pierre led me to a side door. Taking me firmly by the waist, he propelled me to a tall stone column by the stalls, right in the choir, and whispered, "You are small enough to stand here. Keep your back to the column and do not move, and I think you will see the king." Then he vanished, and I do not know where he or his parents or brother stood for the ceremony. But I could see much of it, and what I could not see, I heard, either as it happened or as people near me reported it to those who could not see.

I could make out little of the building itself through the crowd, but I had a sense, even inside, of it stretching toward Heaven, because the gracefully vaulted ceiling was so high above my head. As I stood there, watching the lords and ladies and knights, I found myself wishing for a wonderful dress to wear, a velvet gown, tight to the hips and then flaring in a wide long skirt, with tight buttoned sleeves whose streamers would be of soft flowing silk hanging to the ground, rich with embroidery — and I had never wished for this before. My page's clothes, though I had cleaned them as best I could, seemed ill-suited for such an occasion, though they were drab enough to keep me unnoticed against my column, and for that I was grateful. I found that if I stood on the square base that edged the column's roundness, I could just see between the heads of those who sat in the stalls in front of me. That gave me a good view of the altar and the place before it where knelt the king.

The first thing I remember is a clattering in the rear, and the sound of horses' hooves. Four men, fully armed, among them the Greensnake, Gilles de Rais, rode with their banners held high straight down the center aisle; the people moved to each side, opening a path so they could pass. Among the riders was a holy abbot walking under a golden canopy. I could see only the canopy and the horsemen, but those around me said the abbot bore the sacred ampulla containing the holy chrism — the oil used to anoint the kings of France — which was kept at the nearby abbey of Saint-Remi.

The men dismounted, solemnly though noisily in their armor, which echoed loudly as they walked. Then there was silence and those around me whispered that the archbishop was taking the ampulla to the altar. I could not see it, but a tall knight behind me, who described everything he saw to his short companion, said it was very old and very beautiful. It was in the shape of a golden dove, he said, with feet made of pink coral from deep under the sea, set into a silver plate, all trimmed about with precious stones. In the dove's belly was the glass vial holding the sacred oil.

I could just see Jeanne, in her armor and with her standard. Brother Richard was near her, and I saw him take her standard once or twice, and wondered why it was not Father Pasquerel instead, for surely he should have had that honor, since he had been with her longer. And I saw Jeanne's *beau duc* Alençon, who was, the knight behind me said, taking the place that Philip, Duke of Burgundy, should have held among the peers of France attending the dauphin — but Philip of Burgundy, of course, would not want to see Charles crowned.

There was singing, and the dauphin suddenly vanished from my view. "He is on the floor," whispered the knight. "He must lie there till he is raised — there, he is up now; the archbishop himself has raised him!" Then I could see for myself, though my toes and legs ached from the strain of making myself as tall as I could. Archbishop Regnault de Chartres led the dauphin in a mighty and solemn oath, wherein he promised to defend the Catholic faith as well as our country, and guard the church and honor those who had gone before him as kings, and see that justice was done throughout his realm. I wondered if the archbishop was glad or sorry to crown the king at last, and what La Trémoille felt as well.

I saw Alençon step forward with his sword, looking full of importance. The dauphin knelt, and Alençon struck him lightly first on one shoulder and then the other, knighting him — at which I wondered, for is not king higher than knight, so what need had he of the lower office? But such is tradition among the nobility.

The next part was curious, and gave me more

to wonder at, for garment by garment the dauphin laid aside his rich robes, at which I was surprised and then alarmed, for it did not seem a kingly thing to do before so many people. He stopped, though, when he had reached a simple tunic fastened with silver cords. The archbishop, who had not once looked at Jeanne, though she still stood nearby, opened the cords one by one, touching the dauphin, who was kneeling now, in several places with a long golden needle dipped each time in the holy oil. During this the people sang, and after it the dauphin put on a tunic of a purplish color and then a long and heavy robe — it looked very warm — decorated with *fleurs-de-lis*.

And then the archbishop handed him baton and scepter. "Not the real ones," the knight whispered to his friend. "They're at Saint-Denis, near Paris, and there was no time to fetch them. The same with the crown."

But there was a crown, and even though it was not the real one, when the archbishop put it on the dauphin's head there was a great sigh from the crowd, as if all had been holding their breath. Then he conducted the dauphin to a high throne that had been placed in readiness, and each peer touched the crown. And at last, the archbishop, his miter in his hand, bowed and kissed the dauphin's hand and cheek, as did each of the peers, again our own Alençon among them. How the other captains must envy him, I thought, and

214

then I wondered what La Hire would say of it all!

Jeanne was on her knees, and I could see, from the way the light struck her, that there were tears on her cheeks.

Then came prayers and blessings, and afterwards everyone shouted "Hooray!" and "Long life to Charles the Seventh!" until the very stones of the cathedral's vaults and arches shook with the cry. It was as if all of France was rejoicing.

As the shouting slowly faded and people began to leave, I felt a tug behind me and turned to see Pierre again. "Come," he whispered, "for I have more need of my page than Nicolas has of his apprentice." He took me outside and gave me new gray hose and a short blue tunic woven of a soft, heavy fabric and decorated with embroidered vines, plus a red broadcloth shirt with flowing sleeves to wear under it. Where he got these garments I know not, but he himself was splendid in a long robe with embroidered sleeves. "Borrowed clothes," he whispered, thrusting mine at me, "and we must return them, but we are to attend the coronation feast, and so must look like fancy folk."

We went back to the Striped Donkey, where I changed in the empty house, and then Pierre led me to the archbishop's palace, next to the cathedral, to a great hall there, where he sat at the low table with Jean and Isabelle and Jacques, and I was to wait on them, as his page. But I was in such awe of the silks and damasks, taffetas and velvets of the ladies' gowns, with trailing skirts and ermine trim, and of their jewels and headdresses, some horned, as if a crescent moon had fallen sideways onto a lady's head, and others peaked, with floating saillike veils, that I stared more than I served, I am sure!

At that splendid feast, which cooks and chefs must have labored all night to prepare, there were pies of many birds baked together, confections in the shape of castles, a loaf carved into a horse and knight, delicate soups and roasted pigs and sheep, and much wine. As it ended, Jeanne rose to her feet and said, "Gentle king, now is executed the pleasure of God, who wanted the siege of Orléans to be raised and who has brought you to the city of Reims to receive your holy consecration, showing you that you are the true king and that the kingdom of France belongs to you."

All raised their wine cups to that pretty speech, and cheered and drank. None rejoiced more than I as I turned my thoughts toward Louis, and study, and peace.

But that was not to be.

PART FOUR

Part Four

21

While Jeanne and the captains and the king discussed what they were all to do next, Louis and I explored Reims and discussed the same, for ourselves. I thought often of our dream of Paris, and of the university there — but Paris was held by the enemy, and so was closed to us. Still, Jeanne had sent word to Philip of Burgundy, urging him to make peace with the king. If he agrees, I thought, Paris will be ours, and Louis and I can settle there. Indeed, there soon *was* a truce, but it was not of Jeanne's making. "It is La Trémoille's work," Nicolas said, "and as such I do not trust it to be fulfilled."

It was not fulfilled, and when Jeanne heard that new English forces had landed and were marching to Paris, she said angrily that she would fight them, without the king's support if need be.

"What will you do?" I asked Pierre as we walked through the street of the musicians one evening, past houses decorated with statues of figures playing instruments — a harp, a rebec, a tambourine, and others. It was a street I had come to love, for songs were sold there instead of goods.

"I must follow Jeanne," he replied, "for I have promised our mother to stay with her, and Jean has left again. And what of you?"

"Pierre, I know not!" I cried, in despair — but inside I knew I would go with Louis if he went with the army, and with the army even if he did not, out of duty as a healer, and duty toward Jeanne, and love for her.

And soon enough, Jeanne's army prepared to leave, with the king's reluctant sanction. His advisers were still urging him to negotiate, and it was clear he preferred that to war; perhaps it was Jeanne who had convinced him otherwise. In any case, Louis and Nicolas and I went with them, as did Pierre, marching toward Paris in the dusty heat, for it was now high summer. It seemed to me that the fire had gone out of the army now that the king had been crowned, and many men marched unwillingly, talking of home and wives. They took less care than before about swearing, and encouraged the loose women who followed us in increasing numbers — well behind the carts, though, because of Jeanne's wrath whenever she saw them. I tended one or two of those women in childbirth, telling them I myself was a woman and making them swear to mention it to no one. But I hardly cared if they did, the heat made me so weary.

Some of the towns where we stopped welcomed us, but others did not, and then there was more fighting. Nicolas and I were soon nearly out of linen for binding wounds, and our store of herbs was slender. Still, we did what we could, as always. Once when I heard moans beside the road, I went into the woods, where I found a badly injured Englishman, and I tended him, too. Quarrels seemed less important to me than suffering; I could not make peace where there was none, but I could perhaps ease the pain of war.

One day, when we were setting up our night's camp, Pierre came to where Louis and I were sitting by our meager fire. "Be of good cheer, my friends," he said, easing himself down between us. "It seems they have heard in Paris of our victories at Orléans and along the Loire. Many there are ready to aid us, I am told. And" — he made his eyes round and held out his hands, shaking them in mock horror, reminding me of his boyhood self — "our enemies no doubt tremble. Why," he continued, stretching comfortably, "I have even heard that a great lady called Christine de Pisan, who lives in a convent at Poissy outside of Paris where the king's own sister is prioress, has written a poem praising Jeanne, can you imagine? It seems that she says Jeanne is braver than any man."

Louis raised his eyebrows at this, and looked at me askance, but Pierre continued before either of us could speak; I twisted the stick that held the thin duck we were roasting over the fire.

"She says," Pierre told us, eyeing the duck with interest, "that this is a joyful year, a time of rebirth and peace, because of Jeanne. She praises our men-at-arms, too, and says God has shown He is for France and our cause. Perhaps hers is only a lady's poem," he said, poking the duck, "but if she is right, we will take Paris easily and all will be well. And" — he smiled at us — "I will go home to my wife, and you, I daresay, will have much to do of your own. Imagine living in a house again, and having a quiet life with real meals — I am not speaking against your duck, Gabrielle — and sleeping a whole night through without having to fight the stones on which one lies. That will spur us on, eh, Louis, to take Paris quickly and be done with this war at last."

What little fat the duck possessed sputtered then, and the duck fell off its makeshift spit into the flames.

We laughed, fished it out, and ate it charred.

August had spent itself two weeks' worth when we approached the city of Senlis, not far from Paris. We stopped at Montépilloy, below the high castle there, in dry fields — for there had not been much rain, and I knew the farmers must fear for their dying crops. Everyone was uneasy; we had seen clouds of dust on the road, and scouts had brought word that a party of Burgundians, with their English allies, would soon cross the river outside Senlis, and be in position to attack. Then came word that they were indeed crossing it, and so we reluctantly formed for battle, and rode forward. When we arrived, we found most of the enemy were already across, and so we faced them as we had near Meung and Beaugency, and waited. Skirmishes broke out but no major fighting, and Nicolas and I were thankful that we had little to do. By the time the sun set, our men had made no progress, but neither had they been beaten back.

We spent an uneasy night, for most of us were sure there would be a larger battle on the morrow. I feared for Louis and Pierre, and the other dispirited men. By morning, though, when the king returned from Crépy, where he had spent the night, and when Father Pasquerel and Brother Richard had heard confessions and said Mass, there were many in whom the desire to fight was rekindled. Jeanne rode among the troops, smiling and giving them good cheer, urging them to fight for God and Charles and France. As always, they warmed to her words.

I glanced at her when she neared me, and she stopped and asked, "How now, are you still dove — or has the sword grown more to your liking?"

"Dove," I said, with no hesitation, "as, it seems, is our reluctant king."

"The king is good, but content with too little, and, Gabrielle, my saints tell me we must fight on, lest the English win in the end and take what we have gained. I would rest, too, and return to Domremy, but I cannot."

I found myself regarding her wearily for a moment, without speaking. "Our ways are different," I said at last, "and I have no saints to advise me." I spoke testily, I knew, though I also knew she could not go against her saints. Had I had saints guiding me, I would have done as she did, I am sure.

But I had not, and so I waited with apprehension for the battle to begin, my eyes on Louis, who had ridden up to me and presented me with a dusty orange lily he had found at the edge of the field in which we were camped. "For my lady," he said, smiling. Then, looking up to the castle of Montépilloy, whose towers stood like dark needles against the sky, he said, "I would we were there instead of here, you and I. But be of good heart; we have many men, and will do well."

Indeed, the field was full of men, facing each other. The English commander, Bedford, who was married to Philip of Burgundy's sister, had his men, who were fewer than ours but strong nonetheless, dig ditches and build barricades of brush and thorn to protect them. Jeanne rode boldly up to the enemy, shouting to them as usual to surrender to Heaven or be massacred. The enemy, also as usual, laughed and jeered, and small skirmishes broke out up and down the lines.

As the sun rose higher in the sky, the air grew steamy. We all choked with the dust, which blinded us and became like fog as the fighting grew fiercer. My eyes stung and itched, and I could feel my lips, my arms, my hands, my whole body caked with gritty grime. The battle rose and fell, rose and fell, sometimes raging, and other times at an impasse. But it never included the whole force at once. There were those who grumbled that it would be better to get it over with, to ride in one strong wave at the English, despite their barricades, or so Pierre reported when he came to me with blood dripping from his wrist, to have it bound.

When I had wrapped it in cloth I had taken from the dead, for we had no linen now, and he had left again, I heard a harsh cry for help from the edge of a small skirmish, and saw one of our men fall under his horse; a hoof came down on his chest. Nicolas was cutting out an arrowhead and I was free, so I ran forward, dodging hooves and men. But as I ran, the English surged toward us, and I saw one of them run the downed man through with his sword; he screamed once and lay still. I saw that I could do nothing for him so I turned to go back to Nicolas, but as I did I felt a harsh hand seize the shoulder of my tattered doublet so roughly it tore away its fastenings, laying it and the chemise under it open in front. I pulled them closed again as best I could, but the hand continued to hold me fast, and I looked up into a rough and bearded English face — at least the man spat out words I did not understand, so I assumed he was English. My heart quailed within me when I saw the leer on his lips.

225

His hands grabbed me rudely around the waist and he thrust me away from the skirmish, which was raging anew, and forced me down on the ground a short distance away. I tasted terror in my mouth and my head reeled as if I were losing my senses, even as my hands groped for my mother's knife. The man was kneeling over me, pulling at his hose and mine, when suddenly he lurched and fell to one side, a crossbow bolt in his back.

I lay trembling for a moment, too stunned to put my clothes to rights. But then someone threw a rough cloth over me, and a French voice said, "He will trouble you no more, little healer whose secret I have kept." A friendly hand helped me to my feet, and as I clutched my torn chemise around me, I saw that my savior was the rough, black-toothed gunner who had discovered my sex at Orléans, and whose wound I had tended there.

He led me back to the carts, behind the fighting, and I think I thanked him. Though I never saw him more, I pray for him still, every night, and also for the soul of the man he killed for my sake.

By the end of the day, the dust was so thick, Louis said, coming to me with a sword cut in his cheek, that it was impossible to tell who was French or English or Burgundian, even in those places where men fought hand to hand. "I had this," he said, turning his face so I could see his cheek, "from a Frenchman; at least he who gave

226

it me said, '*Oh, mon Dieu, vous êtes mon frère!* —
Oh, my God, you are my brother!' — and apol-
ogized as he rode off."

"Brother or no brother," I said, dipping a
bloody rag in what was nearly the last of the
watered wine we had been using for cleaning
wounds, "this is a nasty cut, and will pain you
sorely. I must close it with pitch, for I cannot tie
up your face." I had recovered enough by then to
smile at him and attempt to chuckle, hitting his
arm lightly, as if the wound were of no conse-
quence. "If I do not, you will not be able to eat,
or talk, and that would be a great loss, would it
not?"

He tried to laugh, but I could see it hurt his
wound, and I had to stop myself from kissing
him, and from putting my arms around him to
comfort him and to have him comfort me as
well. But I had already decided not to speak of
my ordeal, for I knew it would anger him.

Soon after that came news that La Trémoille
had fallen, and Nicolas, I could see, was at some
pains to hide his pleasure. But before I could
wonder what would happen if he were killed or
taken prisoner, we learned he had been saved,
and Nicolas, sighing, fell to work once more.
The sun at last began to set, and the fighting
eased, then stopped. Men went about burying
the dead in shallow trenches, and we withdrew to
our encampment of the night before, wearily, to
find what food and rest we could.

* * *

227

"I know we cannot, for honor's sake," I said to Louis as we sat that night within the forest, away from the others, "but I wish we could leave, just you and I, and . . ."

"And what?" he asked, his words muffled because he could not move his face for the pain of his wound. "Would my father take us in? He is many leagues from here. Even if he would accept us, we would have to travel through Burgundian lands to reach him, and . . ." He stopped himself and, leaning his head against me, his uncut cheek downmost, he said, "Forgive me, Gabrielle; it is the wound talking. You are right; it is honor that prevents us from leaving. That, and that I am sure it will be over soon. It must be. Once Paris is the king's, it will be over."

"And," I said, "if Paris does not become the king's?"

"That cannot happen," Louis said stubbornly. "I have heard there are Armagnacs still there, men loyal to the king, who merely wait for us to approach. They will rise up from the inside as we attack from the outside, and Paris will fall. And at last" — he bent to kiss me, clumsily because of the pain, and I winced for him, returning his kiss — "at last, changeling, we will escape, you and I. Soon you will be tending to housewifely arts by day and studying with me by night — studying," he said mischievously, "all manner of things . . ."

"Including medicine," I said just as mischievously, for my body had begun to tingle and I knew well what he meant. "But as for housewifely arts, my lord," I continued, putting on a prim air, "I like them little, and so may choose to practice them little."

"Then perhaps I must have two wives."

I reached out my hand to slap him playfully, but remembered his cheek in time, and drew it back. Then we tussled gently, mostly holding each other and tickling and touching, but we were too tired to keep awake long, and soon we fell asleep in each other's arms on a bed of dry moss; it had shriveled in the heat, but was softer, still, than the scorched and dusty earth.

The next morning, we waited for something to happen — some motion or order — but none came, and by afternoon the enemy had turned south toward Paris. We rode north, first to Crépy, where the king had been sleeping at night, and then with him to Compiègne, which had much love for him and for Jeanne. We stayed there, quietly, for several days, though Jeanne was impatient, eager to move on to Paris.

Some lodged in the town, and this time I longed for a town's comfort, but something inside me told me to stay near Louis, and so I did, camping in the field with him, away from Nicolas and Pierre and all others. Had it not been for his cheek, which pained him and which I dressed daily with fresh yarrow and pig's grease, though Nicolas said I fussed too much, it would have been even harder than it was to keep to my resolve of waiting to lie with him until we were wed. Indeed, there was a time when, bathing in the river there, we came upon each other, part by accident and part, I think, by design, and embraced under the water. We would be there still, perhaps, had not a sound in the woods frightened us and made us pull apart. Even now, if I close my eyes, I can feel Louis's lean and slippery body pressed against mine, and mine against his, and there are times I am sorry there was no sin in it.

But I am glad we had those days in Compiègne together, even so. Louis scratched letters on the underside of bark he cut from trees, showing me more of the alphabet that he had begun to teach me so long ago, and I, begging a needle from a woman in the town the one day we ventured into it, and some thread, mended our tattered clothes. I bore Louis's teasing about housewifely arts with good will, for I knew it was just teasing, and that he understood my feelings there as he did in all things. I told him, once when he teased, about my clumsiness at spinning.

We were lying by the river, in the sun; ducks were floating by, dipping upside down to feed. Birds were singing anthems in the leafy trees above, and a swan with her cygnets was sailing by. "We will have," Louis said, chewing gently, because of his cheek, on a long piece of sweet grass, "servants, then, to do the spinning, and you shall sit like a great lady and — embroider." He rolled onto his stomach and flung his arm across my chest, pinning me, or so he seemed to think.

But I wriggled out from under him. " 'Embroider!' " I shouted. "When I cannot spin?"

"What?" he said innocently. "Is not the one easier than the other?"

I pulled the needle from the folds of the cloth my savior had thrown over me, and that I had kept, and handed it to him with a bit of thread. "Here," I said. "Thread this and I will show you."

He squinted, and turned the needle this way and that in his big hands, and tried to poke it into the thread, and then the thread into it, and then, half succeeding, split the thread in twain. At last, pressing his lips together in a way he had when he was bested, he sheepishly handed thread and needle back to me, and said, "*Touché.* Your point is well taken." And I, holding the needle toward him like a dagger, said, "My *point?*" and made to stab him with it. He darted away, and I, quickly securing the needle and dumping my cloth on the ground, chased after him, and we ran and tagged and hid from one another like children till, exhausted, we fell again onto the riverbank. When we could breathe again, we talked, and he described to me plays he had seen at festivals and fairs, making them so vivid I could see them myself. And so we dallied all that day, until the sun went down and we returned to our camp.

I cherish, still, that day's sweet memory.

22

We left toward the end of August, and by then my horse, Anglais, had begun to grow plump with inactivity. By then, also, Nicolas said, the king himself had heard Christine de Pisan's poem about Jeanne; it praised him, too, so he was well pleased, but La Trémoille and Regnault de Chartres were angry. I wondered what kind of woman this Christine de Pisan was, and what it would be like to write words as well as read them; that a woman had written something so many people had heard seemed to me a great marvel.

By the time we left, too, we had learned that Armagnacs had taken Saint-Denis, outside Paris, and that they were so close to the city, and so read to fight for our king, that the people of Paris dared not leave their city's walls to harvest their grapes. The rumor was also that the Parisians had cut their grain before it was ready, to save it from hungry soldiers, and that they were fortifying the town. And indeed, when we

232

drew near Paris, we could see tubs of stones on the city walls, and many cannons for beating us back if we attacked, or for attacking us if we came near.

We stopped at a windmill just outside Paris, near the village of La Chapelle. Our men took several pockets of English outside the city, and Jeanne and the captains met daily to discuss their plans. The king was in Senlis, and Jeanne and Alençon, Pierre said, were much vexed at him, wishing he would come — but La Trémoille and Regnault de Chartres were much vexed at Jeanne and Alençon, for their eagerness to fight. As to Jean, we had not seen him for some time.

At last, at the end of September's first week, the king arrived, and the royal army ranged itself on the northwest side of the city, outside the Saint-Honoré Gate. Spirits soared again, and confidence rose. Everywhere men talked of victory and of Paris's being French again, and of the end of the war.

Then one afternoon, Jeanne rode along the line of men as she often did, talking and smiling, telling them cheerfully it would not be long till victory. When she had come to the end and was turning to go, one of the few women who still followed the army — one of those whose child I had delivered, as it happened — came from behind a cart directly in front of Jeanne. Although this woman was not wed, she was good in all else and loved her man as I loved Louis; they planned to wed as soon as they could. But Jeanne flew in

233

anger at her, saying, "What, is this how you follow your king and help your gallant men-at-arms?" She leapt from her horse, waving the sword she had gotten miraculously so long ago from Sainte-Catherine-de-Fierbois, and had carried with her throughout the war, without ever using it for killing.

Even as I ran to shield the woman, Jeanne struck her with the flat of that sword — and it shattered.

Jeanne froze, as did I, staring at it, while the poor woman slunk off, weeping. I turned to tend her, but as I left, I could not help saying, "This is ill, Jeannette, and ill-omened." I know not what made me speak the words, but I felt a stab inside when I saw the broken sword, as if no good would come of it, and perhaps much evil.

Word of this event spread quickly among the men. Later other word came, too, that Jeanne had taken the splintered sword to the king's armorers and that, though they heated their forges well and pounded the blade and did all they could, it would not mend.

"Superstition," said Louis near nightfall while we ate a scrap of bread and some cheese we had saved. "One should not put store in such foolishness. If the sword cannot be mended, why then it is too old. You told me yourself it was covered with rust when it was found. If it was, then the metal is weakened and thin, too, I'll warrant, from where the rust was cleaned off. And if as you say she has not used it for killing but only

234

for show, it does not surprise me that it broke when at last she struck with it. There is too much talk of omens, good and bad, in this army." Angrily, he broke off a bit of cheese rind and handed it to me; every morsel was cherished among us, since we did not know when we would get the next.

"Even so," I said, "I like it not." I thought of Jeanne's saints, of whom of course I could not speak to Louis, and wondered what they said of it.

I bathed the hurt woman's bruises that night. The next day, which was the feast of the birth of Our Lady, I wanted to mix a poultice of sage leaves to reduce their swelling, but despite the holiness of the day, Alençon rode up and down the lines, ordering us all to make fascines to throw into the moats of Paris, and so I was unable. I never saw the woman again; I think she may have gone away from us that day, and if she did, I hope her man went with her.

At last the order came to move forward, and I wondered if it was from Jeanne, or Alençon, or the king. As usual, Nicolas and I were at the end of the long line, but I could see from Anglais's back that the army was ranged along the length of the city's walls, from the Saint-Honoré Gate to a place they called the Swine Market. We pulled our cart up in back of a hill, and the artillerymen set up their cannons and culverins and other guns. The English and Burgundian garrison inside the city fired at us from the walls, on which we saw many flags, including one bearing the red cross of Saint George, who is to the English what Saint Michael is to us French, I think.

The shots did little harm, being from too great a distance. Though they knocked over those they hit, they did not wound them but for bruises and the minor injuries of falling.

At around midday Jeanne rode up with her standard-bearer, plus Gilles de Rais and other captains. She looked splendid in her armor, as always, but I was shocked to see a different sword by her side, though I should have expected it. She and the men dismounted and strode toward the ditch that formed the outermost moat — a dry one — around the city. I could not help but admire her courage, for stones from cannons were falling around us, with arrows and crossbow bolts. But she and the captains paid no heed, and climbed down into the first ditch, where for a moment they disappeared. I held my breath, waiting to see if they would cross safely to its other side — for I knew that if a stone from a cannon fell on them now, it would surely crush them, and they were within good range of the enemy crossbows as well.

But at last Jeanne emerged with her standard-bearer, on a small hill between the dry ditch and the water moat. She waved her new sword and shouted up to the walls, "Surrender to us at

once, to the King of France. If you do not surrender before nightfall, we shall enter by force
whether you like it or not, and you will all be put
to death without mercy."

"Shall we, you tart?" came the rude reply, and
crossbow bolts rained over the walls. I saw
Jeanne stumble and clutch the upper part of her
leg, and as I ran toward her, I saw her standard-
bearer stumble as well and lift his visor. As he
looked down toward the ground, I think to see a
wound in his foot, he fell back suddenly, and
when I reached Jeanne, I saw that he had caught
a bolt in his forehead and now lay dead.

"My wound is nothing," Jeanne gasped. "You
must leave here; you will be hurt."

"And you, what will you do?" I asked, draping
her arm over my shoulder and struggling under the weight of her armor. "Let me at least
see your wound — here, we can go behind this
ridge, just here." Somehow we managed to cross
to the mound of earth between the ditches. As I
started up the ridge, Jeanne pulled me down,
saying, "If we stand, they will attack us; we must
crawl," and so we did, to the back of the ridge,
where I loosened Jeanne's leg armor and examined her wound, which was only, I was glad to
see, in the flesh. I dressed it the best I could, and
bound it.

No sooner had I done that than she reached
down as if to tighten her armor again. But I
stayed her hand, saying, "Leave it off if you can,

or just strap it loosely over the wound, for the wound will become too hot under your armor, and is sure to fester."

She smiled crookedly, saying, "Friend dove, I will obey you in this, because it is what you know best. But you must obey me in what I know. Go you back to the king's surgeon, so you may be of service to the other wounded, for I fear there may be more this day than there have been for some time. But we will still prevail, doubt not." So saying, she gave me a gentle push, then called me back, saying, "Tell them to bring up the fascines and throw them in the water."

So I crawled back, and relayed her orders to those commanding the carts, and they obeyed. The Parisian defenders fought more steadily now, and more fiercely, and many of our men fell; I was kept busy for some time. Soon Nicolas and I moved to a barn where we could shelter the wounded. But we could do little for them, being very short once more of supplies.

As the day waned, we could see it was going ill for us. I thought of the broken sword, despite Louis's doubt of omens — and thinking of Louis made me worry about how he had fared, for I had not seen him all that day.

Still later that afternoon, more and more of our men left the field, tired, bloody, and dispirited. At last one of them said, "Pack up your wounded, surgeons, for we are about to retreat."

I heard Jeanne say angrily, "By my staff, the place would have been taken!" and I guessed that the order to retreat was none of hers. But it seemed sensible to me, for the walls held and the defenders still had great tubs of stones and appeared to be well supplied with arrows and other weapons.

Nicolas and I moved the wounded, and our men threw their siege ladders and other equipment into the barn and set all alight so the enemy could not use them. A herald rode up, saying, "We have safe conduct to bury our dead; come you with us, in case there are any living wounded among them that need your aid."

As we went, I felt much as I had felt at Patay, though there were not as many dead — but these were French. The slaughter seemed to me as senseless and as wrong as in that battle, and I wondered bitterly why, if God were on our side, He had let so many of our men die. Could it be that He was punishing us for thinking He was on the side of any who fought?

And then I stopped, frozen in disbelief and horror, one foot stumbling against the other — for there on the ground before me lay Louis, flecks of blood on his lips and more blood running from his ear. Although there was no mark upon him that I could see, I knew that boded great ill.

I fell to my knees and touched his healing cheek, afraid to move him or go closer.

"Gabrielle," he said weakly, trying, I could see, to sit. "I knew you would come. But you must leave. They will — fire . . ."

I put my finger to his lips. "Hush, my love," I said, the tears welling from my eyes. "They will not fire. We have safe conduct to . . ."

He smiled, and I knew he was aware that I had been about to say "bury the dead." He raised his arm and let it fall — for such was his great weakness — on my shoulder.

And I lay down, there on the bloody battlefield, my arms around him as well as I could place them.

"It was — a cannon shot," he whispered, his lips close to my ear.

"Where?" I asked him. But I knew.

"On — my head. My helmet — shattered. And — and a bolt, I think, in my back, after I fell. I cannot — turn," he said apologetically, "or I would show it you. But perhaps you could . . ."

"Not now," I said softly, holding him, trying to keep back my tears. "Rest now, my love. Rest." For I knew then that his wounds were mortal, and that not even Nicolas could save him.

And so we lay there silently as the sun sank and the air grew chill. Once I got up to strip a riding tunic from a dead knight who lay nearby, and I put it over Louis, and then lay next to him again.

We spoke hardly at all; I could tell it pained

him, and his mind could not always find words, nor could his tongue and throat and mouth utter them. So I sang to him, some of the songs my mother had sung to babies, and I recited prayers and psalms. He seemed to like the sound of my voice, though I could see his eyes dimming and I suspect he could not understand me, or see me either. I was suspended; I was not myself, but part of the earth on which I lay and the man I held. And Gabrielle, the innocent girl who had longed for adventure, was no more.

As the sun rose again, shedding its pink-and-gold light across the battlefield, I saw that there were fewer bodies. Many, I realized, had been removed, but those who took them had kept away from me and from Louis. At full dawn, Louis's eyelids lifted weakly and he smiled. "Gabrielle," he said quite clearly, "I love you."

"Oh, my Louis, I love you," I said, and hope, which can be the cruelest of emotions, gripped my heart, for he sounded stronger.

But he did not speak again. A few minutes later, his eyes opened wide, as if in surprise. His breath shuddered in his chest, and he was dead.

I made the sign of the cross and then lay there, unmoving, holding him, till the sun was high and warm in the sky, and he was cold. I do not remember thinking, or even feeling. I suspect I would never have moved again, had not Nicolas come to me and raised me to my feet, saying "Come, we will put him on the cart, and take him away. You must come now, Gabrielle, for the army is to leave soon."

Woodenly, still without feeling, I helped lift Louis onto the cart. It was then that I saw the bolt in his back, and I made to pull it out, but Nicolas stayed my hand. I pushed him aside and pulled it anyway, for I did not want anyone to see a bolt in Louis's back and think him coward, not knowing he had been struck down before the bolt found him. The blood that followed it flowed slowly, with no life behind it.

Nicolas talked as he maneuvered the cart across the battlefield. He told me, I think, that Jeanne wanted to attack again and that Alençon agreed. But the king had ordered otherwise, and the army was restless, saying Jeanne had promised a victory that had not come. I heard his words only at a distance, as if he were an insect buzzing near my head.

When we reached La Chapelle, we found Pierre standing near its church. Nodding at Nicolas, he lifted me off the cart and held me, ignoring the stares of those who had not yet guessed I was a woman. "My poor little dove," he said, using his sister's name for me. "My poor, poor playmate and companion. You loved him well; you brought joy to him, do you know that?" He tipped my face up to his.

But I could not respond; I just looked away.

"I fear for you now," Pierre said softly, glancing at Nicolas over the top of my head. "I fear it will go ill with us all. Jeanne is determined to continue fighting, and has some plan with Alençon for going against the king's wishes. She has taken a suit of armor and a sword to the church at Saint-Denis because she was wounded in this battle, and that is the custom, but I fear she wavers in what guides her, or even that she has lost that guidance, and sues to bring it back."

"I fear it myself," Nicolas answered gravely. "And" — he touched my shoulder — "though you are a fine healer, you now must heal yourself. If there were a convent . . ."

I heard a sharply indrawn breath — Pierre's — and then his voice, exclaiming. "But there is! The convent of which the king's sister is prioress. It is, I think, not far from here . . ."

I heard them dully, as they decided my fate, but I did not care. "Christine de Pisan," said one, "the noblewoman who wrote about Jeanne," and "Poissy," said the other, and back and forth they went, settling between them where I should go. But I heeded them only when at last Pierre said to me gently, "We must bury Louis. Surely you do not want to leave him above ground?"

I know I shook my head, but the tears welled up again.

"Come," Pierre said quickly. "I saw some women selling shrouds. Maybe we can beg one . . ." He broke off then, looking at me oddly. "Gabrielle," he said, "have you heard what we have been discussing, Nicolas and I?"

I shook my head again, though I had heard some.

"We think you should go to a convent, and there rest and heal where you will be safe. It is too far for you to go home to Domremy, and I cannot take you. I cannot take you to Poissy either . . ."

Nicolas interrupted. "That," he said gently, "is where the king's sister rules, and where Madame de Pisan, the poetess, lives. Both are friendly to the king and to Jeanne's cause. I think they would welcome you — and it is not far."

"I would see you to Poissy safely," Pierre said, "but I must stay with Jeanne, and so must Father Pasquerel. There is no one save him or me or Nicolas, who is needed here as well, that I would trust to protect you." He hesitated, then said, "But there is one whom no one will molest, for fear of contagion, and that is a leper."

I nodded, remembering the one I had seen on the journey from Le Puy, and realizing now that they truly meant for me to leave them, to go to where the woman was who had written the poem praising Jeanne. I did not care to go, but neither did I care to stay. I wanted only to be dead, like Louis, to be with him in Heaven, forever . . .

"If we can find two shrouds," Pierre said softly, "one for Louis and one for you, you can walk along the roads undisturbed, for all will shun you. You would seem more like an outcast leper if you walked than if you rode your horse. Could you walk, do you think?"

I nodded once more, numbly. I felt no fear at the prospect of traveling alone, for I felt as if nothing worse could befall me than already had. Nothing could ever touch my soul as Louis's death had touched it, and I had little care for my body's safety.

We begged two shrouds of a woman who so pitied us that she gave them to us for a few bits of bread and salt herring that Pierre managed to find among the supplies. We wrapped Louis in one, and dug a grave for him, and out of the other fashioned a leper's garb for me. I held it close to me that night as I slept under the medicine cart, with Nicolas and Pierre nearby. The next morning, Pierre made a clapper for me such as lepers use to warn people of their presence. He and Nicolas then bade me farewell, and numbly, I took my leave of them, and set off toward Poissy.

PART FIVE

23

I remember very little about my journey. I saw few people along the way, for most were afraid of the war, and so declined to travel. I kept to the road Pierre had shown me, and one morning, I saw the walls of a great estate ahead, and I shouted to a passing peasant, "What place is that?"

He, keeping some distance away, called, "Why, leper, that is the Dominican convent of Saint-Louis-de-Poissy, and no leprosarium."

"Thanks to you all the same," I replied, pleased that the convent was named for the saint of my own dear Louis, and I walked toward it.

I came to a low gate set into the wall, so I went aside and pulled off my shroud. From it, I fashioned a rough skirt so at least the nuns would see I was a woman, for of course I could not hope to gain entrance as a man. I tried, too, to comb out my hair, which was full of tangles and leaves and hay, and lice, too, I have no doubt. It had grown, and though it was long for a man, it was still short for a woman, and as unruly as ever.

And then I went to the gate and knocked.

"What would you?" asked a small voice, and then out peeped a head. I saw a nun's dark habit and a white wimple surrounding a fresh young face with refined features. Then came a gasp and a sharp *"Mon Dieu!"* and the nun looked as if she were about to shut the gate again.

"I mean no harm," I told her quickly, "despite my rough appearance. My name is Gabrielle de Domremy, and I have traveled long and far to see Madame de Pisan, who I am told lives here."

The nun looked doubtful. "Madame is very old," she told me, "and often sick, and sees no one."

"Perhaps you could tell your prioress," I said, knowing I should mention her as well, "that I have traveled with Jeanne the Maid and her brothers, and have . . ."

"Ah, the Maid!" exclaimed the nun. "We have heard of her. It was she who had King Charles crowned, is it not? Our prioress is his sister," she went on, "but" — she looked at me kindly — "all are great ladies here, I am afraid."

"I am sure they are," I said, feeling weariness sweep over me, "and I am not one, as you see. But I must speak to Madame de Pisan even so. Say" — I cast about for something plausible that would not be too great an untruth — "say I have come from the Maid."

Well, it was true in fact, although what it implied was not.

250

The nun nodded, and, saying apologetically, "You will have to wait here," she closed the gate and left me.

I sank down weakly upon the ground, hardly caring what transpired next, for all my energy was spent.

But in a while — I know not how long — the nun returned, and opened the gate to me. "The prioress says you may come in," she told me, "and that you may see Madame, for she spoke with her, and Madame is curious. But I did explain that you have been traveling — and she has ordered me to — to take you to our infirmary, there to wash and put on some other garments."

I nodded, wondering with wry amusement if she had noticed that my skirt had begun life as a shroud and my bodice was what was left of a warring page's tattered doublet.

She led me through the gate and across a lawn so green and lush I wanted to lie down upon it and sleep there forever, dreaming of my Louis. Above me I heard the sweet song of a thrush, and I could smell perfume from the tall blue and yellow flowers that nodded at me as I passed. The cruelties of war and want had not touched here; it seemed another world.

The nun led me to one of several gray stone buildings and put me in the care of an older, buxom nun with a heavily lined face and rough red hands. "I am Sister Georgette," she said, with controlled disapproval in her voice, "the infirmarian, and I have been told to prepare a bath for you. Follow me."

She led me past rows of beds in a pleasantly light and airy room. Some of the beds were occupied, and I realized dimly I was again in a hospital. Under my sorrow stirred the thought that perhaps I could work here, could learn. But I said nothing; Sister Georgette, I felt, would not be willing to teach me until she had seen beneath the layers of dirt and until I could show her a mind less stupefied with grief.

She took me into a chamber with fresh rushes on its stone floor and a higher window that let in light but little air, so there was no draft. Lay sisters came with ewers of steaming water, which they poured into a wooden tub. Sister Georgette assisted me out of my poor clothes, averting her face, not for politeness, I think, so much as for the stench that must have come from me.

The water acted as balm to my tired body; I sank into its warmth, and knew no more.

When I woke, I was lying in the softest, warmest place I had ever known, and an elderly woman with a sweet pale face, holding a book in her lap — a book! — was smiling at me. "You rejoin us at last, Gabrielle de Domremy," she said. "How do you feel, now that you have rested?"

"I — I feel better, madame, thank you." I struggled to sit up.

"I am glad. I am Christine de Pisan," she said, putting a graceful hand for a moment on my stubby one, "and when you are better still, you must tell me your story. I see from the medal you wear that you have been to Le Puy, and I am told you have traveled with the Maid, France's fair savior. Rest now; we will talk of all this in time."

Then she left, and I sank back again into warmth, feeling more content than I had in many days.

But later that night, I dreamed of Louis; we were wed, and lying together in a bed as soft as the one in which I now was. And then Death came, with great black wings, and took him from me, and I woke with a cry. When memory returned, I wept sorely.

Soon the same sweet-faced woman was beside me again. Without speaking she took my hand and held it, rubbing my shoulders as I wept. When I was quiet, she said softly, "You have seen much, my child; is that not true? And lost a love, perhaps?"

"Oh, yes, madame," I said, and I told her of Louis as if she had been my mother, and tired her, I fear.

She listened patiently and then she said, "You will not believe me now, but the grief will ease. I, too, have lost a love — my husband, long ago. We must find occupation for you; you said you and your Louis spoke of learning, and you of medicine. I have some books that might interest you . . ."

"Alas," I said, "I cannot read, only a few letters. Louis did not have time . . ."

Here I wept again.

"Perhaps I have more time than he," she said. "I shall help you learn. You are a brave young woman, and" — she smiled and pushed my damp hair away from my face — "you must tell me of the Maid, whom I greatly admire."

"Oh, yes, madame," I said eagerly, overcome by the thought that she could continue what Louis had started, and I could learn to read for him — for me as well, but at that moment, it was for him that I wished to learn, to finish what he had begun. "The Maid's brother was greatly pleased to hear of the poem you wrote about her . . ."

And so began a quiet time, during which I healed, and studied, and began another life.

Christine de Pisan had a small hut, the back of which was set into the convent wall, with a door there as well as in front, so it was reachable from both inside the grounds and out. It was a trusted place, for the convent was strict about allowing outsiders onto its wide grounds. No one but the nuns could sit in the beautiful walled garden with its many fruit trees, or walk in the park among the deer and hare, wild goats and rabbits, or sit by the fishponds. The only place besides Madame Christine's hut where visitors, be they men or women, were permitted was the parlor. Madame Christine herself had been entertained in it, years earlier, when visiting her daughter, who had taken vows there. Then Madame Christine had left, but she had returned to the convent later, seeking refuge from the war, saddened by it — as was I. And because the prioress loved Madame's writing, and wished her to help instruct the young nuns, she let her live in the small hut, which had originally been built for receiving supplies and storing tools.

It was to that hut that Madame took me when I was recovered, and after I had met the prioress, who gave me permission to stay, for she felt kindly toward Jeanne because Jeanne had made her brother king. And it was there, as the chill of autumn came to us on the wind, that Madame taught me the letters Louis had not, and then the words they could form. It was a precious day when she put a book into my hands, its pages thick and beautiful. "This book is French, Gabrielle," she said, "unlike much written about the art you love, so you should be able to read it. I think it will interest you greatly."

When I looked at it more closely, I was amazed to see that it told how infants are delivered, and how to comfort new mothers and care for babies, and how to treat the ills of women.

"A wise and learned woman, Dame Trotula, who lived in Salerno, in my country of Italy, more than three hundred years ago, wrote this," Madame said, smiling, "and here it is in French. Her knowledge is sound, even though she lived so long ago."

I looked up at her, hardly knowing how to thank her, hardly able to speak.

"You will be midwife, physician, and surgeon, too, Gabrielle, if books can make it so."

And so every day, in an uncomfortable gown of thick brown stuff given me by Madame, I sat by the small window in Madame's hut, or outside on a bench by the door where the birds sang sweetly, and I struggled eagerly to read Dame Trotula's book. At first it went slowly, but the more I read, the more I found I could read, and it was like having a midwife like Maman at my side. Dame Trotula wrote of much that I knew, and much that I had seen but did not understand — like the elongated dead twin that time long ago in Domremy — and I stored all that I could absorb in my mind. Madame Christine sat nearby, sewing or writing, sometimes softly singing, and helping me with the difficult words — and always, always smiling when our eyes met. Some days she did not feel well, and I remembered that the nun at the gate had said she was often ill. But she never complained, and I could not diagnose any illness, though she had a swelling of the ankles and feet, and some shortness of breath.

Sometimes she talked of her past, of her girlhood in Italy, where the sun, it seemed, always shone, and of her young womanhood in France, where her father was a physician and astrologer at King Charles V's court. She had married at the age I had left Domremy. Her husband was a man called Etienne, whom she loved as I loved Louis, and she bore him three children. "And then," she said, taking my hand and looking deep into my eyes, "he died when I was but twenty-five, soon after my father had also died, and, Gabrielle, I thought the world had ended, for my world surely had. I had nothing, no means of livelihood, and my children and my mother and my niece were all dependent on me. I was so full of grief I could not think, or move, for a long time.

"But my father had taught me well, and I slowly began finding peace in study, as you are doing even now. I thought much on woman's lot, and men's abuse and also men's kindness, and in time I began to write. God allowed me to earn a modest income with my pen, to keep myself and my family. I still, though I am an old woman, long for my Etienne, as you will doubtless long for your Louis. But I think you will find comfort in study, as I did. You can, if you wish, also find it in work, for our Sister Georgette is not young, and there is no one to follow her. The prioress has said that you may learn her tasks if you wish, and tend the nuns when they are sick. You could perhaps tend the village women, too, when they are with child, for the midwife lives some distance from here, and prefers to stay closer to Paris, where payment is better."

And so work was added to my day's activities, and how I welcomed it! Sister Georgette's hands were, as I have said, red and rough, for she believed in bathing the sick often, in hot water strewn with fresh herbs. Nicolas had spoken of this too, as being beneficial in healing wounds, but he and I had little way to bathe men at the edge of battle and in the open air. Sister Georgette's hands were also painful from an inflammation of the joints, which I was able to ease for her somewhat with flax and honey mixed with oil, and by rubbing at the end of the day. Gradually, she let me do more and more of the work, and the nuns were sweet to me, most of them, when they were ill or needed to be bled, which I disliked doing, for the blood tongs and the blood cloths reminded me too much of tending the wounds of war.

Soon Madame began to teach me Latin, for even though most of the few books the nuns had were in French, she herself had two Latin ones that she was anxious to have me read. They were written by one Hildegard of Bingen, a German abbess, and were very old, but I could see from the one I looked at most, called *Physica*, which was full of artfully drawn pictures of herbs, that this Hildegard understood healing well. The other book, *Causae et curae*, which I could not read till much later, was a study of diseases and their cures. In it she spoke much of how girls develop into women, and how infants form inside their mothers. This book, too, was of great help to me in my work.

One snowy day that winter, when I rose before Madame to make up our fire, and looked around the hut, thinking how content I was and how, in many ways, I had at last found what I sought, though I had lost much in the finding, Madame stirred in her bed and moaned softly. I ran quickly to her, alarmed. "Madame, what is it?" I asked. "How may I help?"

"It is nothing, Gabrielle, except perhaps the infirmities of age."

But her face was pale and her skin was clammy, and her breath came shallowly. I felt her heartbeat, with her permission, for the heart often fails or overworks when one is old, and it was racing, then slowing, with uneven space between the beats. Quickly I made a weak tea of dried foxglove and gave it to her to drink. In time her heart quieted and she wished to go to her table to write.

"I think you should stay abed, Madame," I told her.

"But, child, there is work to do!"

"None that you cannot do in bed," I told her, putting on a severe look to make her laugh, which it did. And I handed her a stylus and her inkhorn and parchment, and a flat board to serve as a table across her lap. "You can write where you lie," I said, and I put all the soft things I could find — shawls, coverlets, cloths — behind her back to support her comfortably. "There, now you are a great lady in her chamber, lying abed all day from dalliance." We both laughed, for of course she *was* a great lady, though she no longer lived like one, and dalliance was unknown to her.

At times I grew discouraged at the amount there was to learn, for it seemed to me that the more I read of illness and wellness and the human body, the more there was I did not know, and the more mysteries there were to unravel. Once, when I put my aching head down on my book, Madame said softly, "You must not give up, Gabrielle. Though you cannot, it seems, study in Paris, you can study much on your own, and so become as great a physician as Jacoba Felicie, or Joanna, or Margaret of Ypres, or Belota the Jewess, or even Dame Trotula, and many others — women all, and learned as you will be. Each one, Gabrielle, helps the next, and so when you are discouraged, you must think of the women who will follow you, and those who will follow them, until the day when women may practice medicine as much as men, and as legally. For I believe that women can do nearly all things as well as men if they wish it and the need is there — though," she added playfully, "until I knew you and heard of Jeanne the Maid, I would not have included feats of arms!"

We both laughed then, and I squeezed her hand, and thought how much I loved her.

We spoke much of war, also, for I was struggling to understand what I had done and what I had helped do, and what Louis had done as well. The picture of him cleaving that Englishman's head rose often in my mind. I felt that Louis's sin that day had been beyond the need of battle, and so I prayed much for his soul. I prayed for Jeanne, too, and for all the good people who fought with her. If war was evil, then were they not all doomed? And if war was evil, surely the Crusades were evil as well, even though the Church called them holy. How could war on God's behalf be good if war itself was evil? Surely the English and the Burgundians thought their cause was as just and perhaps as blessed by God as we thought ours! I knew Jeanne had said she liked not killing, and that she had helped that dying English soldier to confess, but she still led troops into battle, to kill and to maim . . .

I wrestled with these thoughts, but found no answers.

Then one day Madame and I were sitting by our fire, and I was stroking one of the convent cats, a pretty, gentle fellow, orange-and-white-striped, who had come inside out of the winter's cold to warm himself. He was purring, but suddenly the sound stopped, and his body stiffened. He sprang off my lap and onto the floor, where he pounced on a mouse that had scurried from behind the wall, unseen by us till the cat moved.

He batted at the mouse, covering it with his paw, and I leapt to my feet, crying, "No, no!" I ran to the cat, cuffing him aside to free the mouse.

The cat, blinking at me in surprise, sat back on his haunches and cleaned his whiskers.

"You," said Madame softly when I returned to my seat, "are like the Maid after all."

I turned to her, astonished.

She nodded. "Oh, yes, my little Gabrielle, you are. For the cat had in his paw a helpless being, as the English had France, and you made war on him, as our French have made war on the English. Does God frown on you for punishing a bully?"

The thought startled me, and I lay awake that night wrestling with it. I heard the bells ring for Matins, and did not fall asleep till nearly Prime, when it was time to rise again.

24

And so that winter passed, unusually cold, all said, and Madame was often weak with illness, despite my efforts to heal her. But age can only be eased, not cured, and most of her ills came, I thought, from a tired body.

As winter waned, news came that at Christmas King Charles had made Jeanne and all her family nobles — but Paris was still in Burgundian and English hands.

Early that spring, we heard that supporters of the king, Armagnacs who had been making raids near Paris, attempted to enter Paris itself. But they did not succeed; many were arrested and some killed. Soon after this news, Pierre came to see me, much to my surprise and, at first, delight.

I was alone when he arrived, for Madame had fallen ill again, with the fluctuating heart, and I had moved her to the infirmary where I could better care for her with the help of a lay sister who was now my assistant. Sister Georgette did little any longer save give advice, for the coldness of winter had seeped into her hands and would not leave, even though the weather was now warming.

For a moment all I could do was stare at Pierre and, as he folded me in his arms, think what a dear brother he was to me as well as to Jeanne, and how I had missed him.

But the mischief-light that had always cheered me had gone out of his eyes, and he was thin.

"We had a hard winter," he said as I poured him wine and set out bread and salt herring — poor fare, but it was Lent. "Jeanne has been so restless I cannot contain her."

"But you are a nobleman now, I hear," I said, smiling, and cutting him a generous slice from the round loaf.

Pierre smiled back wanly; in other days he would have grinned. "A sop thrown to us by a king who will not fight for what is his," he said bitterly, "intended to make Jeanne content. But it has not done so."

"Tell me of the war," I asked uneasily.

"There is little to tell. We fought against Saint-Pierre-le-Mouton successfully and took it. That was in November, and it restored us much after our failure at Paris. But then we besieged La Charité, and stayed a month outside its walls, as cold and hungry as those within, or more so, and at last we left with it still in enemy hands. And so we went on to Jargeau, where the king gave us the patent of nobility, which means we are now called du Lys, and have a coat of arms, which will pass to all our heirs. For that, I suppose, I am grateful. Our children's lives may be easier than ours because of it."

"What is the coat of arms?" I asked, wondering at it.

"A sword uplifted with a crown at its tip, to show that by fighting we crowned the king, flanked by *fleurs-de-lis*, for France and, I suppose, also for our name. It is a silly thing." Pierre took a great swallow of wine.

"And then?" I prompted softly. "After Jargeau?"

"Back to Orléans for a time — and that was good, though Jeanne was restless, as was I, and also Jean, who still comes and goes as he wishes, sometimes being with us and sometimes God knows where. He puts much store in his new status and in the symbol of it, and acts as if it were he who earned it for us, not our sister. We went from Orléans to Sully, to the king's court, which is a dull life with much meaningless ceremonial foolishness, feasting and gaming and hunting and light talk and entertainment, confection substituted for bread. If it were not for Jeanne," Pierre said, hitting his fist against the table, "I would return to Domremy and my wife, and be content to farm." He glanced around the room, at the books and at the fresh herbs I had begun to gather now that it was spring, and at the few pots of unguents I had devised and was still devising. "And you," he said, "it looks as if you fare well — and learn."

Briefly, I told him of Madame and of my lessons.

He folded my hand in his. "Your Louis would be glad," he said. "He is rejoicing in Heaven, I am sure, to see you so."

Sorrow rose in my throat, stealing my voice; I could only nod.

"But now," Pierre said gruffly, "I come to ask if you will return to us, for we are to wage real war soon, on behalf of our friends at Compiègne. The good Nicolas is dead, and . . ."

"Nicolas dead!" I cried. "Of what wound?"

"Of no wound at all, but an ague, at La Charité. You cannot imagine the cold," he said, and I fancied I saw him shiver, remembering it. "Many died there, of agues and ills of the stomach. It was a horror, Gabrielle; I am glad you were spared it, though perhaps you could have saved some and eased others. But now . . ." He stood, his big frame dwarfing our little hut where only women lived.

"Pierre, I am not sure. I . . ."

He held up his hand. "Hear me first, Gabrielle," he said. "Please."

I nodded.

"The town of Compiègne, which is for the king, has been given by treaty to Burgundy, with no regard for its people's wishes. This was last summer. But the people have steadfastly refused to agree to it, and have resolved to fight, to lose all rather than be disloyal."

I thought of the cat suddenly, and of the helpless mouse, even as I closed my eyes with dislike of what I knew must be coming next.

"Jeanne, rightly I believe, wishes to aid Compiègne. The people love her, Gabrielle; there are songs about her now, calling her *l'Angélique*, the angelic one. Women bring their rosaries for her to bless and name her godmother of their children. The people of Compiègne grow discouraged, but her support and the army's would give them the spirit they need to sustain their fight and win. You have seen how it has been with her, putting heart into the men-at-arms and all whom she comes near . . ."

And I have seen, I thought, how when I leapt at the cat, the mouse, which had been paralyzed with fright, looked at me once in disbelieving gratitude and then ran off to safety . . .

"We tarried at Sully for too long," Pierre was saying, "and so Jeanne, deciding it was time to leave, rode out the other day without the king's leave, saying she was going for pleasure only. But she confided in me that she meant to ride to Melun, where there are many who are for the king, and then to Compiègne itself, if she could summon troops. She asked me to come here for you, for we will have need of a surgeon again, and the king does not seem willing to spare us the man he has chosen to replace Nicolas, nor does that surgeon wish to come, being a pale indoor man, unused to the rigors of armies."

The mouse, I kept thinking, the mouse; it is necessary to free the mouse.

"Is there no other way to undo the treaty?" I asked Pierre.

"Had there been one," Pierre said gently, "it would no doubt have been found." He opened his arms to me. "Come," he said, smiling. "I have need of my page again, and of my companion of long ago. I have missed you, Gabrielle. Jeanne has also. She speaks of you often, and of your Louis, and she has grieved for you, and hopes you are well. And . . ."

"Enough!" I cried, shunning his arms, and trying to swallow the heaviness that was lodged in my throat like a stone. I closed my eyes, seeing it all again — the mud, the dust, the moldy food when there was food at all, the noise of battle and the smell of blood, Louis smiling beside me, Louis cleaving the Englishman, Louis lying dead . . .

I did not want to return. I was well content with my books and with Madame, and with giving what aid I could to the nuns and the village women.

But then I saw the men, ragged, tired, thin, weak, suffering wounds that their squires could not treat, sustaining them for love of France and King and Maid, so that their women and children would not be oppressed under the paws of the English and the Burgundians. I whispered a quick and silent prayer, hoping God would not find my actions ill, and said to Pierre, "Very well. I will go with you."

25

I took my leave of Madame that night, reluctantly. She smiled and stroked my hand softly, saying, "You are right, my child, to go, for you will be needed more there than here. Remember that you will always have a home here; I have arranged it with the prioress. Return when your task is done, if you wish."

"I will wish to return to you, Madame," I said, kissing her hand and then her brow.

"I will always be with you, my child," she said softly, "for I love you as much as if I had borne you, and I am proud — so proud — of your courage and your learning. Go with God, and with my blessing." She brushed back my hair, which had grown out almost to woman's length and would have to be cut again.

Gently, I kissed her once more.

"Smile for me before you go," she whispered, and so I did, though I think it must have been a sad smile. Then I returned to our hut, where

Pierre helped me cut my hair, and gave me page's clothes once more.

It was barely sunrise when we left, on a fine spring morning that promised to warm quickly. I rode a sturdy gray horse Pierre had brought for me, whom I named Smoke, and who was slow and steady. In a purse at my waist, I carried yarrow and dittany and unguents Sister Georgette had taught me to make, and some I had learned about from books; already I was listing in my mind what I must gather to supply my cart. A lark sang in the convent garden as we left, and I hoped it boded well.

We went quickly to Melun, where Jeanne was, and she smiled broadly when she saw me. She clapped my back as if I were one of her men-at-arms, shouting, "Welcome, friend dove, and my thanks for flying back to us. I hope we will not have need of you, but I will rest easier in my soul knowing you are here to care for my men." She looked into my eyes then, and with the sweetness that she had had as a girl, asked softly, "How is it with you?"

"It is well, Jeannette," I answered. "I have grieved sorely, but I have learned much medicine, and have also learned contentment — as you, I think, have not."

"I have not," she answered, "but I am more content now, for soon we ride again for France and for the king. I am a soldier, Gabrielle, a soldier of God, and cannot be content with waiting."

"May there always be battles for you to fight, then," I said for courtesy. Then I wished I could unsay my words, for I knew I did not mean them.

Melun, which was held by Burgundians, was already under siege by forces friendly to us, and when the people there saw Jeanne they rose up with the besiegers against their Burgundian oppressors, expelled them, and opened the city's gates to us. I rejoiced, for there was little fighting. It was as if the very presence of the Maid had been enough to chase the Burgundians away.

That evening I saw Jeanne kneeling apart from the others, praying quietly, and when she at last stood and turned toward me, her face was pale.

"Jeannette," I asked softly, "are you ill? May I help you?"

"Thank you, Gabrielle," she answered, "but no. No one can help me but God."

She turned away with such a tortured look that I could not let her go. I laid a hand on her arm. "Madame de Pisan, my teacher at Poissy," I said, "has shown me books in which it is written that the ills of the soul are as troublesome as those of the body. She has also told me that as bleeding and emetics purge the body of ill humors, so speech can purge the soul. Perhaps it would ease you to speak of what troubles you. I shall tell no one, I promise you."

Jeanne looked at me oddly for a few moments, as if considering it, and she thanked me again, but said nothing further. Many times after that, though, I saw from her eyes and from her laugh, which had become too merry, as if forced, that she was still troubled.

It was only much later that I learned her saints had told her she would be captured before Saint John's Feast, which is near the end of June.

Word came to us that bands of Burgundians were roaming the land near Lagny, stealing, and terrorizing the good people there, and so one day, with what weapons we had, we set out to pursue them. I told myself this was proper, because they were oppressors and were doing much harm and evil. The battle was bitter, and we prevailed, but at great cost of lives and in wounded, and I wished more than once that Nicolas were there to guide me and to help. I enlisted two young pages, whom I saw hanging back by the carts, as assistants, to do for me what I had once done for him. They were brothers, very young, and had come with a knight and his squire, secretly following them for adventure's sake. But both knight and squire had died at La Charité, and the two boys feared punishment if they returned to their lord's lands, and so were willing to serve me. The younger, Antoine, was fair of face and limb, with a ready smile. Claude, the older, was quick-tempered, but brave and willing. The boys had but one horse between them, for the army was poor in beasts as well as in food, but I had Smoke, and so we managed well.

During the battle, when I caught Claude staring at me as we worked, I told them both that I was a woman, and swore them to secrecy. It seemed easier so, and they did not seem to mind. Indeed, young Antoine seemed much comforted, and sometimes snuggled against me at night as we lay under our cart, or near it, and made me think of the children Louis and I would never have.

There followed long marches and several small adventures; they run into each other in my mind. At Lagny, I delivered a dead child, who, when Jeanne prayed for it, came alive long enough to be baptized, and died again. At Pont l'Evêque, we suffered a retreat, at which the men grumbled. Then it was decided we should go all the way to Soissons, where there was a bridge that would enable us to take the Burgundian-held town of Choisy from the rear — but we found the gates of Soissons closed to us. The next day the captain of Soissons sold his city to the Burgundians for gold, and some of the men said this meant Jeanne was not truly from God. Others complained of lack of money and bread, for which I could not blame them. The captains ordered the complainers to leave, and Pierre said this was wise, for soldiers who cannot be paid or fed become rebellious, especially if there are no victories to cheer them.

We were only a few hundred strong when we learned that Philip of Burgundy and his men had set up camps on the northern bank of the River Oise across from Compiègne, which was on the southern bank. We were then on the high hill of

273

Crépy to the south of Compiègne, separated from it by thick forest, and I was not far from Jeanne when the news reached her. Instead of being discouraged by it, I saw her raise her sword with her old fire and say, "We will fight them, then, as we fought at Orléans!"

"We are too few," Pierre answered quietly.

But though the captains around her agreed with Pierre, Jeanne replied heartily, "By my staff, we are enough. I will go to see my good friends at Compiègne."

We stayed till midnight on our hill, restlessly preparing, and the more hours we waited, the more dread I felt. Pierre, kneeling on a patch of dirt, drew me the town, and the river, and the towns nearby, as he had seen the scouts draw for the captains. It was clear to me that we could ride through the forest to Compiègne easily, and that we could enter the city from the south. But what then? The main route into and out of the city, and the route by which it was normally supplied, was over a drawbridge that led across the river to the north bank — which was now dotted with English and Burgundian camps. To free Compiègne, we would have to go through the city, cross the bridge, and take the northern bank. And to do that, we would have to walk into the very arms of the enemy.

"It is a den of lions," I said to Pierre — and he agreed. Nonetheless, we left that night, when it was dark, with clouds covering the stars. Stars would have cheered us, I think, had they been winking at us. We arrived outside Compiègne just as the sky lightened, and were admitted through the southern gates with quiet joy and hope, as we had expected.

I walked around the town with my pages, leading Smoke and collecting what I could for the battle — rags and clothes, dried herbs, unguents, oil and pig's grease, and wine. I had little money, but the keepers of the shops gave what they could to me freely. "For God and the Maid," more than one said, crossing himself as he handed me a bunch of herbs or a vial of oil.

By late afternoon, as I was fastening my pouches and the boys were arranging the goods on the cart, a man-at-arms ran up to us, saying, "We are moving; the attack is about to begin!" And soon we all rode out of the city's main gate, toward the enemy, and onto the drawbridge, which had been lowered for us. Jeanne was at the head of the column, mounted on a dapple-gray horse and wearing a scarlet-and-gold riding tunic over her armor. So mounted, with her standard in her hand, she was a splendid sight, but I still felt fear for her. I turned as we left, for bells were ringing in the town, and I saw on the walls many archers and crossbowmen and culverineers, standing ready to cover us and defend their city.

As we rode, my pages and I well in the rear as always, I saw our small army marching along a causeway that lay beyond the bridge and stretched across the marshy bank of the River

Oise. I waited tensely for the first shouts and shots of battle, but none came, until we ourselves had crossed. The ground beneath was so boggy that I could understand why the causeway had been built, for carts would have sunk without it, easily.

When the head of our band had turned left and reached the Burgundian camp at the village of Margny, I heard sounds of fighting — subdued, as if we had surprised the enemy after all. Gradually, though, the familiar sounds increased, and I braced myself for the wounded that were sure to come.

I saw our men fall back, some onto the drawbridge, and then move forward again. At the same time, I saw a Burgundian force to the right looking down on us from higher ground. They sounded an alarm; soon after, men came riding from all directions, and there was vast confusion. I bound up the arm of one of our archers, and told him he could no longer draw his bow until it healed, and then I saw Jeanne being pushed back toward us and toward the causeway. We were pushed as well, Antoine and Claude and I, nearly onto the crowded drawbridge — and then I saw with horror that the bridge was being raised, no doubt to prevent those who pursued our men from reaching the town. But many of our men, caught on the bridge as it rose, fell from it into the Oise. Antoine cried out at this, and Claude used words that reminded me of La Hire — but then in grateful surprise I saw more than one

Burgundian reach his lance into the water and pull out a drowning Frenchman. Can these truly be our enemies, I thought, when they show such courtesy?

But then a desperate cry drew my attention elsewhere, and I saw that Jeanne and her squire, d'Aulon, with Pierre and Xaintrailles and a few others, had been driven off the causeway onto the boggy ground, where swamp water and grass and sand sucked at their horses' hooves and made them slow and clumsy.

And then — oh, and then . . .

And then I saw Burgundian archers seize the hem of Jeanne's beautiful riding tunic, and pull her off her horse.

26

I did not hesitate; I did not even think, although much later I worried about having abandoned French wounded to squires and pages. But at the time, I could only follow — for was it not Jeanne whom I had sworn to protect?

I saw that not only Jeanne but also Pierre and Jean d'Aulon and Xaintrailles and one or two others were being led away. And where is brother Jean, I thought angrily, as I urged Smoke forward into the bog as quickly as he could go. Could he have saved them, had he been here?

I could see, as Smoke and I struggled over the soft ground, Smoke's hooves sucking mud with every step, that Jeanne's captors were making for the Burgundian camp at Margny. As soon as I was sure of that, I turned, hoping to locate Antoine and Claude, and was glad to see that they had followed me on their horse. As we drew closer I saw a crowd of cheering men-at-arms surround Jeanne and the others; soon I could no longer see them, but I knew now where they were.

My pages and I stopped well outside the camp so we would not be challenged, and dismounted. All was still chaos behind us; there were those of our troops, I felt sure, who did not yet know Jeanne had been taken.

But I knew, and I now had to think what to do.

I knew that important prisoners — and surely Jeanne would be deemed one — who were held for ransom were often treated well, so that they would bring much money to their captors. But Jeanne had been called witch and tart and sorceress and whore by the enemy; they had such deep hate and fear of her that I doubted they would treat her well. And who would ransom her? She was indeed important, but she was not nobly born, nor was Pierre . . .

But then I recalled what Pierre had told me about the patent of nobility, and my hopes rose again. Surely since King Charles had made them noble, and since but for Jeanne he would not be king at all, he would ransom her and her brother with her!

And since it was Burgundians who had captured her, surely they, who were by birth more French than English, would not be as cruel to her as would the English. Had they not just pulled our drowning men from the river?

But Jeanne was a woman; they were not used to having women prisoners, I supposed, at least not women prisoners of war. I had seen how some of our French soldiers treated their own countrywomen when they went into a town, and I trembled for Jeanne.

What could I, myself a woman, do?

I did not know, so I waited, with Claude and Antoine, concealed with our two horses as well as we could manage in a ditch near a crumbled wall. The boys grew restless, but I hardly noticed. The sky in the west gradually darkened, and the sounds of battle eased. All around were the clanks and hoofbeats of an army returning to its camp. I wondered how our own army fared, and how the people of Compiègne would be this night, since the siege had not been lifted, and their hopes, I thought, had no doubt ended with ours.

The night was warm for May, but I felt cold and huddled together with my pages. I could not sleep for thinking what to do. By first light, though, I had devised a plan, and as soon as there was motion in the camp, I roused my pages. "You must," I told them, "return to Compiègne and our cart, and do what you can for our wounded. And then, when you have done all you can, I beg you to deliver a message for me. Know you," I asked Claude, "the convent at Poissy, outside of Paris?"

He nodded.

"Then take this to a lady there called Madame Christine de Pisan." I pulled my pilgrim's medal, which she had admired, from under my clothes. "Tell her I am well, and that the Maid has been captured, and — and that I follow her." I had some dim hope, I think, that Madame could intercede for Jeanne, because of her love for her and because of the prioress being the king's sister.

Claude nodded gravely, and then Antoine, his mouth trembling, asked, "Will we see you again?"

"I know not," I told him as gently as I could, hugging him to me. Then I pushed him a little away and said, "I release you both from my service, when you have treated our present wounded. I am sure the nuns will be kind to you, and will help you find places with a fine nobleman. Or" — I smiled, taking their hands in mine — "with a surgeon, as apprentices, for you have both been good help to me in my work, and I thank you for serving me so well. You will be surgeons yourselves someday, perhaps!" I gave Claude a pat and hugged Antoine again, for he flung himself at me. And then I mounted Smoke, for men were coming out of Margny, and I knew I must be ready to follow them if they were escorting Jeanne elsewhere. They rode directly past us, without, it seemed, noticing or caring that we were there. But I saw Jeanne, pale but straight and dignified, glance my way, and, clearly startled, glance back; I held up a hand to her and nodded silently.

Pierre was no longer with her, nor Xaintrailles; only d'Aulon, who at least, I knew, would look after her well, if their captors allowed. But I had not thought they would be separated, Pierre and Jeanne. Jeanne would, I knew, be in great need of comfort; she would have her saints still, I hoped, but I vowed to go to her myself if there was any way I could, for her mother's sake as well as for her own and mine. When the small party headed north, on the road to Clairoix, I followed.

I lost sight of them when they went within the town. I dared not follow farther, for Clairoix was in Burgundian hands, and I was deeper in Burgundian territory than I had ever been.

While I hesitated, indecisive and fearful, a band of ill-dressed peasants came near me — peasants, I thought, till I saw their bows and daggers and their tattered clothing and knew them for highwaymen. I was on the main road, but just off it there was a wood, and I fled there, dismounted, and huddled behind a tree, praying that Smoke would be quiet and not betray my presence. But soon I trembled for my life, for the band of men came closer, and it seemed they were going to make camp in that same wood, not far from where I was.

I was trapped, like an animal, and worse — or so I thought.

"And so Compiègne is lost, too," I heard one of them say, and at that I listened more closely.

"My poor wife!" exclaimed another, as they gathered firewood. "I was sure I would be able to return to her with food, once the Maid had lifted the siege."

282

I was astonished! Could it be that these men were residents of Compiègne, and had become robbers to help supply their families throughout the siege? I moved closer, and watched as well as listened.

They were clustered around their fire, and the third member of their band joined them bearing several rabbits, which he quickly skinned and cleaned, putting the meat on sticks and holding it over the fire. My mouth watered, and I realized it had been two days since I had eaten.

"I met one of the Maid's soldiers," said one of the men — tall and heavily bearded, with shoulders wide enough to bear an ox. "He said she did not scream when she was taken, but rather crossed herself and prayed, and bore all stoically."

"Ha," said a smaller man with a pale beardless face and a long scar running down his neck. "I wonder how stoic she will be able to remain in their hands."

"Would we could free her," said the third, short and round and ruddy, "and free our city, too."

His companions grunted assent, and they soon took the rabbits from their sticks, and fell to.

I hid there still, beside my horse, hardly daring to breathe or to hope. But if they were friendly to Jeanne, and loyal to France, surely they would not harm me — and I was near fainting from hunger. Besides, I had noticed that the round ruddy one had a filthy cloth bound around his foot, with dried blood on it, and something oozing above the blood; perhaps I could exchange my skill for food.

Hesitantly, I stepped from behind the tree, leading Smoke, and softly said, "*Messieurs* — gentlemen."

They looked up, each man with a hand to his weapon, and then, seeing me, they glanced at one another, and let go their weapons.

"What have we here?" said the tall man with the beard.

"A waif from the battle, methinks," said the scarred one. "Come, lad, we will not hurt you. You look hungry; come. Tie your horse there. Were you at the battle?"

"Yes, sir," I said, fastening Smoke's reins to the tree at which he had gestured. I went toward them and sat carefully, hoping my tattered garments were still whole enough to disguise me.

"Why," exclaimed the ruddy fellow, "it is a very young lad, surely, with no hair on his face and no change to his voice and" — he reached out his hand and squeezed my shoulder — "small bones, light as a girl's . . ."

"And hands, sir," I said quickly, trying to deepen my voice, "skilled at healing, for I served the king's surgeon in many a battle, and follow the Maid even now. Your foot, sir" — I nodded toward it — "looks to be festering. I perhaps have with me herbs that will help, and skill, too."

"And grace in your hands as well," the ruddy

one replied, looking at me hungrily, his eyes dropping to the front of my garment.

I hastily drew my tattered doublet closer around me, and pulled up my chemise beneath it. Too late I realized that of course that very action might betray me, for a boy would have no need to hide his body.

"Leave off your lewdness, François," said the bearded man, "lest you anger our guest so that you will find no help for your wound. We could go much faster had you not that festering sore. Let the lad — or lass — tend it."

I could see they were all looking at me with the eyes of men who have been too long away from women, and I turned cold inside, but I managed to stand and say, "*Messieurs*, I follow the Maid, as I said, and I am from her village, Domremy; I am known to her and to her brothers, and like them, in God's care. If you harm me, no good will come of it. I will not look to your foot," I said to the ruddy one, "unless you pledge that you will do me no harm."

"Pay no heed to François," said the bearded man. "His foot pains him and makes him lose all courtesy. Whether you be man or maid is your concern and yours only." He looked severely at the others, and I could see he was their leader, and that they respected him. "Come, eat with us; the little we have left is yours. And then we will test your surgeon's skill on François's foot. He will extend to you the respect due to a follower of the Maid, or I — I am Guillaume — I will give you leave to cut his foot off."

Here the other man, the scarred one, who I later learned was called Collot, laughed, and handed me the remains of his rabbit, which I ate hungrily and with no daintiness, I am sure. Then I turned to François and unwrapped his foot, which gave off an evil smell from a huge green pustule.

"This must be cut," I told him, "and the poison drained out — or the foot will die without my taking it off," I added as François's hand strayed to my arm, tickling it softly.

He pulled back his arm, and soon his bravado vanished as I heated my mother's knife in the fire, and opened his wound. He screamed and the others had to hold him down as I cleaned it out and rubbed it with an unguent Madame had taught me to make, call *gratia dei*, which I had carried with me. I tented the wound also, as Nicolas had taught me to do, by leaving a small opening and inserting a strip of cloth, made from Collot's shirt, to keep the opening free. This would allow the poison inside to drain out.

Finally I wrapped the leg all around in cloth from Collot's shirt. By then François was sweating; I pitied him, and wiped the moisture off his brow.

"It should feel better shortly," I told him, and he fell asleep soon after, from pain and fever and fatigue.

Collot and Guillaume made a place for me between them near the fire, where I curled like an animal to sleep. Though it was now well after dawn, I was weary, and they were as well, having watched all night for fear the battle would resume. I needed to relieve myself, but dared not until they were breathing deeply, and when they were, I got up quietly and went into the forest to do so.

When I returned to the smoldering fire, Guillaume was awake, sitting up and watching me. "You would be safer," he said softly, "if your doublet and the chemise under it were less tattered." So saying, he pulled off a leather jerkin he wore and handed it to me. "If you pull the thongs tight so the jerkin is closed across your breasts," he said, "you will be better concealed— mademoiselle."

I felt afraid once more, but was reassured before he spoke again, for I could see his eyes were kind, not lustful. I put on his jerkin, and as we talked, he told me of his wife and daughter in Compiègne, and I told him of my quest.

"It is Jean de Luxembourg who has charge of the Maid, I heard from one I met on the road," said Guillaume. "If I am not mistaken, he will take her north to Beaulieu, for that is his nearest castle, where surely he can guard her better than he can here. If you truly wish to follow her, you should go to Beaulieu and wait." He cleared his throat. "I myself," he said, "have a wish to see Beaulieu again."

"Surely not," I cried, "for you and the others

287

are supplying your families in Compiègne with food!"

"I am weary of the company of these rogues," he said, nodding toward his sleeping companions. "And my family can do without me a while longer, and will be glad when I return to hear that I had helped one who has helped their Maid." He then told me he had a cousin, secretly loyal to the king, living near Beaulieu — and later, parting from his companions, he set out to take me to him. I gave Smoke to him in thanks when at last we arrived, and his cousin, Arnaud, took me in. But Arnaud's wife, Marie, grumbled and seemed afraid, even as she helped me bathe.

I soon learned that Jeanne was indeed imprisoned in the castle at Beaulieu, so every day, in a cast-off dress Marie reluctantly gave me, I went to the castle on the pretext of selling eggs, glad to be out of Marie's sight, for she did not pretend to welcome me. At the castle gate I gave out that I was a cousin of Arnaud's, come to stay with him, for my family had been killed by the French. Yes, the French, for all around were Burgundians, and Arnaud went to many pains to keep secret his loyalty to the king. Had his true feelings been known, he would no doubt have been murdered.

I was let into the castle grounds to sell my eggs, along with those selling other goods, and I stopped a page the first day, saying, "I hear there is a great prisoner come to stay with us here."

"Ah, *oui*, *madame*," he replied excitedly, "a

very odd one — Jeanne the Maid, and she is in that tower there, at the top." He pointed to a round donjon with a small peaked roof and a thin slit or two for light. I ached then for Jeanne, for she would hate being kept so far from God's sunlight.

"They say," a young laundress told me on another day, "that her hair is as short as a man's and that she will not wear women's clothes, nor does she eat much, and they keep a close eye on her, for fear she will escape."

"She would have to be very strong and very clever," I said dryly, looking up at the high tower, "to escape from that."

Even so, she tried, I learned one rainy day when I had no need to ask questions, for there were clusters of people all over the castle yard, speaking of her. I had only to listen.

". . . and she stamped right hard upon the wooden floor, until she had made a hole, and down she tumbled. She was about to take the keys from a sleeping guard to lock him up so she could leave, when she was caught . . ."

"No, no," said another. "She did not stamp; had she done so she would have woken the guards. She lifted up the floorboards . . ."

"But how?" said another. "Surely she had no weapons with her, and she is, after all, a mere woman!"

"A woman of great strength, they say. Why, she had overpowered two of the guards by the time the others heard and seized her!"

"No, not two," said someone else, "but ten!"

"There be not ten guards, Jacques, in the whole tower," another retorted, poking his companion in the ribs. "How rumors fly!"

"Yes, and how she herself may fly," added a thin man with a weasely face, "for I hear she is a witch, and that is how she broke through the floor."

When I had pieced it all together, it seemed that Jeanne had indeed tried to escape and that she had nearly succeeded in locking up her guards. But she had been discovered and, as punishment and for security, had been locked in a tiny cell in the depths of the same tower. So now she would have no sun at all — and the only thing I could do for her, it seemed, was pray.

Some days later I heard new rumors in the castle yard. Chief among them was that Jeanne would soon be taken still farther north, to Beaurevoir, which was Luxembourg's main castle, and more secure than this one. "For it is feared that she will attempt escape again," the young laundress said, "or that her supporters will try to free her."

"Perhaps they will come in the night," the page added with considerable relish, "and mine the castle by digging under the tower, and thence break into her cell, freeing her. I know about such things," he said proudly, "for Didier, the gunner, has told me of war."

I could tell you of war, too, I thought, but

aloud said only, "Eggs! Fresh eggs!" and went about my task, listening all the while for when the move would be made, and wondering how I would follow.

But that night when I told Arnaud what I had heard, he looked thoughtful and then said, "As it happens, I must travel to Beaurevoir to — to . . ."

"You know no one in Beaurevoir, husband," Marie said quickly, "and it seethes with Burgundians; it will not be safe for you to go."

"I went to Poissy," I said, not wanting to endanger Arnaud or frighten Marie any more than I already had, "as a leper. If I can somewhere get a shroud, I could go that way again. No one will come near a leper; it is a safe disguise."

They both stared at me with what seemed like new respect, and then Marie said, with ill-disguised eagerness, "It will not be difficult to get a shroud. Leave that to me."

"And a clapper, too," said Arnaud. "You will need that."

"Clappers can be made," I told him, describing how Pierre had made mine.

"This time," said Arnaud, "you will have the best clapper any leper has ever had. The very best and the most beautiful!"

Arnaud kept his promise, and a few days later, after the rumor had proved true and Jeanne was removed under cover of night from the tower —

as I learned the next day, again selling eggs — I put on my leper's garb, and thanked my kindly host and reluctant hostess. I took my clapper, which was indeed beautiful, and set out on the road to Beaurevoir.

27

It was a long journey, but an uneventful one. The summer had warmed and turned dry, and the fields were ripening; I took what I needed from them as I passed, and picked berries near the woods. Twice I snared a bird, and once a rabbit, and so managed to keep myself alive. The few people I passed gave me wide berth and surprised looks, which told me there was perhaps no leprosarium on my route, and so in their eyes I had no justification for being on the road. But none of them asked me where I was bound, so I did not trouble myself about them.

In time, I came at last to Beaurevoir. I could see even from a distance that it was a stronger, larger castle than Beaulieu, with many towers, and I wondered, as I drew near, how I was to gain entrance within its walls, to hear news of Jeanne. Then I realized that I had an easy way, for there is nearly always a woman about to give birth in a castle, and I still had the dress Marie had given me.

And so, one bright June day, I washed myself in a shallow brook and put on my woman's dress. I made a sack of my shroud, lest I need it again, and in it and in my purse, I put childbirth herbs that I had spent two days gathering — lupine and sweet cicely, plus wallflower, for I had no ergot to hasten birth and it was too early for carrot seeds and too late for peony.

My sack and purse full, I went boldly up to the castle's main gate. I shouted till I had raised the guard, and when a man came out, saying, "Well, mistress, what would you?" I smiled my best smile and announced, "There is a woman within who has need of a midwife, and I am one. Make haste, man, for her time is upon her!"

The ruse worked, as I had thought it would, for men are cowards when it comes to childbirth. The drawbridge was lowered and I was ushered in.

"Who is the lady?" a guard asked, and I felt less bold then, for I knew not what to say.

"Marie," I told him, speaking the first name that came to my mind. "Or Jeanne-Marie? Forgive me, sir, but I was summoned in such haste, I remember not."

"Send for Madame Grisette," said the guard who was obviously in charge. "She will know."

So I waited, flanked by two knights, who glanced at me skeptically every now and then but said nothing. I tried to look nonchalant, as if standing by castle portcullises was something I did daily.

At last Madame Grisette, a tall, slender woman, middle-aged, with a stern face, and clad in a rich green gown, came out and looked me up and down with open suspicion. "*Bien*," she said to the guards at last. "Good. You may leave us. But remain nearby; I may have need of you." Her French was odd, as is all Burgundian French, but I could understand it if I listened closely. She inclined her head, beckoning me inside, and she did not smile.

"Now, madame," she said when the great door had thudded shut behind us, "please be good enough to tell me the true reason for your visit. I am lady-in-waiting to the Demoiselle de Luxembourg, and there is no woman here who is near her time. I cannot therefore believe that you are in truth a midwife."

"But I am, madame," I said, dropping a curtsy, and trying to speak clearly, for I thought my French would be as odd to her as hers was to me. "But" — and here I drew a deep breath, deciding to trust her, although another voice within told me that since she was Burgundian and suspicious, I was a fool — "I am not here as a midwife but as friend to one whom you keep here."

"And who might that be?" Madame Grisette asked, raising her eyebrows.

"Jeanne the Maid." Even as I spoke my heart fluttered in my chest in fear at her coldness. I dared not tell her more.

"Ha!" she exclaimed, and walked around me as if I were a horse she was thinking of buying.

295

"Then you are no friend to my master, and have perhaps come to do us harm — or by some trick, to free the Maid. I must call the guards again and search you."

She called them then, and while my heart still beat fast with fear, she searched me, in full view of the guards. I closed my eyes from embarrassment until at last she dismissed them and handed me back my clothes.

"I found," she said watching me closely while I dressed, "a purse of herbs and one small knife; I shall keep them, lest you plan to put them to ill use. Make no mistake; you will be watched here, if I let you go among us."

"The knife is for my protection, madame," I told her, "and for my work, which is healing as well as midwifery."

"You will do no healing or midwifery here, I'll warrant," she said severely. "And you will go no farther in this castle without my mistress's leave. My master the duke hunts this day, so I must apply to his aunt, the Demoiselle de Luxembourg, in his absence. Guard!"

The men returned.

"You will watch this woman while I speak to the demoiselle. Do not permit her to leave this chamber."

While I tried to disguise my growing fear by settling the folds of my dress and smoothing my hopeless hair, the guards ranged themselves on each side of me. Madame Grisette left, and we three stood in a silence so stern and heavy I could feel it pressing on me.

It was not long, thanks be to God, before she returned and, gesturing brusquely for me to follow, led me outside and across the castle ward to a long, narrow building, many-towered. We went in through a wide door, and thence up a winding stone stair to a small chamber, bright with sunshine and colored cushions. There a little dog came to greet me, yapping, and an elderly woman, in a soft gray gown trimmed with pearls, sat at an embroidery frame, with several younger women, also embroidering, near her. They all put their needles down and stared at me, adding greatly to my fear.

"Amé!" exclaimed the elderly lady, calling to the dog, "*Tais-toi!* Be silent!"

The dog ran back to her and stood near the folds of her skirt, eyeing me with bright intelligent eyes. I smiled at it, longing to stroke it, and thinking that both it and I would enjoy a game of ball more than the conversation that was bound to follow.

"Madame," said my escort, her voice steady but disapproving, "this is the young woman of whom I told you, come because of your good nephew's prisoner, Jeanne the Maid, whom she says is her friend."

There were whispers from the ladies ranged around the room, and looks both sharp and curious. But the lady in gray remained impassive.

"Leave me, *mesdames*," she ordered her women. "No, Grisette," she said, turning toward her. "You may stay."

When we were alone, the Demoiselle de Luxembourg — for it was she, of course — pointed to one of the small embroidered stools on which the ladies had been sitting and said to me, "Be seated, child, and tell me your story. But before you do, know that you are in a house of Luxembourg, and that my nephew, Jean, is no friend to the French king, though he bears kindly feelings toward those who, out of only innocence or folly, follow him."

"I know nothing of politics, madame," I said carefully, and as morning changed to afternoon, I told her my story. She seemed so interested that I found myself forgetting both my fear and Madame Grisette's disapproval, and telling more than I had planned. The demoiselle asked many questions, especially about my dear Madame Christine, whom she had once met. But she asked nothing, I felt, that would compromise Jeanne or the king's cause if I answered truthfully.

As the light fled from the windows and the room fell into shadows and became colder, Madame Grisette rose, saying, "Madame forgive me, but I must light the fire. Your hands need the warmth, I am sure. And perhaps you would soon like to dine." I thought at first she had softened a little — but then she turned to me, and I could tell that though she served her mistress well, she was no friend to the king's cause or to Jeanne, despite her mistress's kindness.

The demoiselle nodded, waving her hand toward the door and saying, "Have them bring enough food for two, Grisette."

It was then that I noticed the demoiselle's hands, seeing the twists and knobs at the knuckles that bespeak the joint sickness that comes upon the old, the same that had crippled Sister Georgette. "Madame," I said when Grisette had left, "my pardon, but if your kitchen has flax and honey, and oil or pig's grease, I can make an unguent that may ease your hands somewhat."

"I thank you, child," she said. "Perhaps I will avail myself of that in time. But first you must tell me what you hope to do here."

I hesitated, hardly knowing myself, now that I was there.

"I should tell you," she said before I was able to assemble my thoughts enough to speak, "that I have visited the Maid, as have my nephew's wife and stepdaughter, and although as you have seen, Grisette does not approve, we find her to be truly pious and of good character, and the bravest of women. She is sincere in her dedication to Charles and to France, and, seeing her virtue, I cannot hate her as an enemy. I fear for her safety as much as you — not while she is here, but if she were to be sent away, especially to the English. They, you know, would like to put her to trial . . ."

"To trial!" I said, horrified. "But she has done

no crime, except that of war, which surely is not a thing one is tried for, since so many wage it."

"Ordinarily, no," said the demoiselle, "but the English say she is a witch, or a heretic, and that she acted not for God but for herself, for vanity. Indeed," she said gently, "your own Charles, whom you call king, has done nothing toward ransoming her. There was some rejoicing in his court, I am told, at the Maid's capture, especially on the part of one George de La Trémoille. And Regnault de Chartres, Archbishop of Reims, who crowned your king, has, I am told, sent word to the people of Reims that the Maid was too prideful to listen to those who advised her to make peace — so he is not likely to help her either. Indeed, it is said that your king has found a young shepherd who does miracles and that his attention is now placed there, not on the Maid."

She spoke gently, as if she knew the pain her words would cause me. It was unthinkable that the king would not ransom Jeanne, after she had crowned him and saved France!

And that the English would put her to trial was beyond imagining.

"But," the demoiselle continued, "know that if you speak of your plans to me, you speak to one who admires your friend. Do not, however, speak of them to Grisette, lest you be betrayed."

"I — I have no plans," I said miserably, "except that I wish to stay close to Jeanne in case there is any way that I may aid her."

300

"To escape? I cannot assist you there. Surely you see that."

"I can, madame, and I would not ask it, for you must be loyal to your people as I must be loyal to mine. No, it is more because she has no woman with her, no one from home, that I wish to stay near her, to comfort her. I have not seen her to speak to since before she was captured at Compiègne . . ."

I could say no more.

The demoiselle rose and came slowly to me, putting her gnarled hand on my shoulder. "I cannot take you to her," she said softly, "but I can tell her you are here, and I can take her a message if it is not one that will betray my nephew and his cause. It would be unwise to tell him of yours, but perhaps I can convince him to let you stay here as one of my serving women."

"That," I said, trying to regain control of my voice, "would be most helpful madame."

She smiled. "And what message," she asked, "shall I take to your friend?"

"That — that Gabrielle is here," I said, "and hopes she is well. And that I will stay by her, hoping — praying — for her eventual release. And that . . ."

The demoiselle held up her hand, whispering, "Enough!" Serving women came into her chamber then, with a little table bearing dishes covered with gold covers, in which were soups and roasted birds and fruits and even salads, plus a ewer of water and one of wine. The demoiselle remained silent till the women had left and then graciously bade me eat, which I did, hungrily and with much gratitude.

And so the demoiselle spoke to her nephew about me, and he allowed me to stay and serve her, bringing rushes for her floor, and beating dust from the tapestries that hung in her chamber, and airing the great bed in which she slept. Madame Grisette scowled and grumbled, but the demoiselle delivered my message to Jeanne, and brought back one saying that she was well and kindly treated, and that she, too, prayed she would be released. The demoiselle begged me to ask Jeanne through her to put on women's clothes, for both she and Luxembourg's wife and stepdaughter had urged her unsuccessfully to do so, but I said I could not, for she was guarded by men. I reminded her of what I had told her before: that I had worn men's clothes, too, when among men, for safety as well as for disguise.

As the summer progressed, rumors passed among the servants that Jeanne would soon be taken to the English, and the demoiselle herself grew weak. Although she said the unguent I had made for her hands soothed her greatly, it of course could do nothing for the slowness of her step. Then one night she came to me, a candle in her hand. Without speaking, she returned my mother's knife and my herbs to me, and led me up a steep staircase to the top of the tower in which I knew Jeanne was held. I dared not ask her why she was doing this when she had so long refused, but my heart beat wildly within me.

And then, when we entered the tower, I saw why, for Jeanne, pale and thin, lay on a litter of straw, a great bloody mark on her head.

"Leave us; stay outside," the demoiselle said in a low voice to the guards, who nodded and left, stopping just outside the door.

"She fell," the demoiselle said, "or jumped, or someone pushed her from the tower. My nephew is sorely angry, and will not send for a surgeon, saying that if she dies, perhaps the English will stop hounding him. But I know he speaks in anger only, and will send for surgeons in the morning, for she is too valuable a prize to give up and I think he holds her to command the highest price he can. I am sure, though, that he will move her, if she lives, to another place. But she is in pain now, and in need, as you can see, and I cannot let her remain unattended when I know you love her, and have skill."

I hardly heard her, though I felt a flash of horror at what she had said about price. Before she had finished speaking, I was bending over Jeanne, feeling her head gently with my fingers, which told me her skull was intact, as much as I could discern. But whether her brain was addled, as so often happens when there is a blow to the head or a fall upon it, I could not tell. "Jeanne," I said softly — then, "Jeanette!"

She stirred when I spoke her childhood name,

and moaned, and opened her eyes, which stared blankly for a time into mine and then softened.

"Gabrielle," she said. "Gabrielle — friend dove — the good demoiselle said you were here, but I knew not whether it to be true. Oh, Gabrielle!" She reached up her arms to me, with tears in her eyes, and pulled me to her. I embraced her, and then I gently drew away, saying, "Jeannette, your head — does it hurt?"

"It does. But — but for a moment" — she was whispering now — "for a moment, I tasted the open air again, and freedom, and I would have escaped, Gabrielle, I . . ."

"Shh," I warned her, indicating the demoiselle — but when I turned, I saw that she had withdrawn and had her back to us.

"Do not talk, Jeanette," I said. "You must rest."

But she would not. "What of Pierre?" she asked. "And d'Aulon? And Poton de Xaintrailles?"

"I know nothing of them," I told her. "I would that I did, but it was you I followed. D'Aulon was with you, was he not, for a time?"

"At first, and he comforted me unfailingly. But they took him from me at Beaulieu. I am angry, Gabrielle," she whispered, "that I could not escape from here, and my saints are angry that I tried, I fear. But I had heard that I am to be sold to the English, and I cannot abide that thought. And I heard that the English will kill everyone in Compiègne — even children, everyone older than seven — and I felt I must go to them."

"Were you truly seeking to escape so you could go to war again?" I asked her gently. "Or were you seeking to die?"

Jeanne was silent for so long I thought she had slipped into unconsciousness or sleep, but at last she said, "I know not. Either one, I think, would have pleased me. And now I must be patient, and do as God wills." She touched my face. "Bless you, friend dove," she said, and closed her eyes.

"Bless you, Jeannette," I whispered, "for you have done great good for France, and suffered much for her."

Her eyes flew open again. "But I have failed!" she cried bitterly.

I shook my head. "The good Loire towns are still the king's, I am sure," I told her, "and in them no doubt they pray daily for your release. All over France," I went on, to cheer her, hoping it was true, "people praise and thank you. You are remembered as good, not as a failure."

"It is God who should be remembered, not I," she said drowsily, "for I have only done as He wishes, through my saints."

"And so," I told her, "you cannot have failed. One does not always see God's design till time has passed."

She smiled then, and slept.

The demoiselle and I stayed with her till the sky outside the window through which she had jumped turned gray. Sometimes she woke, and I bathed her head, for the demoiselle had the guards bring us cool water and those herbs that I requested for dressing her wound, for most of those I had brought were better for childbirth than for injuries such as Jeanne's. When Jeanne woke, we talked of Domremy, and of the mist on the River Meuse, which she loved as much as I, and of our parents and old friends. I think — I hope — it comforted her.

But when dawn came, the demoiselle hurried me away.

Not long after that, the demoiselle left Beaurevoir. I suspect she was sent away, for her nephew was not pleased at her fondness for Jeanne, and perhaps suspected she had played a part in Jeanne's leap from the tower, which he recognized as an attempt to escape. I wondered, also, what Madame Grisette said to him of the matter and, indeed, of me. Soon afterwards, Jeanne was taken under strong guard to the Cour le Comte, in Arras. I followed her there, again clad as a leper, but this castle was the Duke of Burgundy's, and I dared not try my midwife ruse there.

Instead I found a hermit's hut, abandoned, just outside the walls, and stayed in that, babbling like a madwoman when anyone passed. Every day or so, I strapped one leg under my skirt as Louis had told me false beggars do. With a stick under my arm, I hobbled to the castle and sat against its walls, mumbling and holding out my hand as if begging, but truly listening for news.

Some passersby gave me small coins, *deniers* and *oublies*, with which, when I had enough, I purchased bread.

And so I passed the first part of early winter, until one cold December day when I heard that Jeanne had been sold to the English, and was to be taken to Rouen, to stand the trial she dreaded.

PART SIX

Part Six

28

How did I reach Rouen? I went sometimes as a
leper, sometimes as a madwoman or pilgrim, and
once in the back of someone's turnip cart, when
he did not know I was there. And at last I came
to Rouen, with no idea of how I was to live, but
much confidence, now, from experience, that I
would find a way.

God must have been pleased with my mission,
for I did find a way, and quickly. Not long after I
arrived, I overheard a woman ask in the street
where a certain midwife lived, and when she had
heard the answer and hurried off, I followed her.
Unknowingly, she led me down many small dark
streets, some with houses still in ruins from when
the English had held Rouen under siege, with
the usual city filth running in the gutters and the
usual city cries and smells. She led me to a narrow, shuttered house, and was admitted, emerg-
ing soon after with a short, stout woman carrying
a large basket — the midwife, I was sure. I waited
for the midwife to return, and when she did, I

311

smoothed my hair as best I could, and my skirt, which was muddy at the hem and rumpled from many days and nights of wearing. Then I went up to her.

"*Madame*," I said as politely as I could, "*Pardon, madame*, but you are a midwife — yes?"

Her eyes dropped along my body as if she were gauging how soon I would need her services, and returned to my face. "Yes," she said, not unpleasantly. "What is it?"

"*Pardon, madame*, but it is not what you think. I have traveled here from Beaurevoir, and before that from Beaulieu. I am Gabrielle de Domremy, and I am myself a midwife, as is my mother, and I follow Jeanne de Domremy, she whom they call the Maid." I feared then that I should not have spoken so boldly, for I knew Rouen was not one of the king's towns. It had surrendered long ago to the English, ending the siege, and the English still held it, and had made it their headquarters. Many of its residents had become more English than French, though whether out of fear or choice, I did not know.

As soon as I spoke of Jeanne, I feared the worst, for the woman's brow furrowed and she looked behind me, up the street and down. Then, putting one hand on my arm, she opened her door and drew me quickly in.

"It is not wise," she said when we were in a narrow passage and she had closed the door, plunging us into darkness, "to speak of the Maid in Rouen" — and I felt weak with relief then, and knew that God had not deserted me. "She lies prisoner here," the midwife continued, "in the Castle Philippe-Auguste, for she has been sold to the English, and people say she will come to no good when at last they put her to trial. She has many enemies among the English." She lowered her voice. "There are, however, in Rouen, a few, like myself, who love her, for she is France."

"*Oui, madame*," I said, smiling at her, "she is France indeed. And I gave my word to her mother that I would stay with her as much as I could, and so I have followed her here."

The midwife clucked her tongue. "You are a loyal woman if nothing else, Gabrielle de Domremy. Come further in and rest, and tell me your story — and eat, too, for you look pale and hungry. I have new bread, and soup as well." So saying, she led me to the back of the house, where there was a thick stew on the fire and a thicker loaf beside it — and thus began my acquaintance with Madame Jacqueline Marret and her two daughters, one of whom loved an English manat-arms and was no friend to Jeanne or, indeed, to her own mother. Madame Jacqueline warned me to be careful of what I said around this daughter, whose name was Marie-Claire. In the months I was in Rouen, Madame Jacqueline taught me some few things Dame Trotula's book could not, and I taught Madame Jacqueline, too, for I had learned some things that she did not know. She and Michelle, her other daughter — her husband had been killed during the siege —

never tired of hearing about Jeanne, though we had to wait to talk till Marie-Claire was absent.

And then one day, Madame Jacqueline took her basket on one arm and me on the other, and we went to the castle, so I could at least see the outside of where Jeanne was.

It was well guarded, too well guarded for us to enter beyond its outer yard. I counted eight peaked towers rising above it, with the narrowest of slits cut in their smooth rock walls for light and defense. I thought of Jeanne in one of them — we knew not which — and wished I were sorceress instead of healer so I could gather sunlight for her and thrust it into her dark prison.

I returned every day, and at last one of the guards asked me what I did there. From his accent I could tell that he was English, so I said, slowly, to ensure he could follow, "Oh, I am come to see the witch, but I know not in which tower she lies."

"Why, in the back one," he said promptly. "See, that one there — the next-to-largest. It is called the Treasure Tower, though the greatest treasure it has now is this Maid — who is so brazen, mademoiselle, and so unwomanly that, unlike you good Rouen girls, she will wear only men's clothes." With that he reached out his hand and pinched me, laughing, and I, afraid to arouse his suspicions by displeasing him, gave a soft scream and laughed as well. But I left soon after, saying my mistress would be looking for me.

For two days afterward I stayed away, but then returned, this time to the street across from the tower. I stood there hoping that Jeanne might look out, see me, and be cheered. But I never saw her.

It was said that an iron cage had been ordered for her, in which she was to be chained so she could not move. I could not bear the thought of such cruelty, and spent one whole night raging at it. The next day, Madame Jacqueline went to see a friend of hers, Lisette, who was a kitchen maid at the castle, and found that though the cage had been made, it had not been used. But Jeanne, Lisette told her, was chained by the legs and often by the waist as well, and guarded night and day by men — and to me this seemed nearly as cruel.

In February, Lisette came to our house one evening, and when at last Marie-Claire had gone to meet William, her English love, Lisette said, "Today they took the Maid out of her tower to the Chapel Royal, and people crowded into it to see her. They have questioned her privately many times, I am told, but now there is to be a public trial."

I felt my breath catch in my throat. "Did you see her?" I asked.

"A glimpse, madame," she said. "She looked tired, and thin, but I saw her smile at one of the soldiers even so. She is a great heroine, and I fear what they will do to her."

Lisette saw her a few times after that, but inside the castle only, for no more trial sessions were held in the chapel; instead, they took place in a small room in the castle itself. I arranged to meet Lisette near the castle wall, for Marie-Claire had grown suspicious of my purpose in Rouen, and therefore watchful. Usually when I met Lisette she told me she had not seen Jeanne, but whenever she had, her description of Jeanne was the same, except once she said Jeanne looked ill and pale. Once, also, she said, her eyes looked red, as if she had been weeping. "But always," she went on, "she has a high courage about her, a lift to her chin and defiance in her eyes, even when they are also red or sad, and the glow of holiness as well. She is brave, that one, an example to all women. I could not bear what she is bearing."

With that, Madame Jacqueline and I agreed.

And so the cold snowy months of winter passed, and eased. With the warm winds came melting of the snow and of the ice that followed it — but slowly, for Rouen is in the north. I wondered how Jeanne fared in her lonely tower, and I hoped they had a fire there for her.

At last the spring days grew longer, and warmer, and soon it was May, but the saddest May I had ever seen. It was as if the newly blossoming flowers and the bright young green leaves mocked my sorrow with their beauty.

The first sign I had that something was about to happen came when Lisette reported much unrest at the castle, and more than usual passing back and forth of the various officials. A great throng of them assembled there one day, but Lisette did not know what for, and then some ten days later, she told me that she had seen Jeanne again, being taken to the castle's donjon where were kept instruments of torture. I cried out at this, fearing the worst, but Lisette said quickly, "I do not think they used them, for I saw her being taken back to the Treasure Tower later, and she was walking, and there was no blood on her. She was pale, still, but no worse, and she looked straight before her, with great dignity and holiness."

Another ten days or so passed, during which time Madame Jacqueline and I attended several births, one difficult — a large baby and a slender mother, who named her child for me, and I dared not suggest she name her Jeanne instead. Then late one night, we were awakened by a beating on our door. Madame Jacqueline, her daughters and I behind her to protect her, opened it, admitting Lisette.

"Madame . . ." Lisette began breathlessly — and then stopped, for Marie-Claire had pushed herself quickly forward.

"Yes?" Marie-Claire said. "Yes? Madame . . . what? What news do you bring my mother at this late hour — when anyone can see you have no need of her usual services?" She regarded Lisette smugly, as if most proud of her own cleverness. "Do you perhaps carry messages against the English, or for their prisoner?" Then she looked straight at me, and my heart quailed, though I think I made no outward sign. "Oh, yes," she went on, "I am not as stupid as you would like to think, and I have told William of your comings and goings, Gabrielle, and he has told the castle guard. So if you" — here she glanced again at Lisette and then at her mother and at me — "if you are developing a plan for the Maid's escape, you will not succeed." She smiled then, triumphantly, her eyes flashing and her hands on her hips.

But Madame Jacqueline remained as calm as she did when faced with the screams of a woman in childbirth. "What nonsense you speak, Marie-Claire!" she said. "My friend Lisette is worried about her sister, who has lost much blood delivering her third child . . ."

"And is bleeding still, madame," Lisette said, falling quickly into the ruse. "I have come in haste to summon you, lest she bleed to death."

Madame Jacqueline reached for the basket of herbs and tools she kept hanging ready above the hearth. "Come, Gabrielle," she said quietly. "We must hurry."

But once we were outside, safely away from Marie-Claire, we dropped all pretense, and Lisette told us there had been a great stir at the castle, and that the Maid would be taken to Saint-Ouen Cemetery the next day, there to publicly recant or — if she refused — to be executed.

Executed — when she had saved France!

Was there to be no hope at all, then, ever, of ransom?

I sat the rest of that night at the window of the room I shared with Madame Jacqueline. It faced the castle, and as I looked out at its towers, I wondered if Jeanne watched that night, too, and what she thought. Recant or be executed — that was no choice at all, for to recant would be to say she had not been sent by God, and that would go against all — herself, and the king, and her saints, and God, and France.

But I shuddered, thinking of the cruel alternative. I would recant, I knew, were I Jeanne, out of terror for my life — and silently, all that long night, I begged her to do the same, and prayed that she would; surely God and her saints would forgive her! If she recants, I thought, she will be freed, and I can take her home to Domremy — perhaps with Pierre, if we can find him.

Comforting myself with that thought, I fell into a restless sleep.

The day dawned, warm and bright. Madame Jacqueline and Michelle — Marie-Claire had gone to meet her William — and I hurried outside and joined the throngs already streaming toward Saint-Ouen. As Madame Jacqueline had said, there was some love for Jeanne in Rouen, despite the English, and where there was not love, there was curiosity.

Saint-Ouen was a pretty church, though still being built, and its abbey was in need of repairs from the English siege. On one side had been erected two high platforms, and we stood between them, in the crowd, and waited.

In time, several men mounted the platform facing the church. "That is Cauchon," Madame Jacqueline whispered to me, pointing to the thinnest of them. "He was the Bishop of Beauvais, but he was driven out of that city when he refused to support the king — so he is no friend to your friend. Before that, he was Rector of the University of Paris. He is one of the judges, and I do not like his face."

I did not like it either; it was pinched, and sour.

There was also a cardinal, which I could tell from his clothes, and a bishop, and several others, all to sit in judgment upon Jeanne. Worst, though, was the man I saw come up behind the platform facing the church door: the executioner, all in black, with his cart. I tried not to look at him, but I found my eyes straying there many times.

At last a side door opened, and under its arched frame, decorated with knobs of stone that resembled flowers perched atop triangular stems, stepped Jeanne with three men, who were in earnest conversation with her. Her eyes went quickly from them to the platform opposite her, and then to the executioner's cart, and at last, I thought, to me. I smiled and nodded, but I do not know if she saw me.

A man in long black robes stood; one in the

crowd said he was called Guillaume Erard, and that he was from the University of Paris. Looking at Jeanne, and then at the crowd, and then back at Jeanne, he began speaking. His words filled me with anger and must have wounded Jeanne, for he talked cruelly to her, saying she was prideful, evil, and a heretic. Erard spoke ill of our King Charles also, saying he only called himself king — he who was crowned in Reims Cathedral by the archbishop, with the holy oil from the sacred ampulla! Finally, Erard said severely, "It is to you, Jeanne, that I speak, and I tell you your king is a heretic!"

Jeanne had been silent until now, but at this her pale face grew red and she said, "By my faith, sir, in all reverence, I dare say and swear, on pain of my life, that he is the most noble Christian of all Christians, the one who best loves the faith and the Church. He is not what you call him."

"Make her be silent!" Erard cried, and went on with his sermon. Then he turned to Jeanne again. "Your judges have remonstrated with you, and have explained to you that according to churchmen, there are many things among those you have said and done which are false and erroneous."

Jeanne answered in a clear voice that I easily heard, despite the restlessness of the crowd around me. She told him that they should send report of her words and deeds to the pope in Rome and let him judge her, but most of all, that God should judge her. "And as to my words and my actions," she declared, "I said and did them moved by God."

There was much talk then that I could not hear, between Jeanne and the men near her and the men on the platform opposite her, while the people in the crowd grew noisier. But at last Cauchon pulled a rolled-up parchment from his sleeve and opened it, reading, although the men near Jeanne were still in earnest conversation with her. There was such a hubbub I could hear only angry shouting among the officials on the platform, as if they had forgotten Jeanne and cared only to abuse each other. Then above it all I heard the words "Sign!" and "Recant!" and "Abjure!" Erard's voice rose again, louder than the rest, shouting to Jeanne, "Do it now, or you will be burned this very day!"

At that, the executioner gazed full at her.

I could see Jeanne shudder. She held out her hand for the parchment, and as she did, someone in the crowd threw a stone toward her. Then someone else threw one toward the platform with the officials on it, and for a while, there was much shouting and ducking and hurling of stones, until guards came and quelled it.

When next I looked toward Jeanne, her hands were joined together in prayer and her eyes were looking Heavenward. I wondered where her saints were and I prayed that they were with her — for she had no one else, clearly.

I found myself saying silently to her, "Sign, please sign; it will not change what you have

322

done. Our dauphin is King; Orléans is free and the Loire towns are loyal. Do not throw away your life!" I thought of her mother, and of the little garden where Pierre and I had first heard her answer her saints, and I ached for her.

At last she did sign, or made some mark, for I do not think she could have learned to write, though some said later that by then she could write her name. I felt weak with relief — but then, as I pushed joyfully through the crowd toward her, she was led away.

Led away!

I stopped, stunned, watching in horror. And my arms, which had longed to embrace her and take her home, felt empty and betrayed.

The crowd began to leave. "Poor child," I heard an old woman say. "It is a cruel fate." Another replied, "Yes, but now she will be given to the Church, who will treat her more kindly than the English officials," and my spirits lifted a little at the thought.

But only a little.

29

I left Madame Jacqueline's soon after that, to avoid Marie-Claire's prying eyes, for though of course I had no plan to help Jeanne escape — would that I had! — I did not think it wise to stay and feed Marie-Claire's suspicion, or, through her, William's. Madame Jacqueline found lodging for me with a friend who loved the king, and gave out to Marie-Claire that I had left, discouraged at Jeanne's recanting, to return to Domremy. I saw Marie-Claire at a distance twice after that, but I do not know if she saw me, or what she might have thought if she did.

Lisette came to me now, instead of to Madame Jacqueline, whom I often met at my new lodging or at the side of a woman in travail. The first time I saw Lisette after Jeanne's recantation at Saint-Ouen, I was at least expecting to hear of Jeanne's happier estate in the hands of the Church, though by then I was full of fury at the sentence that had been pronounced upon her. I had been unable to hear it at Saint-Ouen, for the noise of the crowd was too great, but I learned soon afterward that she was to be kept in prison for the rest of her life. She would never see Domremy again, or walk along the River Meuse, or embrace her parents, and this seemed so cruel that I was for a time unable to speak after I heard it. She had done no wrong, but had only served her king — and where was that king? Why had he not come to her aid? Why had he not ransomed her, as any valuable captain would have been ransomed? Surely King Charles could have raised the money to free his loyal Maid! Had La Trémoille and Regnault de Chartres prevented him? And where were Jeanne's brave captains, those who had been so loyal when all was going well? Pierre had been captured and was no doubt languishing in prison himself — but where was Jean?

I resolved to stay in Rouen until I knew if I could see Jeanne, and then I would decide whether to stay and continue to work with Madame Jacqueline despite Marie-Claire, or leave to look for Pierre and perhaps go home to Domremy, or return to Poissy and my dear Madame Christine.

But the next time Lisette came to me, as soon as she was inside my chamber she said breathlessly, "I have bad news, news so bad I know not how to tell it."

I sat her down, poured her some wine, and let

her catch her breath. I remember hoping she might never catch it, for the despair in her eyes chilled me so that I could not move.

"I have just heard that when they took the Maid back to prison," she said finally, looking everywhere but at me, "she at first put on women's clothes, which is what they wished, those men. But later she took them off again and put on the others. I know not why, although someone at the castle said her guards tried to molest her as soon as she was wearing skirts again, and others say someone hid her women's clothes and let her have only men's."

"What?" I said, renewed anger allowing me to speak. "Was she not taken to a church prison, and could she not there have women with her where no one would molest her or force her to dress as a man?"

Lisette shook her head. "I know not why, madame, but this was denied her." She gave a soft moan and looked up at me, her eyes moist. "And now that she has put on soldier's garb again," she said, "I fear all is lost. They say that they will burn her, for they feel no good religious woman would dress as a man, and she must therefore be a witch. But I fear that is an excuse only; they hate that she serves France and our king."

I felt my head spin, and I reached for the edge of a nearby chest lest I fall. Lisette touched my arm shyly and whispered, "We must be brave for her, madame."

I embraced her then, and we clung to each other in sorrow, for we knew that in truth all was lost — and word came soon that Jeanne was indeed to be burned.

I can hardly bear to think further, and must pause to gather strength before I do.

It was another clear May morning. I remember hearing a songbird when I woke up, and for a moment I lay peacefully in my chamber, listening to it, and thinking what wonders God made when he made birds.

Then I remembered what day it was, and a heaviness came into my throat and my chest and stomach till I could hardly breathe.

I dressed quickly, though, and quietly, and tried not to think. I told myself only that I must be with her, that she must see someone from home on this her last day on earth. Perhaps it would remind her of a happier time, of the misty valley of her childhood and of the sparkling Meuse; perhaps the memory would convey that not all was hateful in this world which was so cruelly punishing her. I did not want to see her burn, and I was afraid that the memory of it would haunt me forever — but I pushed that fear aside. And, as I went out into the nearly empty street, I felt I was not present in my body anymore, not that I had become Jeanne but that I was a vessel for her, for her fear, perhaps, and for her pain. I knew that I would die for her if I could, for I felt that she was far better than I, and

327

more worthy to live, despite her warring. She had fought for God and for France, not for ambition or cruelty. I felt humble before the strength of her faith, and knew I could not doubt or even question it.

I did not seek out Madame Jacqueline for company, or Lisette, or even Michelle, for I knew that I must be alone with Jeanne on this day.

All was in readiness when I reached the Vieux Marché, the square in which the execution was to take place, not far from the cathedral. A few people had already gathered there, and vendors of pies and chestnuts were setting up their stalls.

There were four hastily built platforms, close to the church of Saint-Sauveur, but what filled my eyes most was the stake, high on a square made of plaster, with a board fastened to it, bearing the words:

JEANNE, WHO HAD HERSELF CALLED THE MAID,
A LIAR, PERNICIOUS DECEIVER OF THE PEOPLE,
SORCERESS
SUPERSTITIOUS, BLASPHEMER OF GOD, DEFAMER OF
THE FAITH OF JESUS CHRIST
BOASTFUL, IDOLATROUS, CRUEL, DISSOLATE,
INVOKER OF DEMONS
APOSTATE, SCHISMATIC, AND HERETIC.

It was as if they had taken all the things good men hate most and blamed Jeanne for them, and

I seethed with fury at their lies. Why was this happening? Why?

I must have whispered "Why?" aloud, for a soldier standing nearby gave me a look of surprise, and then said softly, "Because, mademoiselle, she is too good for this earth, and some men cannot bear that she is better than they."

It was I who was surprised then, for I heard from his accent that he was English. When I looked at him more closely, he nodded and moved away.

But I knew that Jeanne's goodness could not be the sole reason. I remembered the courage she had given our men and I imagined how much the English and Burgundians must have grown to fear her. That, too, must be the reason for her sentence, I thought, my eyes fixing on the words "sorceress" and "invoker of demons." If you are a soldier, and are bested in battle by a woman, must you not think the reason is something more than that she is a better soldier than you? If you think God is with her, you must then think He is not with you — and so it would serve your interest better to think she is a creature of the Devil.

The square was becoming crowded, so I moved closer to the stake, for I wanted Jeanne to see me. I told myself I could always close my eyes if I could not bear to watch her pain.

I heard the cart carrying her before I saw it, and then it came into sight at the far end of the square, rumbling roughly over the cobblestones. Jeanne stood gripping one side, clad only in a long black shift, with a cloth over her head like a kerchief. Her mouth was set and taut, but I could see she had wept not long before, though she was quiet now and her eyes were dry. The crowd shouted when they saw her, mostly rough words. I think those few of us who loved her kept silent, praying with her when we saw her eyes turn above the crowd to Heaven and her lips move.

She was led to one of the platforms near the stake, and helped onto it. There was a long sermon, whose words I hardly heard. My eyes were on Jeanne, who stood silently and patiently, looking toward the sky, and then at the stake, and then at the crowd. She appeared puzzled, sometimes, as if she did not understand what had brought her here. I could feel my heart hammering in my breast and I wondered if she felt her own.

The sermon ended, and pinched, ratlike Cauchon spoke directly to Jeanne about her soul and its salvation, which seemed to me ironic; his own, I felt, was in more danger than hers. And then a high churchman, a bishop, read words casting her out of the Church and giving her to the secular officials — but this was ironic, too, for it seemed to me the Church had avoided accepting her ever since her capture. The cloth was removed from head, and I saw that her hair had been shaved off, and then her head was crowned with a miter — a mocking miter, not a holy one, for on it were the words HERETIC, RELAPSED, APOSTATE, IDOLATOR. Jeanne knelt in prayer, for some time, and I could hear her forgiving those who had wronged her, and asking their pardon. The soldiers around her, guarding her, laughed, but many near me wept.

Then she was conducted to another platform and was there for some time; again I could not hear what was spoken. But at last the man nearest her raised his hand. Another man seized her arm and pulled her rudely to the stake, and I heard her call upon her saints and cry, "Rouen, Rouen, shall I die here?" Then, with some of her old defiance and courage, almost in the tone she had used to the Burgundians at Orléans, she shouted, "Ha! Rouen, I have great fear that you will suffer for my death!"

My eyes were wet when she said that, as men piled fascines and logs closer around the skirt of her shift. I heard someone beside me saying kindly, "You know, mademoiselle, that they slip them something, to make the dying easier." When I turned to see who it was and recognized the English soldier who had spoken to me before, another person, who I thought must be a merchant from his dress, said grimly, "I fear they have put the stake too high for that, and the logs too high as well. The executioner will not be able to reach her to help her die. For of course he has to do it unseen if he is to do it at all, and that will not be possible."

I wished that I had not heard either man.

I turned again toward Jeanne, and saw that she was looking out over the crowd, and asking, with both hands and words, for a cross. The English soldier searched the ground near his feet and then I saw two small sticks, dropped from the fascines with which they were to kindle the fire. I picked them up quickly, and handed them to him, for he was taller than I and had better chance, I knew, of reaching her, especially being English and a soldier. He smiled at me, and fastened the two together with a bit of cord he had about him. Then he reached up to her with the little cross he had made, handing it to her. I saw her smile at him, and then, I think, she noticed me and smiled again before she kissed the cross and put it in her bosom.

She asked for another cross, a large one from the church, and when this was brought out and held up for her, she embraced it. But then it was pried from her, and her hands and arms were bound. The cross was moved away, to save it from the fire. I suppose — but she could see it still, I think, for the man who bore it held it high.

And then they lit the fire.

I know I stood there; I think I did not close my eyes, for I still remember her face, reflecting the flames and showing such terror and such agony as I have never seen. I remember praying, saying, "Holy Mary, protect her, save her from the pain" — for that was all I could think of: how it must hurt, how it must burn.

In a while there was so much smoke and the flames were so high that I could see no longer, and there was a great smell of burning wood and cloth and flesh that sickened many. I could hear her calling to her saints, and to God, and asking for holy water, which no one could give her.

And at last she cried, "Jesus!" and was no more.

Afterward, I returned to Poissy. The good prioress told me that Madame had received my message and my medal from my pages, who had found another knight to serve. Madame had died soon after, leaving the medal for me in her hut in the convent wall. She had left all her books for me as well, and, the prioress said, her love.

Much has happened since then. Pierre languished in prison for years, but at last bought his freedom, with Isabelle's help, and became prosperous, as did Jean. Seven months after Jeanne died, the English boy king, Henry VI, was given the crown of France, and the war continued, with fighting and truces, and fighting again. La Trémoille was saved from an assassin's sword only by the size of his stomach, but he left the court and was replaced at long last by one who was more willing than he to fight. Paris went to King Charles in 1435, and in that year Philip the Good of Burgundy at last recognized Charles as King of France, and signed an honest treaty with him. In 1449, King Charles took Rouen from the English, and by 1453, they were gone from all but one town, Calais . . .

"Gabrielle! Are you ready to go?"

I looked up to see Pierre, my thickened, aging friend; it was morning, and I had not slept, remembering. "I am," I told him, "for though I do not like soldiering now, I do not think Jeanne was evil, and all France — all humankind, perhaps — can learn from her cheerful courage. She was sincere; she loved God; she loved France and saved it, though she did not live to see the outcome of her work. And I will swear that to all who ask."

Pierre smiled as we left the hut, and he linked my arm through his when I had closed its door firmly behind me to make one more journey.

War has spanned my life, but though I love Jeanne and did not say this to Pierre, I know at last I cannot believe in it. No matter how much I have thought and read and prayed and studied, I have in the end not been able to find it right that people choose to kill and maim one another, though I understand, I think, the passion, like Jeanne's, that leads them to it, and I respect those who go to the aid of the mouse under the cat's paw. But it seems to me that as long as people accept that this is the way to resolve differences, and as long as they bully each other, there will continue to be wars, and that is wrong. Is there not some other way to settle quarrels and stop bullies? Perhaps I am not wise enough or learned enough to understand. Maybe someday, far in the future, someone will find a way, and thus end war.

But how will there be a future if a way is not found, and if wars continue?

AFTERWORD

Joan of Arc was officially pardoned — pronounced "clean" and free of heresy — in Rouen
on July 7, 1456. Pierre, Isabelle, Father
Pasquerel, and many people from Domremy
testified to her goodness, sincerity, and piety.

And then, for centuries, she was nearly forgotten. But on April 18, 1909, she was beatified, and
eleven years later, in May 1920, canonized —
made a saint.

Today, there are statues of her in most of the
places in France where her journeys took her,
and there are chapels dedicated to her in many
churches. Her village, Domremy — Domrémy-
la-Pucelle — is still lovely, nestled in its
misty valley, and much of her father's house still
stands, as a museum. Every year in May, the
people of Orléans hold a procession honor-
ing her, in which a young girl dressed in ar-

mor rides proudly through the streets.

Joan of Arc — Saint Joan — Jeanne — Jeannette — died nearly six centuries ago. But it is impossible to forget her, once one has heard her story.

About this Point Signature Author

Nancy Garden is the author of many books for young adults, including *Annie on My Mind*, which was an ALA Best of the Best Books for Young Adults and a Booklist Editors' Choice, and *Prisoner of Vampires*, an IRA-CBC Children's Choice. She lives in Massachusetts and Maine.